MW01487741

PRAISE FOR WENDY WALKER

Blade

"Fast-paced and emotionally charged, *Blade* digs into the dark side of elite sports in this gripping thriller. Wendy Walker is at the top of her game!"

—Ashley Elston, #1 *New York Times* bestselling author of
First Lie Wins

"*Blade* pairs intricate plotting and a winning protagonist with an insider's take on the fierce pressures placed on young women in competitive ice skating. Wendy Walker always delivers."

—Alafair Burke, *New York Times* bestselling author of *The Note*

"Set in the world of elite figure skating, Walker's latest thriller is as chilling as it is propulsive. Raw, emotional, and razor sharp, *Blade* kept me breathless until the final page."

—Jeneva Rose, #1 *New York Times* bestselling author of
The Perfect Divorce

"Wendy Walker is an autobuy author for me—I'll read anything she writes. Her books are smart, compelling, and packed with tension from start to finish. Every story is a masterclass in suspense, and *Blade* is her best yet."

—Liv Constantine, *New York Times* bestselling author of
The Last Mrs. Parrish

"Beautifully written and emotionally charged, *Blade* is a gripping thriller that delivers triple-Axel plot twists while pulling back the curtain on the cutthroat, high-stakes world of elite figure skating. Both chilling and mesmerizing, it's a story that slices deep and lingers long after the final page."

—Kate White, *New York Times* bestselling author of
I Came Back for You

"Wendy Walker's *Blade* is riveting, propulsive, explosive, and heart wrenching! I started reading this early one night and didn't stop until I'd finished, desperate to know how Walker's intricate plot would unfold! With Walker's signature scalpel-sharp prose and visionary storytelling, *Blade* is Megan Abbott's *Dare Me* meets Eliza Jane Brazier's *Girls and Their Horses*, a timely and timeless portrait of a female subculture complete with power dynamics, toxic friendships, buried secrets that seethe under the surface, and nerve-shredding suspense. I couldn't get enough of this world!"

—May Cobb, award-winning author of
The Hunting Wives (now a hit Netflix show)

"This addictive, atmospheric thriller cuts deep, delving beneath the sequins and spotlights to take an ice-cold look at the darker side of figure skating. Wendy Walker balances every element in her gripping story with the precision and artistry of a gold medalist."

—Layne Fargo, bestselling author of
The Favorites and *They Never Learn*

"*Blade* is Wendy Walker at her boldest: unflinching, urgent, and unforgettable. This is a deeply psychological, fiercely feminist, and emotionally devastating reckoning; Walker captures the weight of trauma, the pulse of fear, and the aching need for redemption with razor precision."

—Carter Wilson, *USA Today* and *Publishers Weekly* bestselling author of *Tell Me What You Did*

American Girl

"[A] cunning thriller . . . The twisty tale unfolds in urgent first-person-present narration . . . instilling an air of uncertainty that fosters tension and momentum. The exquisitely rendered and emotionally complex characters add depth."

—*Publishers Weekly* (starred review)

"[*American Girl*] will mesmerize readers with brilliant and moving characters . . . not just a good mystery, but a truly enlightening tale as well."

—*Booklist* (starred review)

"A compelling narrator, a suspenseful, complex mystery, and twists I didn't see coming—*American Girl* had me on the edge of my seat for the whole ride."

—Sara Shepard, #1 *New York Times* bestselling author of *Pretty Little Liars*

"This novel is smart, moving, complex, and ultimately hopeful. A highly original work from one of the best suspense writers in the business. Don't miss it!"

—David Bell, *New York Times* bestselling author of *Storm Warning*

"Wendy Walker's unforgettable thriller will stay with you long after you've turned the final page."
—Greer Hendricks, #1 *New York Times* bestselling coauthor of
The Golden Couple

"An immersive and original story that is gripping and tense, with a protagonist you'll root for and won't soon forget."
—Carola Lovering, bestselling author of *Tell Me Lies*

What Remains

A *New York Times* Editor's Pick

"I can't recall the last time a thriller kept me so alert, as though the muzzle of a gun were pressed to my temple . . . absolutely splendid storytelling, a book to entertain, to immerse, and to challenge."
—A. J. Finn, #1 *New York Times* bestselling author of
The Woman in the Window

"Finely crafted characters, great plotting, and so much tension you'll have trouble catching your breath. This is Wendy Walker at her best!"
—B.A. Paris, *New York Times* bestselling author of *The Guest*

"Perfectly plotted and beautifully written. I was gripped from the first page."
—Alice Feeney, *New York Times* bestselling author of *Beautiful Ugly*

"A gorgeous and compelling emotional thriller."
—Jean Kwok, *New York Times* bestselling author of
The Leftover Woman

Mad Love

"Twisty and totally unpredictable, *Mad Love* will have thriller fans raving. Brilliantly narrated by the incomparable Julia Whelan along with a full cast, Wendy Walker's dark and electrifying tale comes to life."

—Mary Kubica, *New York Times* bestselling author of *She's Not Sorry*

Don't Look for Me

"[A] twisty, hair-raising tale."

—*Newsweek*

"Distinctive, well-developed characters complement the skillfully paced plot. This moving look at the bond between a mother and her children reinforces Walker's place at the top of the genre."

—*Publishers Weekly* (starred review)

"Gripping . . . with unexpected twists . . . You've got a cracking mystery on your hands."

—Adrian McKinty, *New York Times* bestselling author of *The Island*

"A nail-biter . . . so much more than a twisty thriller. It's a heartbreaking portrait of a family coping with grief and an insightful study of guilt and blame, gaslighting and agency. If you love fast-paced page-turners with relatable, flawed characters, look no further!"

—Angie Kim, *New York Times* bestselling author of *Happiness Falls*

The Night Before

"Walker's clever misdirection paves the way to a truly chilling finale, and she has plenty of insightful things to say about the blame placed on women by society and themselves for the idiotic, careless, and sometimes downright evil things men do. Twisty and propulsive."

—*Kirkus*

"Walker excels at exploiting multiple timelines and ample misdirection to maximize the suspense of her twist-filled tale."

—*Publishers Weekly*

"Skillfully manipulating tension and using breathless pacing, Walker keeps that question in the air until the final twist unmasks secrets about Laura's disappearance and the murder in her past."

—*Booklist*

"As timely as it is compelling, *The Night Before* gripped me from the first page all the way to its stunning conclusion. Through twist after twist, the story takes you to deep, dark places few thrillers dare to go. A riveting read!"

—Riley Sager, *New York Times* bestselling author of *With a Vengeance*

"A sharp, suspenseful roller coaster of a thriller . . . Walker unravels the hidden secrets between families and friends in this smart, compelling read. Impossible to put down!"

—Megan Miranda, *New York Times* bestselling author of
You Belong Here

"Pulse-pounding action makes you race to the finish of this addictive thriller . . . Just when you think you have everything figured out, Walker pulls the rug out from under you and leaves you staggered. The writing sings, and the twists deliver."

—Liv Constantine, *New York Times* bestselling author of
Don't Open Your Eyes

Emma in the Night

"Twisty . . . a thriller that keeps readers guessing."

—*The New York Times*

"In this searing psychological thriller . . . Walker's portrayal of the ways in which a narcissistic, self-involved mother can affect her children deepens the plot as it builds to a shocking finale."

—*Publishers Weekly* (starred review)

"Both twisted and twisty, this smart psychological thriller sets a new standard for unreliable narrators."

—*Booklist* (starred review)

"Explores the bond between sisters and family dynamics that give new meaning to the term 'dysfunctional.' This thriller aims right for the heart and never lets go."

—*Kirkus* (starred review)

"I love an edge-of-your-seat psychological thriller that feels authentic, current, and keeps you up way too late at night."

—Krysten Ritter, bestselling author of *Retreat*

All Is Not Forgotten

A *USA Today* and *Sunday Times* Bestseller

"[A] dark and twisting psychological thriller that had me guessing until the very end."

—Reese Witherspoon

"Deeply intriguing and provocative, *All Is Not Forgotten* explores intricate family relationships against the backdrop of searing suspense. A novel filled with twists, surprises, and a plot that keeps you guessing. *All Is Not Forgotten* is not to be missed."

—Karin Slaughter, *New York Times* bestselling author of *We Are All Guilty Here*

"An assured, powerful, polished novel that blends suspense and rich family drama. Built on a fascinating scientific premise and laced with moral complexity, it is, in a word, unforgettable."

—William Landay, *New York Times* bestselling author of *Defending Jacob*

BLADE

OTHER TITLES BY WENDY WALKER

BLADE

WENDY WALKER

THOMAS & MERCER

Published by Thomas & Mercer, Seattle
www.apub.com

Amazon, the Amazon logo, and Thomas & Mercer are trademarks of Amazon.com, Inc., or its affiliates.

EU product safety contact:
Amazon Media EU S. à r.l.
38, avenue John F. Kennedy, L-1855 Luxembourg
amazonpublishing-gpsr@amazon.com

ISBN-13: 9781662531927 (hardcover)
ISBN-13: 9781662531910 (paperback)
ISBN-13: 9781662531934 (digital)

Cover design by Olga Grlic and Jarrod Taylor
Cover image: © borchee / Getty; © FotoDuets, © andreiuc88, © Chase Clausen / Shutterstock

Printed in the United States of America
First edition

To Dan Conaway

AUTHOR'S NOTE

When I was thirteen, I was accepted into an elite figure skating program in Colorado. I moved far from my home to live in a dormitory and train with promising skaters and champions from around the world. While this story is a work of fiction, the personal impact of my own experience remains with me to this day.

I know I'm not alone.

Prologue

Run.

This is her only thought as she bursts through the front door. Outside, into frigid air, into darkness. Eyes trained on the base of the mountain, where there is a field, and through the field a highway. Lights shine from cars and semis. They move together like they're on a string and the string is being pulled at a steady speed as they pass by the edge of town.

She knows this mountain, the thick forest of evergreens, the switchback carved into them that winds from the highway to The Palace, Avery Hall, and then Dawn's house—all behind her now.

As she runs.

Over the snowy brush with its dried needles, broken branches, shards of ice tearing into her bare feet.

Through the trees. Limbs catching on her nylon tights, cutting into her thighs, whose strength propels her body like a machine, sweeping forward with each stride. Pushing through the branches.

She hears him now, behind her, chasing her, calling out from winded lungs.

"Come back . . ."

The fear spirals, but her legs keep moving and her feet absorb the pain and her arms sweep into the branches before they can cut her face. She keeps her eyes fixed on the moving lights from the cars and trucks that might carry her away.

She runs.

And when she reaches the field, the lights from the road break the darkness and she can see flashes of baby blue from her dress, the yellow butterflies that dance on its skirt as it moves with her legs, her arms, her hands that clutch the blades.

Faster and faster as she breathes in and out. In and out. Arms swinging, close by her side. A glint of metal catching another passing light.

"There's no way out," he calls to her.

But there is.

The highway with the cars and trucks, and in them people who might save her from this place.

The fear catches up, immobilizes her. It slows her pace as her chest heaves. For the first time, it occurs to her that she's crying. So she says the words in her head. *Fight the fear.*

She spins around as his words echo.

There's nowhere to go.

She releases a skate, and it drops to the ground by her feet. She slides her hand inside the boot of the other, like she knows how to do this, then wipes the loose hair from her wet face, her shaking body, out of control. She repeats the words from her training.

Fight the fear.

When the man reaches her, extending his arms, thinking she might fold into them, the words scream inside her head. *Fight.*

As he takes the last steps to stand before her and she lets him see what he's always seen. A girl, barely five feet tall, with glimpses of innocence that have survived this place.

"Come here," he says, and she does, holding his eyes with her own.

It's the innocence that will save her now. It's all he'll see as she raises her arm into the night sky, the blade shining in the headlights. The blade now a weapon.

The voice in her head. Telling her to fight.

Chapter One

ANA

Now

I see Grace when I turn from the window. I don't know how long she's been there. Silently watching me.

This girl I've been asked to defend, who's been accused of a brutal murder, stands just inside the doorway from the front hall, arms at the sides of her slight frame, back straight, gaze steady—on me, but without expression—dressed in black joggers and a long-sleeved shirt. Her hair is pulled tight into a ponytail as if she's heading to the rink. Her feet are bare, and her toes dig into the carpet.

"You're Grace, right?" I ask. I've been here all afternoon, but she's refused to leave her room.

"I'm Ana Robbins—the lawyer from New York. I'm here to help you."

She responds with a curious tilt of her head as she runs her eyes over me, assessing, judging. Her arms cross in front of her chest.

I know this reaction, the dismissiveness. It's a common response, given her age and what she's been through. What she's now accused of and the charges she might face. I've been working with teen offenders for my entire career.

I turn back to the window so she can observe me but remain, herself, unobserved. Maybe this will get her talking. Maybe not. But it's worth a try. We're running out of time.

"It gets so dark here," I say. "I'd forgotten about that."

I'd watched the night sweep in through the picture window as I sat waiting for her. It was startling, like a portrait of the dark hanging on the wall.

I hadn't seen this night for fourteen years.

While I waited, I read her file, learning about the four strikes to a man's head, made with the heel of a figure skating blade, the scene where his body was found, blood on Grace's skate, a missing dress, and lost hours in her alibi.

The victim is a man I once knew.

I picture Grace behind me now, across the room maybe twenty feet long. Separated by the sparse furnishings, a couch, two armchairs, the coffee table. There's a TV on a stand in the corner. All of it, and everything else in here, is the kind of stuff that arrives in cardboard boxes with assembly instructions and an Allen wrench.

Even the Christmas tree is made of plastic, the lights and ornaments now tucked away in boxes on the floor beside it.

I continue as if we're having a conversation.

"We don't get dark skies like this in New York City," I tell her. "I moved there after college and never left." I stop and take a breath, clearing out the sudden urge to be back home, to be anywhere but here, in Echo, Colorado.

I've spent my entire life ridding this place from my mind.

But now I recall how an Echo night demands attention. The way it covers both land and sky until the line between them disappears. No horizon. No shapes or shadows, not even those of Cheyenne Mountain, less than a quarter mile in the distance. We're in a void, an ebony globe where nothing from the outside world can get in. Or out.

It's the kind of night you prepare for. I remember that as well.

Grace spent the day being processed for release. I know she's tired. She hasn't been formally arrested—not yet—but only because of the deal made by her local attorney, Artis Frauhn. I remember him from my time here. A local kid from eighth-grade science class. Not a skater. Just some boy I barely noticed until he found me on Facebook years later. And now here we are, trying to keep a fifteen-year-old skater from being charged for the murder of her assistant coach, Emile Dresiér.

"I trained at The Palace a long time ago," I tell Grace, trying to steer us in the right direction. "I had the same coach too—Dawn Sumner."

She's not surprised by this, and I suspect it's her mother who's told her. Jolene tracked me down at a conference in Aspen where I was the keynote speaker.

Now the DA's office has given us just two more days to provide a statement while they gather evidence—and decide how to charge her. Which degree of murder, if any. As an adult or a child. Or, perhaps, not at all, if there were mitigating circumstances. They won't want to make a mistake with one of Dawn's skaters.

"I can see the lights from Avery Hall."

Grace still says nothing but walks, step by step, to stand beside me, and I think I've struck a nerve, or a pang of curiosity, with the reference to the place where she was living, and where I once lived.

Avery Hall is the dormitory for skaters who train here without a parent. A rectangular structure with a flat roof and stucco siding, with two wings inside that separate the girls from the boys. I can feel it now more than see it. Rough, commercial-grade carpet in the bedrooms, cold linoleum in the hallways, stairwells, and bathrooms. Steam from the metal trays of food lined up in the small cafeteria. Thin paper napkins and silverware I could bend with my bare hands.

What a strange thing to remember. Bending forks and spoons.

My history oddly mirrors her own. I, too, came here to live year-round when I was just thirteen.

"And that's The Palace—there," I say, pointing to the four specks of light near the base of the mountain. Her eyes are already fixed on them.

They outline the training facility. An enormous windowless structure. Two ice rinks, a gym and dance studio, locker rooms, a snack bar. For decades, skaters have come from around the world to train here because of the altitude. A free skate at six thousand feet felt like nothing at sea level.

But it was Dawn Sumner who put The Palace on the map, producing champions one after the next, like an assembly line of human excellence. The kind of excellence she had failed to achieve herself, though she'd come painfully close—missing her third and last try for the Olympic team by "*two-tenths of a point,*" she would say, as if that could take away the sting.

Away from the rink, snaking up the right side into the dense evergreens, is the residential access road. Avery Hall is the first house along it. Dawn Sumner's, the fifth—a Mediterranean design with terra-cotta tiles, arched doorways, and window frames. It hid from the road behind half an acre of forest, the driveway coming to a fork, the main house to the left. To the right was a second driveway, and at its end, the guest cottage where Emile once lived.

It was no more than one large room with a square table. A love seat against the wall. An unmade bed with gray plaid sheets, always tangled and strewn.

The access road turns at the base, until it ends at the highway that passes along the edge of town, running north to Denver and south to Pueblo.

Hidden in the darkness somewhere between is the abandoned property that was once a dairy farm—the place we all knew simply as the field—where Emile's body was found, frozen in a pool of his own blood, making the time of death uncertain.

And in the other direction from the highway is this rented condo. It's in a complex—one of several that were hastily built when The Palace doubled in size. Gray prefab two-unit structures. I could never tell them apart when I rode past them on my bike on the way to school. No one stayed long enough to place a welcome mat by the front door, add a name to a mailbox. All these years later, they haven't changed, just multiplied.

Thousands of skaters have come through The Palace since it was founded. I try not to think about the ones I knew, though some have found me over the years, on Facebook or LinkedIn—mostly coaches now at smaller rinks. Lesser rinks. They reach out, desperate to reconnect with that past through the people who might hold its pieces. To lasso it, perhaps, and drag it into the present. Rewrite it, even just a few chapters.

In between *how are you?* and *what have you been up to?* was the question they really wanted to ask.

How do I leave this place behind?

That's what they crave when they begin to reminisce, then see that I've truly moved past it, not having skated since the day I left, no longer even owning a pair of skates, not poring over old photos and videos of my performances. When they learn that I have reinvented myself so completely I can stand in this room and look at The Palace and still feel my feet planted firmly on the ground. They want to know how. They want me to show them the way. But how can I? Leaving this place, and skating, behind me has felt like an exorcism.

It wasn't pretty.

I turn my gaze back to Grace.

"My first year at Avery Hall I had a room with a view of the mountain. But I think I lived in every one by the time I left—even the one in the back where your mother stayed. Did you know that?" I ask her. "That your mother and I were here together?"

She answers with a nod.

More reflections about Avery Hall and my time there take shape in short sentences, snippets, but I don't say them. I stop myself because I still don't know how to use this, the fact that I knew Jolene. And because I haven't found a place to contain my feelings about her sending her own child here after everything that happened to us. Me, Jolene, and the other two girls who lived here year-round, alone. Kayla and Indy. The girls they called the Orphans.

Grace walks until she's beside me, and together we look at the lights through the window. Side by side, though every detail about her lingers behind my eyes. The tightly drawn ponytail. The doll-like features of her face. Long dark lashes, delicate nose, a natural blush in her full cheeks and lips. Beneath her joggers and shirt are limbs that are slight but toned. Athletic perfection beneath a facade of youth.

It's the youth that strikes me. And this is good. It's what adults are meant to see. Children should stand out to us. They should be easily recognizable so we'll remember that they're vulnerable and do what we can to protect them. Except for the monsters among us who spy an opportunity.

Jolene used to hover over me at the bathroom mirror, teaching me to cover my face with eyeliner and lipstick. Youth didn't serve us here.

Grace stares at the lights—and I wonder which ones are pulling her in. The Palace? Avery Hall? The fifth house on the access road—the one belonging to Dawn Sumner?

I feel the words and lock them in my head. What I really want to know.

What happened to you here, Grace?

I think about my speech at the conference. I never would have accepted an invitation to come here—to Colorado, just five hours from Echo—had I not been given the main stage and a chance to reach other professionals who treat children. To teach them what I know. Not a chance in hell.

Christ, I'd felt the memories begin to stir as the plane descended five days ago, cutting through the clouds. Exposing the snow-covered mountains.

Over three hundred people heard my talk about the specialty of criminal defense work with minors. How it recognizes their developing brains and gives them defenses that don't always play as well with adult offenders. The so-called excuse defenses, meaning they are excused, for sound reason, from criminal culpability for the crimes they commit. Acting in self-defense, or in the defense of others. Trauma response from prior abuse. Insanity, both temporary and chronic. Intoxication. And the mere fact of being a child—the defense appropriately called *infancy*.

Building these defenses, I told them, requires two things. The what. And the why.

I'm the youngest attorney in our practice of six, but I'm the best at connecting the dots. The firm's founder, Jill Kirk, hired me to do just that, and I've proved myself. The facts, the circumstances—no two cases are the same. What has been done? Why has this child done it? There's always a reason.

Because children are not born evil. We still don't understand exactly how empathy, morality, and compassion develop—except that a child's environment plays a major role. The damage begins the moment we get our hands on them. Some believe it starts in the womb.

I stood on that stage and told them what I know to be true.

"*Children become what we do to them,*" I said.

My eyes linger now on this child, the one in front of me. The stillness of her face as she stares out the window. The murder and the precipitating events, trapped behind it.

"Let's sit down," I tell her. I go first, leaving the window and the night sky I had nearly forgotten.

I find the chair and the file on the table, right beside the cold tea and the pale ring around the bottom of the cup. I sit, again on the edge, elbows on knees, hands clasped together, and wait impatiently. My knuckles turn white as I press them into the backs of my hands.

Finally, Grace turns and walks to the couch across from me. She carefully moves an orange throw pillow to the floor and climbs deep into the corner so she can cross her legs. And it is only then, when her pants move, that I see the black plastic bracelet locked around her ankle.

Patience, Ana.

She's told the same story since Emile Dresiér was found murdered in the field. That she left him at The Palace and walked home. That she didn't kill him and doesn't know who did.

But her story can't explain the blood found on her skate and the dress that went missing. Or the vicious fight she had with another skater the same day he disappeared, caught on video.

I hear the words again. I feel them inside me.

What happened to you?

There's no doubt she was well trained. She had been set to peak for next year's Olympic cycle. Dawn was strategic—from the timing of a career to the placement of jumps in a program to maximize points. But that's not what she was known for.

It was the other bullshit. The subject of her book and her methods to combat fear. It was fear that had cost her an Olympic bid, and so it was fear that had become her obsession when she retired to coach.

Performance psychology was deeply embedded in sports when I trained at The Palace, but Dawn had claimed it as her own, like she'd invented it. Everyone knew that controlling fear in competition was essential. But she went beyond that, to the kind of fear that kept a skater from attaining new jumps. The fear of falling that held them back. Jumps got points—and Dawn was determined to make The Palace a jump factory.

She called her methods Fear Training.

A wave of electricity runs down both my arms, a nervous condition I've had for years. Pathways in my mind that are connected to this place. To being on the ice. To the fear. To the training. To Dawn.

Her hands on my shoulders, pushing me away from the boards. Away from her, like a bird being shoved from the nest. But then came the first stroke, the way the skating itself flipped a switch inside me. It's a feeling that had been there from the very first time my body responded to a blade, gathering speed through an edge. It had become as innate as walking, as breath. Like it was nothing. And yet it was everything. Speed, yes, but also control—such divine control. The slightest move of one muscle and the edge got deeper, or changed direction, gravity bending to my will.

It was how I'd spent six hours a day moving through my life. It's how I sometimes still move in my dreams.

But skating wasn't about that with Dawn. We didn't earn points for rejoicing in the freedom, the control. No—we earned them when we left the ice, flew into the air, made the rotations, and landed on one edge of a blade.

Fight the fear.

I can hear her voice, smell her thick makeup, perfume, hair spray—like walking past the cosmetics counter at a cheap department store. I can feel her jagged collarbones when she pulled me close, the cold air on my chest when she pushed me away. Euphoria to despair, neither reaction there to stay. Always a longing left hungry, a little, or a lot. Starving.

Fear Training. I hadn't thought about that part of my experience for years either, and it elicits another little shock down my arms.

I tell myself to do the fucking job already. *This isn't about you.*

I look at Grace on the couch, her arms and legs crossed, feet tucked beneath her thighs. How she steadies her gaze. Fearless at a time when she should be nothing but afraid. So I cut to the chase.

"Do you have any idea why they found blood on your skate?" I ask her. "In the stitches of your right boot? The nylon absorbed the proteins, so even though they were cleaned, it still tested positive." She sees the file. She knows what's inside. She shakes her head back and forth. *No.*

"What about the dress you were wearing that night? The one from The Palace—blue with yellow butterflies? It's still missing." I wait to see if this gets a different response, but it's the same. A head shake. A *no.*

I pick up the file.

"You left Avery Hall with Coach Emile. You were the last person to see him."

This gets her attention, but only a look. Like she's pissed off this is in the file, recorded as a fact. Suddenly, I know what to ask next.

"Before you left with Coach Emile, did you attack another skater?"

She shakes her head and looks down. "No! That's a lie."

"Someone recorded it on their phone. You looked angry. Like you wanted to hurt her. You pinned her on the ground, between your legs, and held her by the hair."

I wait until her eyes find mine. Until she can see that this doesn't faze me. That nothing she does or says will keep me from defending her. Some people have trouble bridging the mental chasm that forms when innocence collides with violence. But this is what I do best.

And this place is where I learned it.

"Grace," I say in a calm, steady voice. "You have to tell me what happened that night so I can protect you." I'm about to explain how it's crucial for me to understand so I can paint the picture for those who will judge her.

But before I can say another word, she starts to laugh.

"What's so funny?" I ask.

She unfolds her legs and her arms and leans forward on the edge of the couch, motioning for me to do the same. Our faces meet over the coffee table, where I've returned the file that holds the horrific facts of the murder. She's so close, I can smell her bubble gum lip gloss.

Then she says, in a whisper, what she wants me to know.

"It's not safe here."

And before I can make sense of this, she speaks again.

"It's not safe here, and it's all your fault."

Chapter Two

ANA

Before—Day One at The Palace

Ana had been violently ill the night before she left for The Palace. High fever, vomiting. Curled up in her bed, in the same room, in the same house where she'd lived her entire life, she told herself this would be gone by morning.

Her brother, Tim, was sitting on her floor, cross-legged, shoving her clothes into a duffel bag with more effort than the task required. A demonstration of his annoyance at having to help.

"Maybe you don't want to go," he said. "Maybe it's your subconscious trying to warn you."

Tim could be a total dick. Getting a stomach bug the night before she moved to The Palace was a coincidence.

He didn't have a single clue about her skating. How good she was—how good she had to be for Dawn Sumner to agree to coach her. He talked about it like it was summer camp. Like she'd be making arts and crafts, carving woodblocks, canoeing, telling dumb stories around a campfire.

Ana didn't kill time. She used every day, every hour, as a chance to get stronger, faster, smarter. To train her muscles so they would remember what to do when she sent an order. One command, and her body could execute a spin, a jump, an intricate footwork pass.

Tim couldn't even throw a Frisbee.

Connie and Carl were next to appear, stopping at the door to observe the chaos. Connie was still in her work clothes after a late house showing—pencil skirt, heels, blouse, and scarf. Always a scarf. As she was constantly saying, it put buyers at ease when their eyes caught a *splash of color*, especially now that she'd cut her hair so short.

"Jesus. What a mess," her father said. He was in the same tracksuit from earlier that day when he'd left work to fetch Ana from school, feed her crackers and Gatorade, and empty the garbage pail.

The room had been pulled apart—every item of clothing from every drawer in piles needing to be sorted and folded and then either put into a trunk or duffel bag, or returned to the drawers. Shoes, coats, hats, bike helmet, and snow gear, and of course, the dresses, joggers, leggings, sweaters, pullovers, socks, tights—enough for six hours a day, six days a week.

Connie seemed frozen by the chaos. "How are we going to get this done?"

Carl waved her off. "She doesn't have to go tomorrow. I can drive her on Saturday."

But then Connie swung around to face him. "No! I can't go Saturday, and I need to take her," she said, and with conviction that caught Ana by surprise. Her mother had been complaining about all the driving for months. That was the whole reason they'd finally agreed to let Ana try out for Dawn Sumner. It was that, or quit skating, they'd told her. As if quitting was an option.

Making the Olympics had been Ana's dream from before she could remember. After she got the feel of the blade in the center of each foot, and when the blades became a part of her body, and she discovered she could just go and go until the wind made her eyes water and lifted her ponytail in the air—she knew she wanted to spend every second she could with her feet in those boots.

It wasn't her fault that the rinks were so far away.

Connie carefully dropped to her knees beside Tim and began sorting through the piles. Carl joined her, resting his hand on his wife's shoulder.

"It has to be me," Connie said.

And then Carl nodded. "Okay. We'll get it done."

In the morning, Connie drove Ana 289 miles to the remote village of Echo. Today's scarf was shades of blue and orange, and it was neatly tied around Connie's head. A splash of color, ready to conquer the world.

Ana leaned against the closed window, sipping a liter of Gatorade through a straw.

"How are you going to skate tomorrow?" Connie glanced quickly at Ana, then looked back at the road. She looked worried.

"Extremely well," Ana answered.

"Haha," her mother laughed. "You know that's not what I meant."

They took the exit for Echo. Cheyenne Mountain was practically on top of them as they passed an open field, then stopped at the first traffic light. They made a right and were soon passing the entrance to the training facility.

"There's the rink," her mother said.

Ana stared at the enormous, majestic building as her entire body straightened and leaned against the door and the window, like it wanted to transport itself out of this car and through the brick walls and the metal stands and the wood boards right onto the ice. This was where she belonged, and she wanted to be there now. Right now.

Connie drove up the access road and made the first turn into the driveway of Avery Hall. She parked in one of four spots, between a blue SUV and a red Jeep with Oklahoma plates, and killed the engine, staring out the window at the building.

"Jesus," she said, scrunching her face. "Well . . . I guess this is what dorms look like."

Connie always had an opinion about houses and property, since selling them was her job.

"Who cares what it looks like?" Ana popped the hatchback with the button on the console.

Connie opened her door, still scanning the beige box with the flat roof, a green wire with holiday lights affixed to the gutters, half on and half off like someone had started to take it down, but then gave up.

"Even a little dormer, or some shutters . . ."

Ana climbed out and walked around the back to drag the two duffel bags and one trunk onto the asphalt. Her mother followed, slowly, tired as usual, and now worried about the architecture.

"Sometimes you can spruce things up with a nice row of boxwoods."

"Connie—stop!" Ana handed her the strap of one duffel, then another, and Connie heaved them onto her shoulders. She followed Ana, who dragged the trunk toward the front yard.

"I'll picture you there in the spring," her mother said, pointing to a snow-covered bench, as if she wouldn't be here to see it. Which was absurd. Connie would probably visit her every weekend.

The door opened, and a woman appeared, breathless and out of sorts, her heavy frame bursting from the sides of an apron like she was someone's grandmother in the middle of cooking Thanksgiving dinner. Orthopedic shoes, royal blue polyester pants, white tunic. Glasses, short gray hair.

She introduced herself with a hearty handshake.

"I'm Edie—the dorm mother. You must be Ana . . . and Mrs. Robbins."

She grabbed one of the duffels from Connie's shoulder and led them down a long hallway, motioning with her head as she pointed out the attractions—her apartment on the right, where she lived alone because her husband had passed and her boy was in the navy; the TV room on the left; and behind that, the kitchen.

At the foot of a wide set of stairs, they stopped to let two girls wearing Team Germany warm-up jackets scurry by without breaking their side-by-side formation.

"This is Ana. Say hello," Edie said.

The girls ignored her, then walked away, down the hallway to the front door.

"Don't mind them." Edie led them next up the stairs, the duffel bags dragging, the trunk thumping as it hit each new step.

"The girls come and go." She looked back at Ana then. "You'll get used to it. Just don't get too attached to anyone. I tell the girls when they first arrive, but they never listen."

More of them passed by as Edie labored up the stairs, trying to explain things about the dorm while she climbed.

"There are two floors for the girls, six rooms on each, with two girls to a room. Three if we get tight on space, but right now I have you in a double. Toilets and showers are in the middle."

They followed Edie left at the landing, then to the first door down the hall.

"Well," she said, letting them pass into the room across from the toilets. "Here it is."

Ana looked around. Two beds, two dressers. Beige carpet and white paint. Her side was the one with the bare walls. The other belonged to her roommate, Mio Akasawa, and Ana lingered for a moment on the poster that hung above her bed, a cat on a skateboard with some Japanese writing. It was enough to paste a smile right across her face.

Mio Akasawa, the Japanese national champion, could land triple Axels in her sleep—and Ana was now one of probably only a handful of people in the entire world who knew she liked stupid cat posters.

Connie nodded as she took in more information from Edie about this place where she was about to leave her daughter. The boys' wing on the other side of the building, meals and laundry and the car service if the weather got *too inclement* for a bike.

Her face tightened, exposing the worry lines between her eyes.

"Mio keeps this room year-round, though I never know when she'll be here," Edie explained. "But she's older, and I think that will be good in this situation. Ana is younger than the others."

She said this with sympathy, like she felt sorry for Ana. But this morphed into resignation when she heard laughter out in the hall.

"Ana—why don't you go meet the girls in the last room. Those are the other Orphans."

Connie's head jerked back. "Orphans?"

Edie explained how most of the skaters at Avery Hall came for a summer, or a few weeks. Just to get a taste of the training, and, of course, to work on new jumps. "The rest of The Palace skaters are locals," she said. "Or transplants—they usually come with their mothers and live in the gray condos on the road to the school."

Connie scrunched her face and shook her head, like she was confused. Or now suddenly worried because she hadn't looked into any of this and now her daughter was considered an Orphan.

Edie patted her shoulder. "Don't worry. There are a lot of mothers here. And Dawn, of course. She'll be just fine."

Yes. I will. This was Ana's dream, and staying here was the only way she could reach it.

She left the two women and stepped into the hallway, in search of the girls, the other Orphans. Two had stopped by the window at the end, one leaning against the ledge, the tall skinny one with broad shoulders and long legs. She had an enormous mischievous smile that spread clear across her face, framed by a pile of auburn curls. The other one, small by comparison, had hair so black it *had* to be dyed, short and blunt, and her eyes were caked with thick eyeliner. Her demeanor would have made Ana steer clear on her way to her locker at school. She lifted herself onto the ledge and sat down.

"Who are you?" the tall one asked.

Ana opened her mouth only to stumble on the words. Two simple words.

"I'm Ana."

"Cool," the girl said. "I'm Jolene." Then she nodded toward the other girl.

"This is Kayla," she said. "She would have told you herself, but she doesn't say much, and she can also be extremely rude."

But then Kayla did speak. "Fuck off, Jo," she said, like none of this was remotely interesting. Like she was bored even by her own thoughts about it.

Jolene laughed, nudging her with her shoulder. Then she turned back to Ana.

"There's one more of us." Jolene pointed inside the room next to them.

Through that door, Ana saw a petite, fair-haired girl with a long braid, sitting on a paisley comforter and talking on her phone.

"That's Indy," Jolene said.

And then, louder, "Indy! She's here! The new girl."

That name—*Indy*. There could only be one.

Indy Cunningham had just gotten fifth at Nationals at age fourteen. She'd had eight triples in her free skate. Each one in combination. It was unreal, and now she was here, training on the same ice as Ana.

Indy looked up and waved, then turned her back to the open door. Her eyes were red, her face wet with tears, and Jolene was quick to explain.

"She's talking to her old coach. She's homesick. You're not gonna be homesick, are you?"

Ana shook her head. "No. No way," she said emphatically.

"Indy's here to get the triple Axel," Kayla said, as if that somehow mitigated the awesomeness of it.

Jolene echoed her thoughts. "She needs it to beat the Russians. And Mio."

"Yeah—your roommate." Kayla placed her hands on the end of the ledge and rocked back and forth, her legs not reaching the floor but kicking the wall with each swing.

"Indy's from Minnesota," Jolene continued. "Her mom is Patrice Cunningham—do you remember her? She beat Dawn that year when she fell twice at Nationals and missed the Olympic team." Jolene's eyes got wide. "By two-tenths of a point!"

Kayla motioned toward the open door. "Maybe you'll cheer her up."

"Oh my God!" Jolene had a sudden thought. "Indy and Ana—*IndyAna*! It's perfect!"

Jolene smiled, then gave her that same shoulder bump she'd given Kayla. Ana shuffled her feet to hold her balance and took a deep breath to calm her brain—jolted by what appeared to be a sign of affection but felt like a field tackle.

Kayla started to tell her something about sneaking in after curfew, "which isn't hard because the window downstairs won't lock . . ."

But just then, Connie and Edie walked out of the room. Ana's room. Mio's room.

"Shhh," Jolene said to Kayla, who zipped her lips and changed her face.

The adults were suddenly in the hall, looking their way.

Connie started to walk toward them but stopped. "I'll be downstairs filling out some paperwork," she said. "Find me when you're ready so I can say goodbye." The last word emerged like a tremble. Like she might cry as she said it.

And then, suddenly, Ana thought she might cry, too, as she listened to the sound of her mother's heels—clip-clop, clip-clop—fade away. Realizing that her life had pieces apart from skating—Connie, Carl, Tim, the only house she'd ever lived in—and all of that would now be replaced by this beige box that needed shutters and some boxwoods, and these two girls, plus Indy Cunningham, crying on her bed.

But no matter. The second they were out of earshot, Jolene started in about Edie's cooking, the shitty coffee in the snack bar, the unfairness of this place because the boys' wing had a Ping-Pong table, and theirs didn't.

"Have you met Coach Emile?" Kayla asked when Jolene stopped talking.

Ana's head was spinning with the new information, trying to assess what part of it was important to her and what was just important to Jolene and Kayla, and for what reasons, all the while swallowing tears.

When Ana didn't answer, Jolene gave her another shoulder bump, this one sending her a step to the right.

"Emile Dresiér is a former Canadian and world champion. Dawn's head assistant coach."

Kayla rolled her eyes, but Ana also saw a little smile in them as Jolene finished her thought.

"You'll want to know Emile. He dries the tears Dawn makes you cry."

Kayla, shaking her head, said, "Wow, Jo—that's so poetic."

Jolene shrugged. "Just wait, Orphan Number Four. You'll see."

Ana nodded robotically—"okay . . . okay . . . okay"—as each new piece of information was conferred, though her conviction faded in lockstep with her mother's disappearing footsteps.

Chapter Three

ANA

Now

I am stunned. Electrified. Calling after Grace as she leaves the room.

"What does that mean?"

Her pace quickens, and I follow, down the short hall to the stairs.

"Grace—wait! You *are* safe. I promise!"

A door opens at the top and Jolene appears, dressed in sweatpants and a sweater, her hair flying around her face where it's come loose from a clip.

"What's happening?"

Grace reaches her mother. She tries to walk past her to the bedroom down the hall—the one she's been locked in all afternoon, since the moment she got back from the police station, where they took her fingerprints and installed the bracelet around her ankle.

Jolene grabs her arm. "Grace! Stop. Talk to us. Please!"

But Grace pulls away, her face showing the same anger that was captured on that video.

"I can't skate with this thing on my leg!" she screams, bending down, taking hold of the thick plastic. Trying to rip it from her ankle.

Jolene takes a step closer, reaches out and grabs her daughter's arm before she hurts herself. "Stop, sweetheart—please," she says, her voice shaking. "You can skate again when this is sorted out."

But Grace doesn't seem to care about any of this—the charges that might be filed later this week. The evidence against her. The man who's been murdered.

"Get away from me!" she screams. "I can't miss Nationals!"

Jolene looks to me for help, but I shake my head. I know this kind of rage. It hijacks the brain. We won't be able to reach her until she calms down.

"Sweetheart!" Jolene says, ignoring my cues. Her voice is steeped in desperation.

Grace walks down the hall, then stops and turns, looking at her mother and then to me. "You don't understand. Neither of you even came close to what I have!"

And with that, she silences us and disappears into her room with a slam of the door.

Jolene covers her face with her hands and shakes in disbelief, staring at the empty hallway. I grab hold of the rail, close my eyes, and take a long breath.

Grace is not my child. She's a client. And I haven't seen Jolene for sixteen years. I think about what I know. What I just talked about in Aspen for five days, in endless seminars and workshops. I can't be derailed by what Grace said. Kids say all kinds of things when I first meet them. Because as much as I tell them I'm here to help, I'm still part of the process connected to what is likely the greatest trauma they will ever experience.

This is normal, I remind myself.

There's work to do. Focus on the work.

First and foremost, I tell myself, is making the list, the agenda for the defense—we need a psychological profile. An explanation for why she keeps telling the same story that doesn't add up. Why she shows no emotion, then erupts into rage. Is it the shock of a trauma? A mental break? Calculated manipulation? Antisocial personality disorder or another sociopathic illness?

Yes, I think, centering myself as I open my eyes and walk up the last few steps to stand beside Jolene. I fight the urge to take her in my arms, this woman who was once a girl I loved so much her unraveling became my own.

She glossed over their history when she first called me in Aspen, and earlier today while Grace hid in her room. A bitter divorce when Grace's stepfather had an affair. His move to California from their home in Oklahoma. Even back then, Grace had been one of the most talented skaters in the country, something I might have known sooner if I still followed the sport. Jolene didn't want her distracted or possibly derailed. So she sent Grace to The Palace twenty-two months ago, hoping to save her career from the domestic chaos.

I feel a jump in my chest, my pulse quickening as I remember my own mother driving away from Avery Hall, leaving me in this unimaginable place where nothing I'd learned in my thirteen years about life applied. I couldn't see the dangers around me. The peers who were also my competitors. The mothers in the stands who weren't like any mothers I'd ever known. Dawn and the Fear Training. The strangers in the field where we went to escape.

And Emile Dresiér.

Jolene said she'd given Grace a checklist, a survival guide, thinking that would be enough. But knowledge isn't the same as experience. She had to know that.

I hear a breath labor inside her chest. Her hands fall to her sides as she turns her head to look at me.

"Did she say anything?" Jolene asks, wide eyed.

I lie by omission.

"More of the same—she says she doesn't know anything about the murder."

"God . . ."

I take her arm, lead her into the bedroom, and sit beside her on the edge of the mattress.

"I don't understand any of this."

"I know," I tell her. And that's the truth. She has no idea.

The first thing Jill taught me when I was hired was that parents, like their children, are not evil. They didn't want this outcome, their child accused of committing a crime. They didn't see where their parenting, their personal decisions, their own behavior setting an example—even just their benign neglect—might lead. How nurture (or its lack) was the predominant factor in children becoming criminals—and that nurturing was their job.

It's a tired analogy, but we don't let people drive without obtaining a license. Yet anyone can have a child, raise a child, and not know what the hell they're doing. No particular preparation, no training beyond whatever modeling they had from their own parents.

When they crash that child into a tree and claim they didn't know how to steer, well—I sometimes choke on my disdain.

Maybe that's what this is. The weight pressing on my heart. Somehow I thought we'd all felt the same way about this place. The four of us. The Orphans. If that wasn't true, which one of us was wrong?

Jolene can see these thoughts as they march across my face like an army headed to battle.

"It was a gift to be here," she says. "To have the chance for this kind of dream."

I draw a breath and push it down, hard, into my lungs.

"You know how good she is, right? She landed two triple Axels at Sectionals. Next year she could have a quad. And she's so beautiful out there . . ."

Jolene gets up to find a box of tissues.

"She's right. I never got close to what she has."

I release the air from my lungs and feel these things swirl in my memory. The Axel—the hardest of the triple jumps because of the forward takeoff, the extra half rotation required to land backward. More speed. Faster spin in the air. When we were here, the triple Axel was a novelty among the women skaters but also the future of the sport. A future that is now here.

Jolene folds one leg under the other, the way she used to when we lived together at Avery Hall. And for a split second, I see her there, the long red waves of hair, the mischievous smile.

"What do *you* think happened to Emile?" I ask.

Jolene doesn't look at me but reaches for my hand, and suddenly the comfort she once gave me is back, racing through my blood. Filling my bones.

"If I thought she was in trouble, I would have brought her home."

"I know."

"I always looked after you, and Indy . . . and Kay—I tried to . . ."

"I know." I close my eyes, jolted by the mention of their names.

Then she laughs before the tears come.

"*IndyAna*," she whispers.

I pull my hand away, stand from the bed as if it just caught fire.

"This isn't about us," I tell her.

I explain how I have to *clinically* understand Grace's mind. "We need mitigating circumstances—which I can then shape into a defense as an expert. This is what I do now. We need the story, Jo. Not our story, but hers. What happened to *her*. To *Grace*."

Even as I say these words, I feel split in two. Two chapters of my life. Two entirely different selves. The defender of children. The helpless Orphan. The one I love. The one I hate.

Grace's words ring in my head. *It's all your fault.*

I recite the evidence. She was last seen getting a ride from Emile Dresiér, from Avery Hall to The Palace. She was wearing the signature blue skating dress with yellow butterflies—the same one every skater got when they walked through the door, even for a one-week summer session. It was brilliant advertising—wherever those skaters went to train next, The Palace would go with them.

"And the skates," I say now. "They were in her locker, cleaned, but with traces of blood on the right boot. The lock was intact."

Jolene gets up, shaking her head. "You're talking like she might have done this."

"That's what I do, Jo—I'm not an investigator. I build defenses."

"No!" The softness, the vulnerability drains from Jolene's face as she becomes a warrior for her daughter. And this, too, brings me back. Jolene had tried to protect us for as long as she could.

"Grace didn't do this," she insists. "She left Emile at the rink and came back here. Anyone could have taken her skates. Taken the dress."

"And the video?" I remind her.

Jolene gets off the bed and starts to walk, pacing the room, bare feet pounding the blue specked carpet.

"Four strikes to his head with the heel of her blade? No—she adored Emile. Just like we did." Jolene weaves her fingers through her hair and closes them into two fists. Then she walks to the window and looks out to the night sky. The pitch black with the flickering lights.

And I wonder, as I did with Grace moments before, where they land, her big blue eyes. On The Palace? The fifth light on the access road—Dawn's house and the guest cottage where Emile lived? Or the patch of darkness before the highway? The field where Emile's body was found, buried in the blood and snow?

Or does she see Emile? His dark eyes. The wave in his hair. He towered over me but stood eye to eye with Jolene. Maybe she's remembering the way he walked, the distinctive limp from the fall that ruined his career, relegating him to a life coaching beside Dawn Sumner. Beneath her, as her assistant.

Dawn. I see us on a couch in her living room, watching my programs on a large television screen. I see the rich colors on the walls and fabric, reds and blues. Soft velvet and candles burning. Sinking in, safe. Warm.

But then, her voice. *"There! You see? You slowed down before the takeoff. You were afraid."* And then silence as the music played, and I stroked around the edge of the boards, cut into the middle. A turn, a toe pick jabbing into the ice, a catapult sending me into the air. Dawn beside me, so close I can feel the heat from her body as my back stiffens, watching myself on the screen, knowing what's about to happen and what I felt when it did happen. The relief when the edge of my blade dug in for a landing. And the shock when my body slammed into the ice.

I can see me now, my younger self, watching as Dawn frowned, or smiled, assessing my performance. Her feelings about me becoming my own. A flood of joy. A flood of despair that I think just might kill me.

Dawn Sumner.

Her voice is in my head. *Don't tell the others. This is our special time. Our secret.* I didn't understand why she brought me to her house for dinner. I didn't understand why Emile joined us, walking up from the guest cottage where he lived back then.

I wonder now about Grace. If Dawn sneaked her out of Avery Hall, too, brought her home for stir-fry and orange soda. Videos of her programs, smiles and hugs that left her with the same desperate swells of joy and despair. And if Emile Dresiér was always waiting for this to break her down into pieces so that he could pick them up off the ground.

If Dawn did bring Grace to her house, singled her out for conditioning or training or whatever the hell that was, Grace might be afraid to say anything that would hurt The Palace—even if it meant saving herself. And now Grace's words take on new meaning.

It's not safe here.

Jolene tells me the facts she's been clinging to.

"Nothing was ever reported about this place. There was no abuse, no sexual misconduct, no neglect. It's different now, Ana. After what happened."

Jolene walks toward me, stopping just far enough so she can see my whole face but still take my hands in hers.

"Your life turned out okay, didn't it?" she asks.

And this catches me off guard.

I left this place at sixteen, spent two years at boarding school on the East Coast, went to Middlebury, then NYU Law. I was an acclaimed defender of traumatized children. Practically a celebrity, according to Artis, who has followed my career. I'm the children's mouthpiece. I win back their lives. All of those things have been said about me. How ironic that I was, in the end, hailed as a kind of champion.

And a walking endorsement for The Palace.

Her question hangs in the air. *Your life turned out okay . . .*

I stayed at The Palace after Kayla and Jolene both left. I stayed with Indy. Me and Indy. *IndyAna.*

Grace's other words play again, this time with new meaning.

It's all your fault.

My fault.

Me—Ana Robbins. The skater from The Palace. The Orphan at Avery Hall. The one person who also knows the truth about Emile Dresiér. About the field. About the room next to Dawn's office where we learned how to fight our fear.

And who hasn't told a soul. Not even Jolene, who might have understood. And who could have foreseen the danger it still posed to Grace.

I'm the one who didn't try to stop it, even though helping children is my life's work.

It's all your fault.

And I think now, *fuck.*

Maybe it is.

Chapter Four

Excerpt from Testimony of Dawn Sumner

ADA OLSON: Ms. Sumner, you've compared your methods for eliminating fear in your athletes to military training. You said, and I'm quoting here, "When a person's identity becomes solely dependent on the institution, that is when they subordinate their own self-interest to that of the collective."

DAWN SUMNER: That's correct.

ADA OLSON: And what is the collective in the context of an athletic program?

DAWN SUMNER: The collective represents the end goal—winning. In the short term, that means overcoming fear and committing to the demands of the training.

ADA OLSON: And the institution? That would be you, in this scenario, correct?

DAWN SUMNER: Yes, and the other coaches under my supervision.

ADA OLSON: And do you ever worry that this kind of conditioning might have repercussions off the ice? In other aspects of these young girls' lives? If you become their only source of self-identity?

DAWN SUMNER: I train them to skate and to win. That's my only concern, Ms. Olson. If they aren't equipped to handle that, they shouldn't be here.

ADA OLSON: One more question about your methods, Ms. Sumner. Did you ever hold the back end of a blade to a skater's head as a way of summoning fear?

DAWN SUMNER: No. Those girls are all liars.

Chapter Five

ANA

Before—Five Months at The Palace

The dream was always the same.

Ana lies flat on her back after falling on the triple flip. It's days before the Midwestern Sectionals, and she needs the jump to place in the top five and make Nationals in the junior division. She hasn't landed it once, always short on the rotation. It's become the bane of her existence, Kayla says, a phrase she now understands and plays over and over in her mind.

Everyone has seen her fall. Jolene, Kayla, and Indy, who are on the ice. Other skaters, too, for the morning session. Seven a.m. Coach Emile stands by the boards, shaking his head. He's disappointed, and this stirs something inside her.

It's a vicious cycle, Indy says. They all know the theory—the one spelled out in Dawn's book. Making Champions. *Ana keeps it by her bed like a Bible. Fear makes you hesitate, slows your speed, and then there's not enough height and then you fall. And the fall makes you more afraid.*

Indy has it, too, this vicious cycle with the triple Axel. The bane of her existence.

In the dream, all of this flashes by until she sees Dawn come out of her office between the stands and walk down the steps and open the boards.

Always in the big blue puffer coat and beige skates like they had in the Ice Capades when that was a thing, and gold blades, not silver.

Fear crawls into her stomach, and it clenches tight, and this spreads up and down her body like a shiver until she's unable to move a single muscle. Dawn is on the ice, skating right toward her. The mothers from the stands gasp as they strain their necks to get a good look. And Ana's mother, Connie, cowers behind the plexiglass, her head wrapped in a scarf and her eyes tearing up.

Because Ana couldn't fight the fear, and now she's fallen. Paralyzed on the ice as Dawn barrels toward her, and will she even stop? And then no! *Ana screams. Then a spray of shaved ice covers her face when Dawn's blades dig in for a hockey stop just before they reach Ana's head.*

"Ana," Indy whispered, her hand on Ana's back. "Wake up—you're having a bad dream."

Ana opened her eyes, still in the dream, but then here, in the Orphans' room down the hall. In Indy's bed.

She sat up and rubbed her palms into her temples as reality set in.

They were still six months—not two days—from Midwesterns. There was plenty of time to get the triple flip, and maybe even the loop or the Lutz—the harder triples requiring three full rotations. *Thank God.*

But then here she was, not in her bed, but in Indy's. Not in her room, where she'd been living alone while Mio was back in Japan, but in the room at the end of the hall. The Orphans' room.

And now it all came back. Each pathetic moment. Waking up alone. The random thoughts of home that had crept out while she was asleep, small things like the smell of Connie's warm banana bread and the crinkle sound when Carl turned the pages of the paper. Tim's car—the worn leather seats, the gross smell of stale pot smoke, food wrappers everywhere—as he drove her to school.

Then the tears, and the walk down the hall that turned to a run because the lights cast strange shadows. Opening the door slowly so it wouldn't creak, tiptoeing across the room and curling up at the foot of Indy's bed like a little baby.

"I'm sorry," Ana said.

But Indy shrugged it off. "I don't mind." She was buzzing about in the morning light shining through the window. On the other side of the room were two unmade beds. Jo's with the fuchsia comforter. Kayla's with the brown wool blanket.

Ana swung her feet around and planted them on the floor.

She heard footsteps thumping from down the hall, then Kayla's gruff voice as she returned from the bathroom. "Get up, dummy."

Jolene was right behind her, dressed for the morning session.

And Indy, too, was almost ready to go. Black leggings, yellow sweatshirt. Hair combed and braided as she put on lip gloss in front of the mirror above a shared dresser.

Ana swallowed the panic left over from the dream but also from new thoughts creeping in about her lesson with Dawn. It was a big deal at The Palace. The Saturday morning session was reserved for the best skaters—the international champions, the Americans who had made it to Nationals, like Indy—and the boarders at Avery Hall.

To skate with the best in the world, and to have the first lesson from Dawn on that session, was evidence of her progress, in spite of the triple flip she couldn't land. In spite of the dream. In spite of her being a big baby who missed home. She'd promised Jolene that very first day that this wouldn't happen.

Indy was on the bed now, beside her, pulling on her sneakers. "Was it the same dream?" she asked with a grin.

Ana nodded.

"Did Dawn do a hockey stop and spray your face?" Her smile widened as she leaned closer.

"Yeah," Ana answered. The dream was losing its power in the light of day.

"I keep waiting for her to skate right over your face, in front of everyone . . ."

"Indy!"

"And there's blood everywhere, shooting out of your neck."

Ana let out a small laugh, though it felt like a betrayal of the woman who filled her dreams. And whose affection she'd started to crave.

Indy continued. "After Dawn skates over your head and kills you, you turn into a zombie."

Her eyes lit up with amusement, her voice deep and theatrical. "You chase her through the stands, back to her office and into the training room. Your hands have turned into skates, and you swipe at her head with the blades . . . and then she falls and starts crawling on her hands and knees, trying to get away from you, because you keep saying, in your zombie voice—*Fight the fear, Dawn! Fight the fear!*"

Now she was laughing, hard, not caring who joined her or didn't.

"Jesus, Indy," Kayla said. "That's twisted. Even for you." Indy let out one last burst of laughter, pleased with her story and the images of Dawn's suffering. Her heart was filling with hatred for Dawn and The Palace, drop by drop, like a pail beneath a leaky pipe. It was almost imperceptible, until moments like this one.

Indy had been at The Palace for almost a year, and she was no closer to getting the rotation for the triple Axel. It was the only reason she was still here—at the insistence of her mother, Patrice Cunningham, Dawn's nemesis.

She was here against her own will. Separated from Bobby Stark, her coach back home. It had become a matter of fixation for Indy, and *God*, were they sick of hearing about it. Especially Jolene and Kayla. It had become *a symbol of her defiance*, Jo said, because Bobby was the antithesis of Dawn, and the reason she'd gotten this far.

Indy swore that Bobby could help her get the triple Axel with his kindness and encouragement. Not a brutal course of falls and Fear Training.

No one, not even Indy, questioned that she needed the jump, failing to outscore others in her field, always finishing fourth or fifth, and for reasons no one could quite explain. If Indy had the triple Axel, she would be one of only four women in the world who could land it—becoming an irrefutable contender for a medal in the next Olympic cycle. And that was just eighteen months away. Her mother said she couldn't come home until she landed one in competition—proof that she had it *under her belt*. So Indy jumped and fell. Over and over. And let the drops of hate drip into her heart.

Indy grabbed Ana's hand and pulled her to her feet. "Come on."

They went to Ana's room down the hall, where she changed into her favorite dress and tights, a sweatshirt, sneakers. Next, to the bathroom to brush her teeth and pull her hair into a band, her mind shifting from where she was, nestled inside Avery Hall with the Orphans, her new family with the roles that had been firmly established, to where she was going, a knot forming in her stomach as she thought of Dawn and the dream and the triple flip.

Then outside, the four Orphans in rows of two, walking to the rink along the start of the access road, a quarter mile of mountain air and views that caused tourists to stop and take selfies. When had things like that stopped mattering one single bit? Ana's focus was always ahead, to the ice inside, to The Palace. To Dawn. To the triple flip. To her dream.

They went in through the side door to the snack bar, and the familiar smells of burnt coffee and rubber mats, then pushed through the maze of mothers and local skaters who swarmed The Palace on the weekends but had to skate on the earlier sessions and were now having a breakfast of donuts and shitty coffee. They unlaced their skates, getting ready to yield the ice to the ones who mattered. Maybe that was harsh, but it was the truth.

They passed by the opening to the arena, and the break in the stands where the mothers liked to sit, in the bleachers around the edge of the boards, as the Zamboni made its oval sweeps, the engine loud, fumes rising, black to white all the way to the rafters. The sound of it, the smell of the gas triggered a pang of nerves. Every single time. Fresh ice. Time to perform.

They walked from the locker room together, skates laced tight, rubber guards hugging the blades, and stood among the herd. Indy smiled and mouthed the words *good luck* because Dawn was already there, on the ice, before the Zamboni had cleared into the dock, finding her spot on the side across from the snack bar entrance, away from the mothers so they couldn't hear, close to her office where she could easily retreat.

Ana felt the urge to take Indy's hand and never let it go.

But the doors opened and the herd began to move, pulling off guards and taking the ice, stroking counterclockwise like horses on a track as they warmed up.

This wasn't the dream, the nightmare, Ana reminded herself as she gathered speed. Her spine straightened and her shoulders pulled back as she made the first turn at the end of the boards. She felt joy moving this way. Freedom. She lifted her right hand over her head in a perfect dancer's arc as she turned backward.

Dawn was standing at the boards, and Ana wondered what she was so afraid of. Why Dawn had grown so ominous.

"Ana!" Dawn called her name, summoning her for the lesson.

This is not the dream. She wasn't lying flat on her back, unable to move. Dawn was just a woman, barely five foot two, her navy blue puffer coat unzipped and hanging loosely from her narrow shoulders. She reached out and took Ana's face in her hands, her skin cool against Ana's flushed cheeks.

"How are you today?"

Ana answered, "I'm good."

Dawn let go of her face and smiled with her thin lips and nearly perfect white teeth—save for the crooked one in the bottom row.

"I was thinking about this dilemma with the flip," she said. "And why you can't get the height—I can see it, Ana. I can see the exact moment when the fear takes over."

The word—*fear*—entered Ana's mind like a storm warning. A trigger.

"I see everything."

Ana followed her gaze to the session, where skaters moved in and around one another, jumping, spinning, stroking into footwork passes or spiral sequences. It became innate somehow, the way they all knew where each body was heading and cleared a path.

She caught a glimpse of Jolene in the center, working on her flying camel spin, slow and labored by lanky limbs.

And then Kayla gathering speed by the Zamboni door, too much speed. Out-of-control speed, because—Jolene said—this was the only thing that stopped the thoughts in her head. Thoughts about her old life in New York that she never spoke of.

Ana knew only what she had pieced together—that Kayla had been rescued from her evil grandmother by some charity in New York that gave her a sponsorship to train at The Palace. And that whatever else had happened there, her unrest was big and unruly, and quelled by adrenaline from the speed and cigarettes and Jack Daniel's that she kept in a metal flask under her bed.

And, finally, Indy, procrastinating by the boards with Coach Emile, pulling on neoprene gloves. Not wanting to be here. Not wanting to fall, but there was no way around any of that.

"That's where it counts—out there," Dawn said, her words perfectly enunciated and delivered with an extra burst of breath, like she was narrating a movie. "It's easy to stand here and make promises. Anyone can do that."

And now Dawn opened her hand and pressed it again to the side of Ana's face. "I don't think you're ready."

Ana froze, not knowing what this meant. *Not ready for what?*

Dawn looked from the rink, the ice, to the break in the stands that led to the offices. Standing there was a man in a cardigan sweater, with gray hair and glasses.

He waved at Dawn, who waved back. And then his eyes shifted to Ana.

"I've decided you shouldn't have any more lessons until you stop slowing down," she said.

"What? No . . ." Ana protested. She felt like she was pleading for her life. Skaters who stopped getting lessons were not making the Olympics. Not ever.

"I'm sorry, Ana—I think you need to work on what's going on in here," she said, knocking on Ana's head with her knuckles. "I know you cry in the closet. I know you miss your sick mother."

How did she know that? About the times Ana sneaked away to the closet in the basement, sat in the darkness, with the mops and the brooms and the Pine-Sol, leaning against a wall and letting herself cry? Because she was alone, and because her mother was sick, maybe more sick than she even knew because they'd kept it from her with lies and colorful scarves for months before she'd left. All of them. Carl. Connie. Even Tim. She would never believe them again. But, also, they'd lied so she could come here. So she *would* come here.

And now it was all for nothing? Because she was a big fucking baby? "No!" Ana said again. "I can do it. I can!"

Dawn sighed like she was exhausted by Ana's pleas. Like she'd heard this all before. It was in her book. Chapter 7. "Denial—the Fourth Response to Fear."

Ana looked at the man in the stands. The work they did in his office was covered in Chapter 12. "Turning Flight to Fight."

"Go on," Dawn said. "Take off your skates and meet with Dr. Westin. When he says you're ready, we'll try again."

Ana felt a wave of electricity fly through her body. "No!" she said again. "I can do it."

And with that, Ana skated out into the session, the adrenaline surging, tears forming in the corners of her eyes, screaming at herself, *Just do it! You're such a baby!*

And she was a baby, crawling into Indy's bed. Missing home after swearing she wouldn't. Slowing down at the takeoff. But this—nothing was worse than losing a lesson.

She could feel the eyes on her, the other skaters, the mothers in the stands, as she picked up speed and hugged the boards all the way around to the other end.

Past Indy and Coach Emile, she cut into the center. Past Kayla, who slowed down to watch as she moved onto a left outside edge. *Don't slow down . . . fight the fear.*

Jolene was watching, too, as Ana made a three turn, then jammed her toe pick into the ice . . . *Don't hold back . . . fight the fear . . .* pulling in tight, arms crossed at her chest, right leg tucked behind the left. The blur, a split second, *Don't be a baby . . . you're a freaking baby!*

And then—no! It wasn't there, the height, she felt it like an instinct, but she had to make it around. She tucked her legs higher, squeezed them tighter as she descended, every muscle turning to the left, until she felt her right blade slam into the ice and pop her backward, onto her tailbone, so hard she thought it must have shattered.

And as she lay there, taking in the shock, she heard a clap and a holler. "That was it!" Dawn yelled. "Three rotations!" Before she could get up, Dawn was there, looking down at her with a giant smile and a hand reaching for hers.

"That's not the right way—you know that—but you made it around," she said. "Come on—I'll show you the marks."

The marks on the ice—the takeoff and where she came down, on a straight backward edge, her body twisted, the edge unsustainable, but evidence of the full rotation.

Then a hug, so tight, and the words that hugged her tighter.

"I'm proud of you," Dawn said. Then, without even a beat, "And I'm sorry about your mother." The messages bleeding together to form just one. She was sorry about the malignant lesion in her mother's head. But if that drove Ana to cry in closets and not hurl herself higher into the air, her dream would die, and all of this would have been for nothing.

She felt Dawn's words leave her mind and burrow deep inside her, in her gut, where she suddenly felt a rush of something good, for a change. Something euphoric. And she wanted to wrap her arms around it and never let it go.

I'm proud of you.

No more tears, Ana thought. *You big fucking baby.*

Chapter Six

ANA

Now

I lie in bed early in the morning, staring at the ceiling as the memories play. I see the ice at The Palace, the way it was in the summer months, softer, slower. How my blades would disappear through the shallow puddles that remained after it was cleaned. I hear Mio explaining about the humidity in the air and how the water takes longer to freeze again after the Zamboni melts the top layer, evening out the grooves.

I see Avery Hall and the other Orphans. Jolene with her red hair and pink warm-up jacket. Pink lip gloss. Pink everything. A *girlie girl*, Kayla would call her, sometimes with affection. Other times like an accusation.

And Indy. She comes to me in flashes of bright eyes and long, powerful legs that stroke around the bend of the rink like they're separate from the rest of her. Like her upper body is attached to an engine.

Flashes, too, of her sadness and the defiance it bred. How I could feel it rise and fall in her chest as I lay beside her while she slept. Heaving in and out, breath that sometimes carried a faint moan. A cry. A longing to leave this place.

But it is Emile who steals this show that plays in my mind.

Emile—standing by the boards next to Dawn. I can almost see him here, in this room I've never been in before. And then, finally, lying in the field on a slab of frozen blood. Four strikes to his head from the heel of a blade.

I shake it off—grab a sweater and wool socks, and go to the kitchen.

No—I won't let the past break through walls I built long ago. I won't. I'm stronger than that.

My thoughts turn to my work, to the other children and crimes that have crept beneath my skin. The most tragic. The most preventable. The most shocking transformations from innocence to violence. Young lives hobbled before they could begin. There's always a reason. Abused, misused, neglected.

The clock is ticking, I remind myself. I need to focus. Be strategic. Treat this like any other case.

I shake off what's left of the memories and think about the next twenty-four hours.

Jolene told me she never saw any signs of change in Grace. But then there's that video. Grace attacking another skater at Avery Hall. The housemother there, a former skater named Shannon Finch, witnessed the altercation. She's young and far more involved than Edie ever was—the old woman who ran the place in my day.

I have to get to Avery Hall, then The Palace, and Dawn. I feel bile churn in my gut, a small burst of adrenaline at this thought. But there's no time for my own apprehension. This is what has to happen. We need more facts. And we need them quickly.

The local attorney, Artis Frauhn, has already been crucial to Grace's defense. Making the deal with the prosecutor. Buying us these two days to come back with a statement before she decides about the charges.

I didn't know Artis well when I lived in Echo. But he remembered me from our eighth-grade science class, had followed my career after I left because he, too, had become a lawyer. I remember when he reached out on Facebook, how I couldn't place him until he spoke about a lab we were assigned to, as partners. We were dissecting frogs, and I made him do the cutting of the skin and sorting of the organs while I hid behind pen and paper, taking notes and making drawings.

The skaters and the locals didn't mix. Other than the few hours we spent at school with them, excused from all nonacademic classes and having no time to hang out, our lives rarely intersected.

But now he was a big fish in this little pond. And the first call Shannon Finch made when Emile's body was found and she knew the police would soon be at the steps of Avery Hall, looking for Grace. Artis then called Jolene, who was still here after the holidays, staying in this condo until it was time to take Grace to Nationals. Jolene tracked me down at the conference in Aspen.

In the kitchen, I make coffee, bring it to the living room, and sit in the chair with my back to the window, remembering what Grace said to me.

It's not safe here.

It's all your fault.

I close my eyes and see that blade striking Emile's skull.

Emile is dead. This hasn't reached the places inside me I know it will go as soon as this is over, this fight to save Grace.

Emile is dead.

This thought will go to those places. And make me feel good.

There's a knock at the door, startling me away from the image of Emile's crushed skull. I walk to the foyer, where a wall of cold slams into my face. Two men walk past me before I can close the door. We stand and shiver as snowflakes float to the ground.

"Hey," Artis says, hanging his parka on a hook. He's wearing a blue suit with a red tie and smells of aftershave.

"I thought you were going to court this morning," I tell him, remembering that we'd made a plan. He was supposed to be in court up in Denver on another case, using the opportunity to have a conversation with the state's attorney. Maybe lay some groundwork before we have to report back to the local prosecutor. Face-to-face, leaning into personal relationships. Trust. The intangible, often invaluable part of the legal system.

We had plans to meet later, after lunch. It's barely eight. I haven't heard a sound from upstairs, the two bedrooms where Jolene and Grace are staying.

"Canceled," Artis says now. "Because of the storm."

But his explanation is swallowed by the presence of the second man. The recognition crashing through me like a tsunami.

"You remember Dr. Westin, don't you?" Artis says.

My eyes fall on his soft pale skin. The way it hangs looser from his cheekbones, framed by gray hair that was once sandy blond. Those sharp blue eyes, piercing through the lids that now weigh them down.

Yes, I know this man.

But I don't speak. I can't. There's no air in my lungs.

"I thought he might be able to help," Artis says as he kicks off his boots. Westin does the same, both men making themselves at home.

"Jolene said Grace is still not telling the truth about that night," Artis continues.

I feel defensive now—like my skills are being questioned. But also, as if I'm a young girl sitting in a chair, across from Westin, in the office next to Dawn's.

I make a note to myself about how Artis has framed things—that Grace is lying. A possibility, but we don't know that yet. There's still work to do.

Finally, words form and leave my mouth as I stand there in my sweats and a sweater, wool socks on my feet. "I didn't realize you were still here," I say to Westin.

Both men look confused now.

"Didn't Jolene tell you?" Artis asks.

I shake my head. "Tell me what?"

The flesh around Westin's mouth begins to pull up at the corners. The smile that is so familiar, and yet I see it now through a different lens. I see it for what it is. *Condescension.*

"Oh yes," he says, tilting his head. "I'm still here!"

I look at Artis, but his eyes are fixed on the doctor.

"You still work with Dawn's skaters?" I ask, feeling my feet on the ground. Finding my bearings.

Westin explains that he's never left. He was here before I arrived, so he laughs, that makes it over two decades, and *how about that!*

I remember the first day I saw him at The Palace. Walking from the offices in the arena, across from the snack bar. He was right behind Dawn. Indy followed behind them both, her head hung low. Face red. I was standing next to Kayla on the ice.

I remember what Kayla said. The exact tone of her voice and what it implied about this man.

"Mindfucker." And then. *"Poor Indy."*

Westin keeps talking as this memory plays.

"I've been seeing Grace for several months," he explains. "She's working on the quad."

I steel my face as my heart pounds and the blood flushes to my cheeks.

"Let's sit down," he says, leading us into the living room. He knows the way. He's been here before.

At the kitchen, he stops, smelling the coffee.

"Can I get you a cup?" he asks us.

I remember this about him. How calm he always seemed. How he normalized whatever it was we told him. Whatever it was that had happened. And the things he told us. About our fear, and what to do with it. How to channel it.

Fear into rage. Rage into action. Fight—not flight or freeze.

Christ.

Artis and Westin carry their white coffee mugs into the living room. Mine sits on the table, and I find my seat in the chair that faces the doorway. Westin and Artis sit on sofas, facing the window, facing me.

We used to call him Dr. Fear. That thought now fills my head as Westin continues with his casual chitchat, acting as if no time has passed since we last sat together in a room. As if I haven't rid myself of this place and the damage it did, and then gone on to help dozens of children out of situations like the one Grace is in.

"They say we're getting a lot of snow. Maybe six feet."

"That never stopped Echo before," Artis chimes in. "The plows will clear the roads."

Westin agrees. "Right—and the two of you are making the rounds. A couple of detectives."

"If we had time, I'd recommend hiring someone," Artis says. "I know a few guys. But with the storm . . ."

"Of course." Westin nods. "I'm sure you two can handle it. First stop—Avery Hall? A stroll down memory lane, right, Ana?"

Mindfucker. Still at it.

I draw a long breath, nod, smile. "I'm afraid there's not much time for strolling." Like Grace last night, I dig my toes into the carpet.

"We need to speak to Shannon Finch."

"Indeed," he says. "I have to say—I found the video quite shocking. I'm curious to see if Shannon can provide more context."

Westin takes out his phone and opens the video, turning it so we can all watch as it plays. The altercation between Grace and another skater, Tammy Theisen, recorded on a cell phone moments after it began.

A group of skaters was in the TV room at the dorm, and even though the decor has changed, the layout appears to be exactly as it was when I lived there. The TV on the wall to the right, the couch under the window that faces the front yard. A few chairs along the path to the dining room, the kitchen, and the boys' wing on the left.

In the video, Grace screams at Tammy—"*You're a liar!*"—her face bright red. Tammy whispers something inaudible, then tries to leave, but Grace lunges forward and grabs a fistful of her hair. The other skaters gasp. A few are caught on the screen, hands covering their mouths.

Grace, who stands a foot below Tammy, dominates her with this one fistful of hair, pulling her to the ground, climbing over her in a straddle. She's wearing the dress from The Palace, blue with yellow butterflies. Light-beige tights. Puffy boots.

I can't see her face in the video, just the back of her head and her prisoner, trapped between her powerful thighs, beginning to cry as she yields control of her body.

"I'm sorry! Let me go!"

Grace climbs off her, slow and steady like she's made of steel. Like nothing can break her.

Finally, she turns, sees the phone filming her, grabs it, and throws it to the ground. That's where the video ends, on a frame of her face that holds an expression I've only seen once before. The complex intersection of defiance and despair that belonged to my best friend. Indy Cunningham.

"Jesus," Artis says. "That's gonna kill us. She left with Emile right after that. Demanded to see him."

Westin spins his thumbs, his hands folded in his lap.

"I know how it looks," I tell them. "But she's a child."

I stop myself from leaning on my script. I'm an advocate for minors—I know the arguments and the science behind them, about brain development and decision-making and emotional maturation.

But those are just conjecture until we know what actually happened. To *this* girl. In *this* place.

"Why were you seeing her?" I ask now. I picture Grace, sitting across from Westin in the office next to Dawn's. Two chairs in the center of the room. His deep, soft voice. Tugging on her brain like a puppeteer.

Fear into rage. Rage into action.

He looks at me with curiosity. "Oh, nothing out of the ordinary—sports conditioning. I use many of the new techniques for mindfulness," he says with a casual shrug.

"The thing is—these athletes are on a different trajectory. The discipline, the drive, the exposure to complex feelings and relationships. I don't think we can compare them to other adolescents. They aren't like most children their age. But that doesn't mean what they're going through is somehow damaging them or turning them violent."

He takes a sip of the coffee. "Do you have any theories—from your experience here, and your work with young criminals, that might help us understand the face we both saw in that video? Because"—he pauses for a moment—"that looks like a girl who could kill someone."

He stares at me like I should know—and not from my work. But from the time I spent here. With him.

Artis answers before me. "Shannon told Jolene that Grace was an angel. Up at five a.m., going to the morning sessions. She took her bike unless it was pouring rain or sheet ice. Got straight A's in school."

I remember my own schedule now. I also rode my bike to The Palace in the dark of morning and then home in the dark of night. I sat on the same bench, pulling on nylon laces with raw fingers, drawing blood from the cracks in brittle skin that refused to heal, licking them dry. The blood in my mouth, the ache in my muscles and joints and bones. The sting of Dawn's words after that first fall. And the second. And the third. Thousands of falls.

Every skater has done the same.

Westin shifts gears. "You know that Grace's stepfather left them."

"Yes—Jolene told me."

Artis stands up. He needs more coffee. The second he's gone, Westin lowers his voice, leans closer to me.

"You know," he says. "It reminds me a bit of your situation."

I look at him with surprise.

"You didn't feel like you had a home to go back to either. Remember?"

I'm about to answer but then stop. *This is a trap.*

"When you first arrived and learned your mother was sick, right?" Westin reminds me. "You would cry in a closet—in the basement, if I

48

recall correctly. Your father kept you away from her, away from home, so you wouldn't have to see it."

It took years of therapy for me to understand my parents' decision. To forgive them for it. Being away from my mother didn't make it any easier for me. But they couldn't have known this.

How I would stifle tears anytime I called and heard my mother's voice. How my brain clung to the attachments that, as a child, I still desperately needed. I don't remember when I turned instead to what was in front of me.

When I became a scavenger for affection.

They couldn't have known what this place was like. The place they'd sent me to live at thirteen so I wouldn't have to watch the progression of my mother's illness. She would lose her speech, her mobility, her memory as her tumor grew. The treatments to cure her would wreck her body. Hair loss. Weight loss. The skin on her face would turn gray and hang loosely around the bones.

But—wait. I feel a wave of adrenaline, waking me up before I walk into the trap Westin's set.

"How is this relevant to Grace?" I ask.

"You were very attached to Dawn," Westin says. "Grace was as well. Dawn tried to fill that void for girls like you and Grace. The so-called Orphans. But maybe it wasn't enough."

His gaze wanders off toward the ceiling. "The video—the rage it exposes." Now a sigh. "The training we do—it can't be blamed," he says. "Otherwise, the place would be overrun with this kind of behavior."

There it is—the party line rearing its ugly head. *Of course,* I think. That's what this is.

Westin has been here forever. *Dr. Fear.* The Fear Training. Indy used to make up stories about him and Dawn being lovers, painting vivid images of them in bed together, Dawn screaming her favorite mantra when she came—*Fight the fear!* She would send us into fits of laughter, none louder than hers.

Westin reaches into his bag, resting on the floor by the chair, and pulls out a copy of Dawn's book. I glance at the title, *Making Champions—the Power of Psychological Training to Conquer Fear and Win*, struggling not to roll my eyes.

"They were selling it at the conference," he tells me.

Wait . . .

"You were there?" I ask.

Westin smiles. It's more of a smirk. "Yes. I saw your speech. You have great compassion for troubled children."

My mouth is bone dry as I try to carry on.

"It's science—that's all. I'm sure you've kept up on the advancements that have been made in the study of trauma."

Westin sighs. Leans back again like a Cheshire cat. "There's always a new study, isn't there? I couldn't keep track of them all at the conference."

Now a pause. "I didn't see you on the second day," he says. "I thought for sure you would join the workshop on youth sports."

I think back on the five days before I came here. I was at the opening reception. I gave a talk on the last day, in the morning. Then I got the call from Jolene.

I try to remember when I got the text message on my phone. The one I didn't understand and still don't. The number was a burner. The message was just one picture. An emoji of a skating blade.

I thought it was someone at the conference who remembered me from Echo. It was a shock, being pulled back for the first time.

Was that the second day? I know I was there. And I also know that I didn't see Dr. Westin.

"Here's the thing," Artis says, returning from the kitchen. "All we need is a story. That's it," he tells us.

I shake Westin off me and launch into the first line of defense we're going to use.

"Grace didn't kill Emile. Someone else did, and they're framing her. That's it. Simple."

"Okay. So who wanted Emile dead?"

"He was a damaged man when I was here. I doubt he changed."

Westin knows the story. How Emile had been struggling with a quad toe loop in the middle of competition season. How Dawn was training him to stay on his feet no matter how he came down from the air. There was an automatic point deduction for a fall. He had to fight his body, make it bend to his will. Another rendition of her theme song. He went up for a quad toe, then came down twisted, fighting his body, which needed to fall.

Then *pop*. And just like that, his knee was wrecked, and his career was over.

Emile lost his everything with that one fall. And he blamed Dawn and the way she'd trained him. But then she turned around and saved him, taking him on as a coach, giving him a place to stay.

"Emile was damaged when his career ended," I remind Westin. "And damaged people . . ."

"Damage people." We finish his thought in unison. It's a common expression in the field of trauma psychology.

Westin lets out a slight laugh. "The profession could use some new material."

"It is true, though."

"Well," Westin says, shrugging this off. "The skaters all loved him. And he was an asset to Dawn and the program. I think we have to consider the possibility that Emile got in the sights of a deeply disturbed young woman. I know you want to believe she's innocent, but the truth is, Ana, we haven't had any issues at The Palace since you were here. Until now—with Jolene's daughter."

And then he says, "I was surprised when Artis told me you'd agreed to come."

"Of course I came. Jolene and I were very close."

"Yes, yes, I know," Westin says, his hands patting the air like he's soothing a small child. "And Jolene has been here for two weeks—visiting Grace while she trained for Nationals. Celebrating the holidays with her."

A burst of wind smacks the window, drawing our attention outside, where an army of gray clouds has gathered.

I grip the arms of the chair as I try to follow his train of thought.

I was just five hours away when Emile was killed in that field. Jolene was here, in Echo. So was Grace, and she was the last person seen with Emile. And what did he just say? *Damaged young woman.*

My eyes return to the book. It's a new cover from when I first read it years ago. Something about it had caught my eye, and I see it now, at the bottom. A line of print that says, *With a foreword by renowned sports psychologist Dr. Gerard Westin.*

Westin's entire career, his life's work, is tied to Dawn and The Palace. To the training methods he implemented. This all makes sense. And so does the new conclusion that I arrive at—Westin shouldn't be anywhere near Grace or her defense team. Maybe he's thinking the same thing about me—I could be a suspect. Or Jolene. He was subtle when he slipped that pin from his grenade.

"We're expecting half a foot of snow," Westin says, filling the uncomfortable silence between us. "I hope you and Artis can get where you need to go. Plows notwithstanding, we could easily get snowed in here."

And now I think, *here*—in this condo. With Grace and Jolene. With Westin. A dead coach. A murder investigation. The truth hidden behind a young girl's silence. Clues to that truth maybe buried somewhere in mine. Roads about to close. Keeping all of us, all of this, here. *Here.*

Grace's words come back to my mind. *"It's not safe."* That was the part that sounded an alarm. But it wasn't just that.

What she actually said was—

"It's not safe here."

Here, at The Palace? In Echo? That's what I thought.

Or here—in this condo?

Westin notices the change on my face. "I'm wondering if Grace had any issues before arriving. Maybe because of her childhood. You spoke about it at the conference—about inherited trauma. Jolene left The Palace before you did."

He pauses, draws a breath. Then tilts his head as he pulls the pin from another grenade.

"Do you know something about her time here, or why she left, that might shed some light? Maybe even from one of your famous theories that help get kids off the hook for violent crimes?"

I slowly place the book back on the table.

I'm about to answer, but then something catches my eye. I'm facing the doorway that leads to the foyer, so I'm the only one who sees her standing there, half of her body hidden behind the wall.

Grace. How long has she been listening?

"Ana?" Westin says when I don't answer.

Right then, Grace lifts her finger to her lips, her eyes wide and her cheeks flushed with panic.

And I swear I can hear it from across the room.

The whisper. *"Shhh."*

Chapter Seven

Excerpt from Testimony of Dr. Gerard Westin

ADA OLSON: Would you say the skaters were afraid of Dawn Sumner?

DR. GERARD WESTIN: In a sense. It was part of the training. They feared Dawn more than what they had to face on the ice.

ADA OLSON: And you helped them turn that fear to rage? Is that accurate?

DR. GERARD WESTIN: It's not quite like that.

ADA OLSON: Okay—what is it like, then?

DR. GERARD WESTIN: Fear causes three responses. Fight, flight, or freeze. I help the skaters channel the fear into a fight response, which helps them take the necessary action on the ice.

ADA OLSON: You don't work with them to calm the fear? Isn't that the most common practice in sports psychology?

DR. GERARD WESTIN: For competition, yes. But for training—to override the innate fear of falling, of speed and height—no amount of mindfulness can stop the brain from a real and immediate threat, like hurling your body into the air over a sheet of ice. That requires a kind of fire in the belly. In the mind.

ADA OLSON: The fight response?

DR. GERARD WESTIN: Yes.

ADA OLSON: And fight is born of rage?

DR. WESTIN: Yes. Rage at the obstacle. The threat.

ADA OLSON: Of losing Dawn's approval? Her affection?

DR. GERARD WESTIN: Yes.

ADA OLSON: Like the kinds of things a girl might face in the field?

DR. GERARD WESTIN: I wouldn't know about that. The training is about what skaters face on the ice.

ADA OLSON: But did you ever consider what might happen off the ice—if you started that kind of fire in the mind of a child?

Chapter Eight

ANA

Before—Eight Months at The Palace

Avery Hall smelled of bacon and syrup. Edie always made pancakes on Saturday mornings, and the heat of late August had taken hold of the odors and followed Ana and Mio right up the stairs after breakfast.

Mio was standing on a small stool so she could see herself in the dresser mirror, checking that her underwear wasn't showing when her skirt moved.

When she was satisfied, she climbed down and gathered her things into a small backpack. Ana sat on the edge of her bed, still listening to the lecture that had begun the second they'd returned to their room.

"I know they're your friends, Ana. But don't go to the field with them."

Mio had become like a substitute teacher—she had a lot to say but wasn't here very much to say it.

"The things they think they know are wrong. Nothing good ever happens at the field."

The field had been the topic of conversation at the breakfast table. And not just among the Orphans but *everyone*, especially the trio of men from abroad who'd been here all summer. Ivan from Germany,

Hugo from Spain, and Travis from South Africa, though he was an American with dual citizenship, skating for another country so he could make it to the international stage in the next Olympic cycle with Mio and, fingers and toes crossed a million times, Indy.

Hugo was twenty-one, and he'd been taking orders for the beer, vodka, and gin—Jack Daniel's for Kayla—over a mountain of pancakes smothered in Nutella. His eyes had remained fixed on the door to the kitchen, where Edie was inside scooping leftover batter into plastic Tupperware, loading drink cups into the dishwasher, until he saw her approaching and told them all to *shhh! Shut up!*

Mio couldn't stand those boys. She'd warned Ana to stay away from them.

"You still have a lot to learn about this place. The Orphans—all of you—you're just playing a game of being grown-up."

Maybe that was true, but Ana felt like she'd been through a transformation. No more crying in the closet down in the basement. No more sleeping in the Orphans' room every time Mio was away.

It had not been easy.

There were nights when she'd woken up and lost track of where she was, expecting to be back home in her room, Connie clip-clopping down the hall with a scarf around her neck, Carl humming a song from behind the bathroom door, the water running while he shaved his beard. There were, it turned out, endless memories like these that had to be seen and felt to then be mourned and sent scurrying away, because home was not like that anymore. There was no clip-clopping. No humming. She was certain, though she had no idea what had come in its place.

And while she lay there, alone, she'd taught herself the trick of making a list—all of the things she'd learned, all of the things she'd conquered since she'd arrived at The Palace and Avery Hall.

She could now manage a bank account, shave her legs, use a tampon, fix the chain on her bike that was always slipping off. She'd found comfort with the Orphans—her new family that did new things together. Things that filled her up, like gossiping about the boys downstairs or driving around town for no reason at all, just because. Singing at the top of their lungs. Jolene's perfume. The clove cigarettes that lingered on Kayla's clothing. And Indy—everything about Indy had started to feel like home. Her new home.

"Don't go to the field," Mio said again. Her face was serious as she stared at Ana, eye to eye because even at eighteen, Mio was not a centimeter taller. She shook her head quickly, her short black bob swinging side to side.

"Nothing good is happening there. Do you understand?"

Ana nodded, though she didn't understand. Everyone was going to the field that night. It was the last night of the summer program, which was ending with a big show. And it was also the last night before the start of school. The entire town of Echo would be there—not just the skaters.

"We can watch a movie instead," Mio promised. "I'll drive us to get ice cream first."

But Mio had never been to the field. It was just a bunch of kids drinking and messing around. It had already become one of the things that felt good to Ana, simply because it was something the Orphans shared. Mio was wrong—and besides that, Ana's mind was on the solo that she was going to be performing in less than two hours.

She told Mio, "Don't worry. It'll be fine."

Mio smiled, but with concern, maybe even disapproval. "Oh—Ana. Be careful. Please! I'll see you at the rink?"

Ana watched as Mio bounced out of the room, glad to have that out of the way. She had to get to the rink.

She headed next down the hall to assess the situation with the Orphans.

"What are you guys doing? Costumes and makeup are starting in five minutes!"

Kayla looked up from her bed, where she was laying out clothes for later, after the show, when they would forget about skating and go to the field.

"Chill." She plucked a T-shirt from the pile and set it aside on her pillow with a pair of jean shorts.

For Ana, this night was more about the show than the party. They'd been rehearsing for two weeks, the entire training program virtually halted so they could learn their group numbers, choreograph their solos, not to mention an entire day to transform the larger of the two rinks into a stage. Props and lighting and a curtain blocking off a quarter of the ice for staging each number. They'd already had two dress rehearsals to get out the kinks.

The show always borrowed themes from Disney movies, recreating the story with skating numbers set to their songs, with costumes for the different characters. This year it was *Pirates of the Caribbean*. Ana had never seen it but assumed it was self-explanatory. Pirates. Their ship. On an ocean.

Ana had a solo—ninety seconds alone on the ice, in front of every skater, coach, parent, and judge who lived nearby and came to watch. Tonight. In two hours. And now they were already officially late for costumes and makeup because Jolene and Kayla were obsessed with the field.

Jolene was at the mirror, slowly brushing her hair. It wasn't even pinned up yet, and with Jolene's hair that could take forever. She turned and smiled, a seductive expression sweeping over her face.

"Up or down tonight?" She grabbed the thick auburn waves and gave them a twist and a pull to the back of her head, paused, then let them fall around her face.

Kayla glanced, then decided. "Down."

Which satisfied Jolene, now shoving it all into a band, a sloppy ponytail that was not going to work with her costume. It had a headpiece, and all her hair needed to be hidden inside it. They'd have to fix that at the rink.

Indy's voice echoed from down the hall. "We're late!" she said as she burst into the room. She ran to her unmade bed and grabbed the bag she'd packed for the day. "My mother is going to kill me!"

"I know!" Ana was grateful for the reinforcement.

"Fucking Patrice," Kayla said, a little louder.

Indy sighed, with extreme exasperation.

"*Fucking Patrice* is going to kill me. I can't be late!"

And then Jolene also sighed, with aggravation, because to her the show was a nuisance she had to get through until the party at the field.

Bag on her shoulder, Indy charged toward the door, grabbing Jolene's car keys from the dresser and tossing them to Ana.

"We'll go without you! Ana knows how to drive."

Ana felt her heart jump. Jolene had let her drive a few times, but that didn't mean she actually knew how. And she was two years away from even getting a permit. She looked between her two friends, the keys in her hand, not knowing what to do. But then Jolene folded.

"Fine," she said to Indy. Then she turned to Kayla. "Come on. Let's get this over with."

She took the keys from Ana's hand and, finally, they headed down the hall.

They drove to The Palace with the top down, music blasting, sun shining. The show just two hours away, and Ana's solo, and the costume that made her look twenty and not thirteen. Everyone had noticed at the dress rehearsal. Hugo told her she looked *sexy*, and Travis tried to pinch her ass, true to form. No one liked Travis.

They parked in the back of the already crowded lot and made their way like a proud band of thieves through the door to the snack bar, then to the big rink, which was decorated with fake palm trees and strips of sand-painted plastic, and the red velvet curtain at the far right end that opened to the locker rooms.

Kayla mumbled, "This is a total shit show," and maybe it was. But Ana had never felt this kind of excitement.

The Orphans walked to the other end, out through a set of swinging double doors, to the second rink that was being used for makeup and costumes.

The second rink was smaller, about two-thirds the size of a normal arena. Years ago, skaters would practice compulsory figures there, before they were eliminated from competition. Now it was used for practicing spins and choreography, and giving public lessons for little kids.

This week, for the show, the ice was covered with rubber mats and racks of costumes. Headpieces, suits, dresses, capes, and skate covers shaped like pirate boots.

Ana could barely sit still when it was her turn to have her makeup done, and then have her costume zipped and strapped and buttoned by the skating mothers who had volunteered to help with the show. She just wanted to be on the ice.

Normally gathered in the stands just outside the snack bar entrance, the mothers would be everywhere now. In the second rink doing costumes, and later outside the locker rooms with clipboards of pages listing the numbers and the skaters performing in each one. They would stand behind the curtain, lining them all up in the right order and shushing them because it was hard to stay quiet with so much excitement in the air.

There were two kinds of skating mothers at The Palace—another thing Ana had learned in her time here. The first—the locals—were the lesser of her worries. They lived close enough to Echo to drive to the rink and stay for hours until the sessions were done, thinking that their kids had any remote chance of making it past Regionals. As if the odds of winning the lottery were better just because you lived next to a gas station that sold the tickets.

The second kind—the ones who could cut you with a single look—were the transplants who'd moved to Echo from far away. They'd left the rest of the family back home with a father, aunts and uncles, brothers and sisters. Their lives, their sole purpose, and the reason they were so vicious, so annoying, Jolene said, was to justify the sacrifice to the families they'd abandoned. Their kids had to succeed. So they spent their days watching every move of every skater—their own and their child's competitors. They kept notebooks on each session. What their kids practiced—jumps, spins, footwork connecting required program elements, choreography, run-throughs, maybe twice to build stamina.

Jolene called them bleacher bees. "*Steer clear of their nest,*" she said. "*They'll sting you until you're dead.*"

When Ana walked by them, it was sometimes hard to remember what she'd been told, because they were mothers, and in her old life, mothers were always looking out for kids. It was one of those things that she had to keep in the front of her mind, like a Post-it note of something you're likely to forget.

Ana repeated this to herself now, as they zipped her up and pinned her hair and painted one eye with a black circle that was supposed to look like a patch. She reminded herself not to let her guard down, not to be fooled by their smiles and the words that turned into knives, spoken with voices that were sweet and soft.

Like the one doing her makeup, Shannon Finch's mother, who smelled of stale coffee from the snack bar and the unmistakable scent of the rink—ammonia, gasoline, and sweat.

She studied Ana's face, smoothing the makeup with her thumbs.

"There," she said, pulling her face back a few inches to admire her work. "Adorable!"

The woman looked her over, head to toe. She brushed a trace of lint from Ana's shoulders. Straightened her headpiece.

"It's such a shame no one's here to see you."

She knew what Mrs. Finch was really saying—that Ana's family didn't care about her—but Ana wasn't going to be taken down by this woman with her gray roots and saggy underarms, who had left her husband and son back in Oregon so Shannon could train with Dawn. Shannon didn't even have a triple-triple combination.

So Ana took a breath, like she'd been trained to do by Dr. Westin, and let it fuel her anger.

"They'll see me when I make Nationals."

Shannon's mother smiled wider, but her eyes got smaller and her teeth clenched together so tightly Ana worried she might break one in half. Shannon would be lucky to make it out of Regionals this year. Maybe that was cruel to even think. Shannon had been sucking up to Ana since she got here. Trying to be her friend, since they were the same age.

So it felt good, but then bad, using her own words as knives. But this wasn't about Shannon. It was her mother. And if one of them had to leave costumes and makeup bleeding, better this bleacher bee than Ana. The *new* Ana. The one who'd stopped climbing into Indy's bed at night.

She skated her solo in the pirate-girl costume, her joy unfettered by the bleacher bees and her parents MIA and the triple flip she still couldn't land but needed for the upcoming season.

The song was from the movie, a quick tune, and her choreography matched the scene where one of the pirates swabbed the deck. She made the most of it, a bounce in her strokes, quick arm moves, one hand on her hip and one stretched high into the air, *ahoy!*—then landed a gorgeous triple-toe-triple-toe combination for everyone to see—including the judges who would be at Regionals in the fall.

Her heart was still racing when she neared the end of the ninety seconds, because she had never performed like this—in a dark arena with a spotlight following her every move. Skating a solo for a packed crowd. Killing the performance. Bursting with satisfaction as the audience applauded.

Then the music ended, and new music began, the claps fading as the spotlight moved from her to a new trio of girls who'd just taken the ice.

She exited stage left, with a shiver from a kind of elation that she'd never felt before. Not even when she'd won a medal. There was something about doing it here, as a Palace skater, that resonated deeper.

Behind the red velvet curtain, a bleacher bee checked off her name on a clipboard. Indy was there, too, waiting with Mio and the top three men training at The Palace—the ones who'd also been at breakfast. Ivan, Hugo, and Travis.

Mio smiled and waved. *Great job,* she mouthed, following the shushing orders from another bleacher bee.

Ana smiled and waved back, then looked toward Indy a little farther away, hoping to catch her eye as well. But Indy was distracted, staring into the stands. And when Ana followed her gaze, she saw Dawn at the boards by the entrance to the snack bar, next to Indy's mother. The two of them watching the show side by side, former rivals now enlisted in the same cause—to make Indy a national medalist this year and then the next one, too, leading up to the Olympics. A second chance at a dream neither one had fully realized. Lifelong rivals in a tenuous détente.

Ana skated around the back to find her way to where Indy stood, but one of bleacher bees grabbed her arm.

"Exit that way, dear," she said. Ana pulled away, tried again, but then her path was blocked by a swarm of younger girls being lined up for an ensemble number.

"Indy," Ana whispered.

But the bleacher bee was angry now, giving her an evil eye, pointing to the boards and the exit from the ice.

So Ana left just as the music for the trio signaled the end of their number. She grabbed her skate guards, almost falling over as she put them on in the dark, then walked, hugging the boards so she wouldn't block anyone's view of the show, to a spot where she could see the skaters who were watching in the stands, Kayla and Jolene and the others who were done and already out of their costumes.

The audience applauded again as Indy's name was announced, and Ana looked back to the ice and watched Indy skate to the center, then stop, arms overhead, right toe pick planted behind her left skate. Her starting pose.

The music began. A dramatic action scene from the movie that showed off Indy's power. No one moved faster on the ice. Not even Mio.

A tickle in her gut, and not the good kind that had been there before, Ana glanced back at the stands and caught Kayla's eye, then Jolene's. She waved at them to come down.

"What's wrong with Indy?"

Kayla shrugged. "We think she had a fight with Patrice. She was crying in the locker room. We had to put her head thing back on and shove her out there."

They all watched then, as the music played and Indy moved. She rounded the corner and hit a triple flip. Ana's gaze went back to the two women by the snack bar entrance, clearly visible under the light for the exit. Dawn was watching Indy with her *fake face*, the one Indy told Ana to watch for whenever Indy had a lesson. This face, she said, was proof that the détente was a ruse. A cover. And that Dawn was just using Indy to torture her mother, not to help Indy land the triple Axel and make the Olympic team.

"She hates me," Indy had sworn a million times. "Coach Emile told me."

She said Dr. Fear had told her the same thing. And then asked her what she was going to do about it. Cry like a baby?

Standing beside Dawn was Patrice, oblivious to the fact that Dawn wanted to annihilate her daughter, but instead watching her daughter with freakish intensity, her arms actually moving in sync with Indy's, knowing the program by heart, her face changing expression with the music, like she was the one on the ice performing, landing the jumps, soaking up the applause. A champion once again, and right under Dawn Sumner's nose. Just like she'd done twenty-three years ago. As if that one lucky moment had failed to seal her lifelong victory and she still needed more.

Now all eyes were on Indy as she finished a footwork sequence, a spiral, then started to pick up speed.

"What's she doing?" Kayla asked. "Is she trying the Axel?"

Indy hugged the boards, then turned backward—Kayla was right. This was her approach to the triple Axel.

"But she can't land it!" Ana said, a gasp filling her lungs. She'd been falling, crashing all summer. And hard.

Then Indy was turning, stepping forward, flying into the air off her left toe pick.

The entire arena froze as Indy spun like a top. She came down hard, catching her right blade, then flipping off it again into the air, this time almost sideways, landing on her right hip, sliding into a fake palm tree that fell over on its side with a dramatic thud.

"Oh my God," Ana whispered, her hand over her mouth as the rink quieted to a hush. The music changed abruptly as the spotlight shifted to the ensemble that was taking the ice early, Indy's solo cut short by the fall, the show disrupted, the audience buzzing within a hush.

When Ana finally exhaled, it was Jolene who put the pieces together, just as Mio slipped out from behind the curtain, skated to Indy, and helped her up and off the stage. Hugo followed after putting the palm tree back in place as if nothing had happened.

But something had happened, even if it was only the Orphans who understood.

"That was a message," Jolene said. "To her mother—and Dawn. She'll do anything to get home to Bobby Stark."

Chapter Nine

ANA

Now

I watch Grace slip away, out of sight, then wait for a moment to follow her that won't raise suspicion.

"We should go before the roads get bad," I tell Artis and Westin. "I need to change."

I leave the two men to sip their coffee and spin theories about Grace—and me and Jolene. I bound down the hallway, then up the stairs to Grace's room. I knock. Once, twice. But she doesn't answer. I try the knob, but it won't turn. It's locked from the inside. I hear the shower running.

Frustration takes hold, and I feel my body wanting to break down the door. First, those cryptic messages last night. And now this? The *shhhh* when Westin asked me about Jolene and why she left The Palace.

Panic rises as I force myself to remember that I am not a child alone in the dark. Or out in the field. I'm not about to fall on a jump, or wait for Dawn to yell at me or dismiss me or surprise me with a hug and a *good girl, try again*, then dinner at her house, because she's a skilled manipulator. And then the night when Emile joined us. When she invited him.

I am a grown woman. An accomplished attorney. Getting the truth out of traumatized children is what I do for a living, but it is also my calling. And I'm damn good at it.

Deep breath, Ana. I can't force it out of her.

I turn away, ready to head downstairs, dig some jeans from my suitcase. A fresh sweater. Maybe comb my hair. But then I hear music playing.

It's coming from down the hall. From Jolene's room.

Music I know.

I find her door cracked open and go inside to see Jolene sitting at a small desk, watching a video on a laptop.

It's music that I remember well—*Rhapsody in Blue*, the Gershwin piece from 1924 that pairs a piano solo against the backdrop of a jazz band. Controversial in the day. Challenging the rules, blurring the line between classical and pop genres.

On the screen, a girl in a royal blue dress stands in a starting pose, right foot draped behind the left, bent knee, blade resting on its toe pick. Her arms form a crescent on each side of her body. Her head tilts down, eyes closed. Waiting to begin. And then, suddenly, she opens her eyes, like a warrior called to battle, and pushes right into a layback spin.

I know this music—and this girl. I know the program—it's *mine*! My music, my free skate from an exhibition the one year I made Nationals. I'm stunned.

"Where did you get this?" I ask as I step inside the room. She seems startled and then defensive. She hits pause.

"It's on the website. The Palace has hundreds of programs . . . even ours."

I walk closer, stand behind her. I can see the logo in the corner of the video. Then my name and the year. The music. On the right side of the screen are two paragraphs of text.

"What does that say?" I can't read it, but I'm consumed now, with my image on the screen and the new facts worming their way inside me. I knew Dawn recorded our performances. I remember watching them with her as she pointed out every flaw, or every moment of *sheer brilliance*. Riding the waves of her affection. Drowning in them. Starving without them.

Jolene looks from me to the screen, clears her throat. And begins to read.

"A bold program with music to match, beginning with a layback spin rather than the triple combination . . ."

I can hear Dawn explaining the program to me as we stood together on the ice. The one o'clock session. It was fall. I had just started ninth grade.

I can see her skating in front of me as I follow her steps, copying the movements. *The layback here, right in the center* . . . then around the boards, crossovers and simple footwork, arm variations to match the music but nothing that might slow the speed going into the jump combination at the other end of the ice.

Jolene reads from the screen, about the placement of the jumps. Most skaters started with their most difficult jumps because they were harder to execute on tired legs. But if you could do them past the halfway mark, you'd increase your score.

The description of my program continues, and I find myself almost immobilized by what I'm seeing. Is this really me?

Jolene hits play, and I watch my scalloped skirt float like a ribbon, pulled away by the centrifugal force. My body bent backward, one leg stretched to the ice, spinning on the front of the blade, the other at a perfect ninety degrees. Ten perfect turns, then on to the jumping pass.

The triple here . . . land, right into the double, land and hold—two beats— did you hear that in the music? Hold the landing longer than they expect. A long hold made a statement about the jumps being solid, the body in perfect alignment on that outside edge. So perfect you could hold it forever.

And I see it now on the screen, my eyes focused on the stroking pass that set up the jump, backward around the corner, cutting into the center, then forward, stepping onto the left outside edge, a push into the three turn, then onto the back inside edge. Right toe pick digs in, propelling me into the air. Legs crossed at the ankles, arms over chest—it happens so fast, muscle memory in complete control, but then my foot is on the ice before I complete the three rotations. I force the landing, then spring up again for a double loop, just making the rotations. I'm on my feet but I know I've lost points.

Moving next into the double Axel, then a spiral sequence, combination spin. One by one, I execute the elements, and each time I pass the end of the rink where the boards break into two swinging doors, closed tight during the program, there's Dawn, her face taut with anticipation, her entire body from her scrunched shoulders to her fisted hands, holding the emotions that I am not allowed to feel—not until it's over.

Then the music stops, and I skate to those doors, desperate to fall into Dawn's arms.

I'm back there now, remembering how she would open her coat and fold me inside it, drawing me to her body, where I could feel her heart pounding with joy—for me and what I'd just accomplished.

I feel Jolene's eyes upon me, waiting for a reaction. I don't want to give her one, but I'm reeling. I can't take my eyes from the girl now frozen on the screen, wondering if Dawn will hold her tight or turn away because the jump was cheated. A flaw in the program.

Jolene sighs. "You were a beautiful skater."

"Why are you watching this?" I ask her.

She shrugs, not sure how to answer.

"I . . . I don't know. I suppose I was curious."

I feel the anger stir.

"Curious? About what?"

Again with the shrug. "About what happened to you here. Why you see this place so differently."

A gust of wind thick with snow rattles the window, and we both turn our heads. It clears to reveal the gray sky and the white coating over the parking lot, cars, garbage bins. I search for the outline of the mountain and then the lights of The Palace, the access road, the fifth house. The clearing that is the field.

"You know what happened," I remind her.

Jolene stands, takes my wrists in her hands and pulls them together so we are arm in arm, unified in our mission.

"Do I?" she asks.

I try to pull away from her, but this only makes her hold on tighter. The way she used to do when we were girls.

"What happened?" she asks again, her voice quivering. "What happened after we left?"

She stares at me, searching for answers.

"It doesn't matter," I tell her. But she won't relent.

"You were so excited to be here. I remember the day you arrived." She gives my arms one last squeeze before letting them go.

"Of course I was," I admit. "Because I had no idea what was coming."

This memory is right there for me to see and feel. The way I saw and felt it then, but also now, after fourteen years of close examination, intentional and unintentional healing. From my years racking up achievements to replace the dream I'd left behind.

My entire life has been defined by the days, weeks, months, years that came after I was dropped off at Avery Hall.

"Don't you remember when I used to cry in the closet—down in the basement? And how I would sneak into Indy's bed when Mio was traveling? How I couldn't be alone?"

Jolene's face grows curious. Perplexed, even. "I thought that was because you missed home. And then your mother got sick . . ."

I shake my head. "No—it was more than that," I try to explain, though in my mind they all knew. The Orphans—me, Indy, Jolene, and Kayla. They all felt the same way about this place. How alone we were. How ill-prepared for this world.

Jolene walks the carpet, back and forth. "You stopped doing all of that—the crying and sleeping in Indy's bed. I remember, Ana! You grew up—we all did."

"It's not normal, Jo," I tell her, desperate for her to share our history. "It's not really growing up—I know that now. I've studied it. I . . ."

I look at the computer on the desk and the girl frozen on the screen. The blue dress with the low scoop neck. The tight bun. Bright lipstick and dark eyeliner. I think about that program and how it made me feel. The longing I carried in my body, not for my family, or even for my dream anymore. I can feel it now, seeing that girl. Living on scraps of what I was taught to crave. It makes me want to punch my fist through the screen.

Jolene skips forward to the very end, when I finish the program and skate back to the boards, where Dawn is waiting.

But with a sinking feeling, I realize it's not just Dawn.

She freezes the frame at the point when my head stops turning. When my eyes can't find Dawn because she's turned away, angry about the underrotation of the triple flip, the cheat that will reduce my score, they land on the man standing beside her who was always there to pick up the pieces.

"Do you see that? The way you're looking for him. And the way your face changes when you see him? This is what I was searching for."

I pretend not to know.

"That's Emile Dresiér," she says quietly.

Jolene looks back at me now. "That's the piece none of us knew about, isn't it?" She pauses, waiting to see if I'll volunteer an answer. When I don't, she tries again. "Ana—tell me what happened after we left?"

I step toward the door, deflect us both away from the past. *My* past.

"What matters for Grace is what happened to her. She was seeing Dr. Westin. Did you know about that?"

Jolene nods. "I didn't think it would do any harm—he's a joke, right? Indy always said so. And Kayla—my God. She tore him to shreds, the way he tried to therapize her over her childhood. Her mean grandmother—remember?"

Of course I do. I can see Kayla's face imitating his concerned stare. The way he draped one leg over the other and pinched his chin with his thumb and forefinger. She had his voice down too.

"Well," I tell Jolene, "sometimes a hack therapist can do damage. Grace looked pretty angry in that video—it's the worst piece of evidence, in my opinion."

"You think Westin taught her that? In their sessions?"

"That's what he used to do. Turn fear into rage that could be channeled into action—on the ice."

I can hear the mantra in my head.

Fight the fear.

When he told me to get up from the chair. To close my eyes.

Christ. The things he would say—about Dawn leaving me. About my mother, my family sending me away.

"Are you sad, Ana? Does that make you angry? Where do you feel it in your body? Where does it live in your mind?"

And now, where did it go, I wonder?

"Westin is how I knew you were in Aspen the night Emile disappeared."

She wipes the tears from her cheeks and steadies her gaze as I choke on the air I've just sucked into my lungs.

"He told me you'd been there for five days."

"Yes," I admit. "And he told me you've been here since Christmas."

We lock eyes for a brief moment. Both thinking the same thing. Until, finally, Jolene says it.

"Jesus, Ana. Emile is dead. He's *dead*, Ana—and the way he was killed . . ."

"I know . . . with the blade . . ."

"We were both there when Indy told that story."

Jolene shakes her head. "Oh, fuck him. *Dr. Fear,*" she says in a mocking tone. "Fucking mindfucker, right."

I nod, see a flash of Kayla's face.

Jolene stands, walks to me, and pulls me close, her hand cradling the back of my head.

"You changed that night—after what happened in the field. We never talked about it again."

I shake my head as I hold back tears. That night was the start of everything.

"You turned out to be the strongest of us all."

"No," I tell her. "That wasn't strength. It was terror."

Chapter Ten

ADA OLSON: Why was it so hard for these girls? The Orphans?

MIO AKASAWA: You have to understand something about The Palace. Dawn wrote that whole book about her Fear Training, like she could build an army of loyal robots. But girls are not machines. Their bodies get hurt, and their brains long for things that have nothing to do with skating. No one was there to help them with any of that. But even worse—some were just waiting to take advantage of them.

ADA OLSON: Like who? Emile Dresiér?

MIO AKASAWA: Emile, the other skaters, the mothers in the stands, the world outside—something bad was bound to happen.

ADA OLSON: You mean what happened in the field?

MIO AKASAWA: Yes. But first, what happened to Indy.

Chapter Eleven

ANA

Before—Eight Months at The Palace

As on the other nights they went to the field, they started at Avery Hall, in the bathroom where the mirror was big enough for all of them to stand before it, putting on makeup like Kayla's—thick stripes of black and red. Eyes and lips transforming. They wore shirts that fell off one shoulder. Jolene said this was always sexy and had not, according to Kayla, "*gone out of fashion in the 1980s.*"

And now the conversation continued from the locker room, where they'd practically kidnapped Indy after one of the bleacher bees helped her off the ice and all the way to the bench by her locker. Not to be kind, Jolene reminded them, but to revel in Indy's epic fall, which had taken down part of the set and disrupted the entire show.

It had felt like a spy mission, getting her out of The Palace without Patrice or Dawn seeing them. Ana had to get her own skates off, and the costume, then help Indy with hers, while she was crying, sobbing so hard she couldn't tell them what had happened. Why she'd tried the triple Axel, knowing she couldn't land it. Knowing that the ice wasn't big enough for one of her falls tonight with the curtain and the props.

Kayla shoved her costume, and Ana's, into Shannon's hands and told her to take them back to the second rink. Indy was supposed to meet Patrice there after her solo. Shannon agreed, even though she'd already returned hers. She wanted to be their friend, and this was a chance to prove it.

From there, they crossed over to the men's locker room. The back door exited to the parking lot, and Jolene ran ahead to get her car.

It was then, in the back seat of Jolene's Jeep, that Indy finally caught her breath and told them about the fight she'd had with her mother.

"I can't go home," Indy said, wiping her runny nose with the back of her hand. "I tried to talk to her about Bobby, and she wouldn't listen."

Jolene turned around when they got to a stop sign. "We know, Indy," she said.

Kayla looked back, too, from the passenger seat. "But what the fuck with the triple Axel?"

"I was just so mad at her!"

"But you hurt *yourself*, Indy. Not your mother," Jolene said, stepping on the gas.

Indy laughed through the tears. "Don't be so sure."

They were quiet until they reached Avery Hall, then slipped past Edie's apartment, where the door was closed anyway, a reality show blaring—big surprise—and up the stairs to the bathroom, where Indy went right into a stall, locked the door, and started crying all over again.

Twenty minutes later, she hadn't budged.

"Indy—come on. We have to go," Kayla said, while Jolene twisted her hair, up and down, up and down. A sign that she was losing her patience. Ana knew—the field was waiting for them, the two sixteen-year-olds who'd been looking forward to this night for weeks.

"Just go without me," Indy said.

This sent a shock wave through Ana—she and Indy usually banded together, *IndyAna*, not drinking more than a few sips of beer and avoiding the rest of it, except to take it in, as observers. Not that they didn't wonder, didn't think about the boys they saw there and who saw them. But for Ana, it still felt like she was playing at all of this. The same she'd felt trying on her mother's clothes when she was little. Wrapping every single scarf around her like a tapestry. The scent of her mother's perfume spilling into the air. Clinging to her skin for hours after she'd put them away.

Jolene bit her lip. "We're not leaving you behind. Just open the door."

Kayla was more direct. "Open the damn door, Indy!"

Ana leaned against the row of sinks, catching a glimpse of herself in the mirror—long hair falling around her one bare shoulder, painted eyes and lips and cheeks. She looked every bit as old as Kayla and Jolene, minus the subtle curves, but that was hidden beneath the part of the shirt Jolene hadn't cut off.

She realized, now that the show was over and it had gone so well, that there was more excitement left in her stomach. Excitement for the field, and the party, and the possibilities—of what, though? Being someone else, maybe? Not Ana the skater rounding the corner, fighting with her own mind, her fear. Not Ana the Orphan at Avery Hall who cried in closets. Who *used to* cry in closets. Whose mother was sick. But Ana—a teenage girl, a *pretty* teenage girl, about to go to a party.

Come on, Indy. Giving advice was usually Jolene's job, and being tough was Kayla's, but they were sucking at all of that tonight. Their brains had been hijacked by yearning.

So Ana stepped away from the sink and said, "Indy—you knew Patrice wasn't going to let you go home. What else happened? Just tell us."

Indy inhaled a huge sniffle, then coughed. Then blew her nose into a wad of toilet paper that she dropped to the floor with a pile of others.

"Indy?" Ana said, Kayla and Jolene now holding their hands like they were praying, apparently happy to cede their roles in their Orphan family if it would get them to the field faster.

"Come on, Indy—it's me!"

Finally, Indy started to speak in a long ramble.

"I told her how I was falling. And that Dawn didn't care and that Bobby would never make me fall like this, he would find another way, and she said that was never going to happen. Even if I came home, she wouldn't let me train with Bobby, and I asked why. And she just said *because* . . ."

Another sniffle, another wad of toilet paper hitting the floor.

"And then we both just kept saying that, *why, because, why, because*—and she never gave me an answer."

Jolene's maternal instincts were suddenly piqued, because she stopped twisting her hair and said, "So you went for the Axel to show her how bad it was? How hard you've been falling?"

Then Kayla rolled her eyes. "But she's never letting you leave. I don't know why, but you have to stop obsessing about Bobby Stark. It's just making things worse."

They were all sick of hearing about Bobby, who'd been Indy's coach since she was five years old and who believed in her not just like a coach, but "*really believed in her*" like no one else ever had. They'd seen him before at competitions. To Ana, he looked like a tired old man, especially next to Coach Emile.

Still—they'd seen something else tonight. The way Patrice had almost teleported herself into Indy's body while she performed, and the way Dawn's face had lit up a little when Indy fell, so hard the entire arena gasped. The whole situation was a rivalry dumpster fire that had been burning for decades, and now Indy was right in the middle.

The room went quiet.

Indy sniffled, loud as thunder. But then she said in her most quiet voice, "I don't want to fall anymore."

Ana, Jolene, and Kayla looked at each other, shaking heads and shrugging shoulders, and Indy blew her nose, sniffled, blew again, until finally, the lock slid open, then the door.

She stood there in her bra and underwear, lean muscle head to toe, one hand braced against the wall. The other holding down the top of her underwear, exposing her right hip—and a giant plum-colored bruise—and stunning them into a collective silence.

It ran from her waistline all the way down her thigh to just above the knee, with shades of red, yellow, purple. Some spots appeared to be popping out, protruding from beneath the skin like they wanted to explode.

"Holy shit, Indy," Kayla said, as Jolene reached out to touch it.

"What do I do?" Indy asked.

Ana stared at her best friend, at her bruise, and wondered how she hadn't noticed it before.

Jolene and Kayla shifted into their roles, performing their duties. Jolene wrapped her arms around Indy and let her bury her face in her neck.

Then Kayla pulled the flask of Jack Daniel's from her purse. Only this time, she didn't take a swig herself, but handed it to Indy, who shrugged, not sure whether to drink or not drink from Kayla's flask, but the indecision stopped her crying.

"Going once . . ." Kayla said, waving the flask between them. She'd started to pull it away when Indy reached out and grabbed it with both hands.

Without a single beat she opened her mouth and tilted it back, wrapping her lips around the metal rim as she took a drink.

"God!" she blurted out, her face twisted and her throat gagging. But she swallowed it, only to have Kayla tell her to take another.

"Trust me," she said. "Just take one more."

Which Indy did, and then her face grew curious, and then she took a third sip, this time prepared and determined.

"It'll kill the pain," Jolene said.

"Which one?" Indy asked with a devilish smile. "The bruise—or my mother?"

Indy held on to the flask, drinking until she got a good buzz, while they spun plans and solutions to the problem of the bruise. They had no idea what to do about Patrice, who hadn't even bothered to chase

Indy down. Hadn't come here to look for her. Apparently, she was more mad than worried.

Ice packs, heating pads, ACE bandages? What would help heal a bruise? A bruise that kept getting injured every day. Suddenly, Jolene knew.

"Wait!" she said. "Hugo told me about something he did back home. Something he used on a bad bruise." Hugo—the Spanish skater who had a crush on Jolene and was bringing the booze to the field tonight for the underage skaters. Not exactly a reliable source for medical advice.

"He's there—with the other guys from Avery!" Jolene continued, making her case for leaving now, for the field, because everything could be solved, satisfied, relieved—at the field.

And this was enough. This and the Jack Daniel's were enough to get Indy into a pair of loose shorts and a T-shirt. Sandals and even some lipstick and then down the stairs and out the front door.

Jolene drove. Kayla sat beside her in the front, Indy and Ana in the back. The top was down, the wind drowning out Jolene's singing until they were stopped at a light, and again until another light, and then a final time when they reached the field.

It was total chaos, cars everywhere like in a parking lot where someone forgot to paint the lines. Music blasted from a speaker propped up in the trunk of a hatchback. It was so loud the bass notes shook the ground. One giant party on the last Saturday before the start of school.

They found a spot between a black windowless van and a silver sedan. Everyone could see them with the top down. *IndyAna* with cans of soda they'd sneaked out of the kitchen at Avery Hall. Kayla with her Jack Daniel's. Jolene lit a cigarette.

The passenger door to the black van opened, and a wiry boy hopped out, his jeans falling from his narrow hips. He pulled them up, tucked in his T-shirt.

The driver's side door opened next. Another boy. Then the double back doors, two more boys.

It was dark, well past nine. And dark in Echo was *dark*, even with all the parked cars, and the headlights of a gray pickup behind them. Even with the overhead lights shining from inside the van.

And in that darkness, the boys were just shapes in jeans and T-shirts. Still, they were boys, and Ana felt her brain out of sync, like she, too, had taken three swigs of Jack Daniel's and her emotions were now drunk, not doing their job.

The show was over. Indy's bruise crisis was over, for now, because Jolene had convinced her that they could make it better. The getting-ready part was over, the drive with the singing and wind in their hair—also over. It was time for *this*—boys getting out of vans in the dark—and where were the emotions *this* required?

Ana tried to analyze the boys like a science project, because the thinking part of her brain never failed her.

The tall wiry one. The sporty one. The two from the back, somewhere in between. Short hair. Long hair. Straight, wavy. One wore a jean jacket.

Then Jolene, with a different, more astute observation, said, "There's four of them . . . and there's four of us."

"Cool," Kayla said, taking another swig of Jack Daniel's.

Indy leaned over, her eyes still red and swollen from crying, her breath smelling of alcohol and her face relaxed. "I need to find Hugo," she whispered, as if she hadn't noticed the four boys and what was about to happen.

Which then did happen when Jolene opened her door, and then Kayla opened hers, and the wiry boy from the passenger side said, "Want to party?"

They were around them in a second, Wavy Hair by Indy's door, Wiry by hers. Jean Jacket went to the front to meet up with Jolene, and Sporty went straight for Kayla. As if they'd decided all of this beforehand.

And there they were, at last, Ana's emotions catching up to the facts. Excitement. *Check*. Curiosity. *Check*. Anticipatory humiliation. *Check*. Fear. *Check*. *Check*.

"We've got some cool shit inside . . ." Sporty said.

Jolene liked the sound of that. "Really?" she said. "Like what?"

Kayla walked to the back of the van, and then Jolene followed. "Come on!" they shouted in unison.

Indy looked at Ana and shrugged. Like she was silently saying *it'll be okay if we stay together*, and also like *maybe it will be fun*. But Indy was a little drunk, and away from The Palace and Patrice and Dawn, so there was no telling what part of Indy she was seeing, and if she'd ever seen it before.

Excitement and curiosity won the battle of emotions, and both girls climbed out of the back seat.

The inside of the van was set up with beanbag chairs and a shag rug and two enormous speakers. Wiry put on Led Zeppelin, and Kayla shook her head and whispered louder than she realized. "I think we've been transported to the seventies."

"Shhh!" Jolene gave her a shoulder bump.

But Kayla didn't shush. "We're a decade off with the shirts," she said. "We should have gone with some bell-bottoms. And clogs maybe."

Jolene ignored her, plopping down in the red beanbag. And when Jean Jacket plopped down next to her, Jolene's smile was so big Ana thought it might devour her whole face. Because *this* was happening. Boys were happening.

"What do you think?" Sporty asked, his face beaming with pride at the party room they'd created in their motor vehicle. He sat on the floor, cross-legged, and Kayla sat next to him. Ana watched Kayla's face change, slightly, the way Indy's had. Her disdain for life taking on more feminine attributes. What was that look, Ana wondered? Pouty—that was it. Kayla, of all people, looking *pouty*.

This was going to be trouble.

Jolene asked Sporty, "What do you have to drink?"

And there they were. Kayla and Sporty, now sitting side by side on the shag rug that lined the floor of the van. Jolene and Jean Jacket on the beanbags. That left Ana and Indy, trying to stand, their heads brushing the roof, next to Wiry and Wavy Hair, waiting for someone to decide what would happen next.

And then, like gusts of wind:

"Wanna score some weed?" And Kayla was gone.

"Wanna go for a walk?" Then Jolene was gone.

"Be good!" she said, winking at Ana.

Indy was next, hopping out right behind Wavy Hair, telling him she wanted to find their friend from Avery Hall, the Spanish skater named Hugo.

"You're skaters?" Wavy Hair asked. And then, "Cool," and then they were gone.

Leaving Ana alone in the van with Wiry, and all of her emotions, excitement and curiosity still in the lead. Fear coming in next, but the other one—the anticipatory humiliation—was right behind it. Saying things to her like *don't do anything stupid*, and by *stupid* it meant things that would expose her ignorance, her inexperience, her age.

Because tonight she was not a skater. She was not an Orphan with a sick mother. She was not lying on the ice waiting for Dawn to slice her neck, turn her into a zombie.

Not being any of those things felt like a giant stone had been lifted off her chest.

And then, before she could hear the rest of the chaos going on inside her own head, Wiry moved closer, grabbed her wrist with his bony fingers, and pulled her onto the beanbag left vacant by Jolene and Jean Jacket.

Then, "Want a beer?"

Then, "What's your name?"

Then, as if by magic, the opening bars of "Stairway to Heaven."

And the sound of metal on metal as he closed the doors.

Chapter Twelve

ANA

Now

Downstairs, I find Westin gone and Artis waiting for me by the door. He's slipped on his boots and tucked the pant legs of his suit inside them. The fake fur on the collar of his parka frames his face. The rest of it seems to swallow him whole.

"Did you see Grace upstairs?" Artis asks.

I shake my head. "Let's just go."

The dark clouds are here now, along with the wind that tears right through my coat and sweater, to my skin and into my bones as I walk from the front door to the parking lot.

I shiver as I climb into Artis's SUV.

"You got soft in New York," he says with a smile.

We take the long way to Avery Hall so we can drive by the field. The scene of the crime. I want to look at the layout again, the proximity to the dorm and The Palace. And, also, the highway that runs along the other side.

With the town hunkered down for the storm, the roads are deserted.

"Does Shannon know we're coming?" I ask Artis.

"Yeah," he says. "She remembered you right away. You skated here at the same time."

My entire body recoils—not at the thought of Shannon, but at her mother and the other bleacher bees who tormented us. I remember how they would sit in the stands above the snack bar. The lessons I had to learn about them. How their words turned to knives. How they were always looking for ways to hurt us, undermine us, come between us. Anything that would weaken us so their daughters would have an advantage, especially over Indy.

"A lot of skaters are still here," he adds. "It's a cool town."

I nod, thinking it has nothing to do with Echo. They couldn't let go of this world and now cling to it for dear life. But what do I know? Maybe they're happy here, hiking and fly-fishing.

Artis turns off the engine. "Looks like they've removed the police tape," he says, pointing to the field. "The body was found just beyond the tree line."

I let myself see it now. *Really* see it, the way it was. The field. The cheap beer in plastic cups, spilling on my hands. Wiping them on my jeans, or the dead weeds. Pot smoke. Fires burning. Music playing. Cars and kids. Finding a place to pee behind a tree, girls laughing, standing guard on wobbly legs.

"What goes on here now?" I ask.

Artis shrugs. "Same as before—small-scale stuff. Kids coming to score, drink, make out in cars. There's still that truck stop about a quarter mile up the highway, so we get some riffraff from that."

"Is that a possibility, then?" I ask, wondering. "That Emile was killed by a stranger—a trucker maybe—or maybe he was involved in something, like drugs?"

"That doesn't explain the blood on her skate. And I'd bet good money Grace came here to party like we did, which means she knew her way around."

His smile fades as he looks from me to the window, out to the field.

"But why would she come here with Emile? In the middle of winter?" This doesn't make sense to me.

A gust of wind rocks the car as Artis turns the ignition. "We should get moving," he says, making a U-turn to head back to the access road.

The car moves, and the field disappears, and I look ahead to the storm clouds and the deserted road.

Artis draws a long breath and holds it, like he's not sure how to say something.

"Westin's kinda odd, right? Or is it just me?"

I don't know how much to tell Artis about Westin. I remember Grace with her finger to her lips. The whisper, *shhhh*. Why she didn't want me to answer his question about her mother. And why Westin brought up the conference in Aspen.

"Did you know about his name being on the new edition of Dawn's book? His whole life is tied up in this."

"When you say *this*, do you mean Dawn?"

"Dawn, The Palace, the training," I say, pondering the possibilities. "The point is, Westin has an interest in protecting the program. And that could be at odds with helping Grace."

"You think Westin is involved somehow?" he asks, raising his eyebrows.

I can tell he doesn't agree. "I think anything that hurts The Palace hurts him, and I don't see a way around it. If Grace knows something about the murder that implicates another skater or parent—or even something about Emile—that would damage the program."

Artis sighs. "Look—that applies to pretty much everyone in this town. It wouldn't survive without the skating center. I sure as hell wouldn't be here," he says.

"Okay, then," I say. "That's our first line of defense—Grace is being framed. And it could be anyone—even a stranger. That will buy us time."

"And if the evidence keeps pointing her way?"

I shrug. "You've read my cases. You know how I operate."

I see the skepticism on his face. I've seen it before. Not everyone believes in trauma psychology. "You disagree with the defenses I use?" I ask him.

"Nope," he says. "Look—I'll argue whatever the fuck I can to get my client off. Even the guilty ones."

At the first stop sign, Artis makes a right-hand turn, then drives past The Palace—too fast for my mind to orient itself, to linger. Next, we're at the short driveway that leads to the rectangular beige building.

I can hear my mother's words now, something about the landscaping and dormers. She didn't want to leave me in a place that looked like this. A beige box. An older woman in an apron, too tired to climb the stairs. And the other Orphans luring me away and down the hall. Pulling me into their fold. The family that would replace her, and my father and brother. Stand-ins that would have to do because she didn't want me to see her illness progress. Or the side effects of the treatments.

Artis turns into the empty driveway and parks the car. He gets out like this is nothing, to him or to me. Like these memories aren't quicksand.

I follow him silently, up the stone steps with the metal rail, to the front door. It's open, and he walks right in, with me close behind.

It's the smell that gets me first, drags me back in time. I can't pin it exactly. Industrial cleaning products. The distinct must old houses take on and can't shake. The decor has changed. Beige paint on the walls, and wood floors replacing flowered wallpaper and pale linoleum. But the smell lives deeper than that. Too deep to be stripped away by the redecorating or the Christmas tree in the TV room, still flickering with colored lights and ornaments.

Artis keeps moving to the door on the right. The apartment where Edie used to live, which is now inhabited by Shannon Finch.

He appears steeped in anticipation as he knocks, his parka rising and falling with his breath. And I fight to catch mine. Everywhere, I see the ghosts. Kayla. Jolene. Indy. Mio. Dressed in leggings and sneakers, hair pulled into ponytails and buns. And back up the stairs at the end of the hallway, to my room on the left, and the Orphans at the end. And the bathroom across the hall—which brings a smile as I remember caking on makeup, Kayla with her Jack Daniel's, teasing us. But then other things creep from my mind, where they've been hiding, and I stop before I sink deeper.

Thank God the door opens, and a woman stands before us.

Shannon Finch.

She looks surprised when she sees me, not because she didn't expect us. But maybe because I'm nothing like the girl she knew fourteen years ago.

"Ana Robbins!" she says, moving toward me with open arms, pulling me into a halfhearted squeeze.

"Shannon . . ." I say, not wanting to finish the thought that sits on my tongue. *You're still here.*

She looks exactly the same to me. Corkscrew curls. Round face. Petite body, only now with curves and some extra weight.

"I know," she says, answering the question I didn't ask. "Weird, right? But I always loved it here. Even after I quit skating and moved back to Oregon." Then she shrugs like this is somehow inexplicable, her inability to move on.

"Come in," she says, leading us past a small foyer with a desk and an actual phone, a landline, to a small living area in the back.

In my three years at Avery Hall, I never entered this space. Edie kept it locked, with the key attached to a coiled chain that hung from her neck so she wouldn't lose it. So we couldn't get our hands on it. As if we'd ever want to.

We sit on stiff sofas, like the ones at the condo. Take off our coats and lay them beside us. I hear cartoons playing through the walls from another room. There's a LEGO set on the floor in the corner. I don't ask questions about her personal life. I don't want to answer any about mine.

"It's so awful about Grace," she says. "And Emile. I can't believe he's gone."

Artis bows his head in reverence to Emile's tragic passing, though something about it feels contrived. A lawyer down to his bones.

Shannon appears unfazed. Maybe even excited by the drama this has created, and that she's now a part of it.

"What are they saying?" she asks.

Artis launches in about the meeting tomorrow with the ADA, and how Grace still claims that she didn't kill Emile in the field.

He runs through the timeline—the one that's in the file. Emile picked up Grace after her fight with Tammy Theisen. Dawn was still at the rink—witnesses place her there through early evening.

Grace returned in time for dinner that night, having changed out of her dress. Her skates were back at the rink, in her locker, though she claims she accidentally left them in Westin's office after her session.

Emile didn't show up for training the next day, and his body was found three days later by a local resident walking his three black labs in the field. There had been snow, then freezing rain in the days leading up to the discovery. Emile's body and the pool of blood were frozen, discovered by the dogs after they were let off their leash.

Questioning followed, the missing dress, the search of the locker, the blood found on the skates. How Jolene, who was still in town after the holidays, tracked me down in Aspen, and I came the same day. Shannon called Artis. He was one of the few criminal lawyers in town.

Shannon listens, riveted like she's watching a true crime show.

"I remember seeing her at dinner. She'd changed out of the dress—the blue one with the butterflies—remember it, Ana? I still have mine after all these years."

I tell her that I do remember. But mine is long gone.

Shannon shrugs. "She couldn't find it when the police asked her. It was all so horrible," she says. "That's when I called Artis."

"Right," I say. And now I wonder—"How did you know him?"

Shannon laughs. "Grace isn't the first of my kids to get into trouble."

My kids, I think. Edie never would have called us that.

Artis chimes in. "I talk to the skaters every season. Tell them how to stay out of trouble. What to do if they get pulled over. If they're caught buying weed, using a fake ID at the liquor store. I do the same for the private school in Colorado Springs."

I get it now. "And they put your number on speed dial?"

Artis laughs. "Something like that."

And I think about what he said earlier—how he wouldn't be here if it wasn't for The Palace.

Shannon exhales a heavy sigh. "Artis said you wanted to talk about that video? And about Grace—her . . . personality?"

I nod. "Yes."

Shannon takes a beat, like she doesn't want to tell us. But then, suddenly, she does. "Look. I love Grace like my own child. She's not like that. And Tammy—well, that had been coming for a long time. They were rivals on the ice, living together here. Then Grace made it to Nationals and Tammy didn't. It came down to the triple Axel, like it always does—even when we were skating, right, Ana?"

"I remember," I tell her, and for a second I think she's going to talk about Indy. But she doesn't. Maybe she knows better. Maybe she can feel the embers still smoldering inside me.

"Only now, several girls have it. They just don't always land them when they need to. And that's what happened at Midwesterns. Tammy fell and Grace didn't."

"But that day, and that night," Artis asks. "Why did it suddenly come to blows?"

"And why did you call Emile?" I add.

Shannon shakes her head. "I guess it doesn't matter now."

"Why don't you let us decide?" Artis leans forward, hands in a prayer.

"California—you know about that, right?"

"What about California?" Artis asks.

"You really don't know? My God—Emile was planning to move some of the top skaters there. He was hired to take over a program in San Diego. The place is already set up, training top skaters from around the world, but they're about to lose their head coach, Eduardo Patteli—you know him, right, Ana?"

I did. Eduardo Patteli was one of Dawn's rivals. He'd been around forever.

"Emile was stepping in to replace him."

"Ah," I say as it all comes together. "Was he taking one girl and not the other?"

"Yes—but probably not what you're thinking. Grace, right? Because she made it to Nationals?"

She's right. This is what I'm assuming.

Shannon smiles. "Nope. He was taking Tammy. Go figure."

And now I think about the house up the hill, the guest cottage I could walk to from here. The night Emile joined us for dinner, and everything that followed. Emile always had his own agenda.

"Maybe he knew Grace would never leave. She was in deep with Dawn and *Gerard*," she says, referring to Dr. Westin with disparaging intonation.

"Was she in deeper than the others?" Artis asks, reading my mind.

Shannon looks at me. "You remember what it was like, right, Ana? How Dawn had her favorites?"

The secret dinners at her house. Emile in her guest house. Yes, I remember.

"Anyway," she continues, "Emile was trying to keep it under wraps. He didn't want Dawn to have time to change anyone's mind about leaving."

"Did you see the fight?" I want to get back to Grace and Emile.

"I got there right after Grace slapped the phone away. That's when Tammy said, 'Ask Emile—he knows the truth,' or something like that."

Artis looks surprised. "So that's why you called Emile to get Grace?"

"No—Grace demanded it. She said she had to see Emile. After the fight, she broke down crying. I brought her here, to my apartment. Closed the door. She just fell into my arms and sobbed, asking for him over and over."

This was all making sense until right now. "Why was she so upset?"

Shannon looks at me like I'm the one who should know the answer. "She was an Orphan. And the only one. I knew what it was like for her. Because of—well, you and the others when we were skaters together. She had trouble regulating her emotions. Tears to temper tantrums. I tried to help her. It's—well, to be honest. It hasn't been easy."

I think now that this was always her nature. Shannon tried to be friends with us, but we didn't trust her. Her mother was dangerous.

"Were they that close?" I ask now. "Emile and Grace?"

Shannon shakes her head. "No—I mean—all the skaters loved Emile. He's older now—so it's different. The girls don't have crushes on him the way they used to. But you remember—he was the antidote to Dawn. Still—Grace would never have left The Palace for him."

"Well," Artis says. "This just opened up a whole can of worms—and by 'worms' I mean suspects." He smiles like a little boy, and I have a flash of him dissecting that frog in eighth grade. "Dawn would have been beside herself if she knew."

Shannon leans back, crosses her arms. "Damn straight. Trying to steal her students? That's a declaration of war in our world."

I think about how Emile used to live in Dawn's guest cottage. She had ruined him and then saved him. At least, that's how he saw it. I wonder how she felt about their relationship. If this betrayal would have been a knife in the back.

"So you think that's what Grace wanted to hear from Emile? The truth about him leaving and not taking her with him?"

"That's all I can think. Look—Emile was very paternal with her. Maybe she was triggered by his leaving—because of what happened to her back home."

Jolene had told me about Grace's stepfather leaving them. She framed it around the skating—like that was her only concern when it happened. She made it sound like her husband and Grace weren't close enough for Grace to care.

"Do you have any of her medical or school records?" I ask now. "I remember Edie getting them when I lived here."

Shannon nods. "The police already requested them. But I told them to come back with a warrant, right, Artis?"

"It'll take a few days, but they'll get one."

"Can I see them?" I ask. Shannon nods, then walks to a small file cabinet hidden beneath a tablecloth. A vase with flowers sits on top of it like it's an end table. She pulls a file and gives it to me.

"You can take it," she says. "It belongs to Grace, and you're her lawyer now."

I take the file. Artis stands to leave, and I do the same.

"Thanks for your help, Shannon," I say. "And for being so kind to Grace."

She lets out a small laugh. "Well, like I said. She's one of my kids."

When we get to the end of the hallway, to the front door, Shannon stops. Looking at the ground as she shakes her head.

"The way he was killed," she says. "With the heel of a blade . . . it made me think."

The current runs down my arms.

"What about it?" I ask, remembering Indy and the story she told us. How we laughed about the image—me turning into a zombie and chasing Dawn. Shannon couldn't possibly know about that.

She scrunches her whole face together like what she's about to tell us is incendiary.

"Kayla Johnson," she says, out of nowhere. "Do you remember her? Why she was asked to leave?"

Artis looks puzzled, his head swinging between the two of us.

"What does Kayla have to do with any of this?"

"She still lives in Pueblo. That's just an hour from here," Shannon says.

Artis is perfectly still like he's making more calculations, adding suspects to the list. Suddenly I wonder if he's already placed me and Jolene there. If Westin put the idea in his head. I begin to wonder if my trust in him is misplaced, a fellow lawyer, dissecting the facts, speaking the same language.

I can hear the ghosts coming down the stairs from the room on the second floor, all the way in the back. Down the stairs and the hall until they stand right outside the door. Shannon knows something about why Kayla left. Something I don't.

"Why don't you tell me, Shannon," I say. "Tell me what you know about Kayla Johnson."

Chapter Thirteen

Excerpt from Testimony of Kayla Johnson

ADA OLSON: Two months after that night in the field, you left The Palace. Is that right?

KAYLA JOHNSON: I was asked to leave, to be more specific.

ADA OLSON: After you had an altercation with one of the mothers in the stands—a bleacher bee I think you call them. Is that right? Can you say what happened?

KAYLA JOHNSON: I heard them talking about the night in the field. But it was more the way they said it. They spoke like we were beneath them. They had no fucking clue what we went through and what it did to us. To me.

ADA OLSON: And what did you do?

KAYLA JOHNSON: I'm not proud of it—but at the time, I couldn't contain my anger. I walked up into the stands and started screaming at them. Telling them how pathetic they were, how their kids couldn't skate and Dawn just wanted their money. Then one of them—Mrs. Finch—said something about my mother, and that's when I lost it. I raised one of my skates in the air like I was going to kill her with the blade.

ADA OLSON: And did that idea just come to you—using the blade as a weapon?

KAYLA JOHNSON: No. It was an image I had in my head that never left—from a story one of the girls made up. It felt ridiculous when she told it.

ADA OLSON: Which girl?

KAYLA JOHNSON: Indy Cunningham.

ADA OLSON: And did you ever tell any of them about the way you threatened Mrs. Finch—Jolene, Ana, Indy?

KAYLA JOHNSON: No. I left and never looked back. I couldn't let myself think about them. I loved them too much, and I'd learned that lesson before I even came to The Palace.

ADA OLSON: What lesson?

KAYLA JOHNSON: That love destroys you.

Chapter Fourteen

ANA

Before—Eight Months at The Palace

In the back of the van, the wiry guy tossed Ana a beer, then dropped back into the beanbag next to her.

"What's your name?" he asked.

"Ana," she answered, popping the tab on her beer. She took a sip, swallowing a gag because it was warm and bitter and also because she couldn't find the nerve to look at him.

He was tall and skinny, his fingers digging into her arm when he'd pulled her down to sit, bone on bone. Who was this guy, and where was he from? He smelled like sweat, and now cheap beer, and this was not at all what Jolene and Kayla had described. Butterflies (Jolene), heat (Kayla)—either way, Ana was supposed to *want* things now. Like him moving closer, leaning into her, turning her face toward his, lining up for a kiss.

And how many times had she imagined her first kiss?

Back home, before she left for Echo, it was with a hockey player whose name she never knew. The way he moved on the ice—with an even pace and steady gaze. Like he knew what he was doing.

She had pictured that face gazing at *her*. Strong hands around her cheeks, not one moment of doubt or hesitation as he leaned closer, and then his lips were on hers. Sheer, utter confidence, like *don't worry, I've got you, and this kiss is going to shake the earth.*

Earthshaking. That's how Indy had described her first kiss with a boy back home, a pairs skater named Brian, behind the rink. She'd been thirteen as well.

This wiry boy with his bony hands and smelly concert T-shirt, and the warm beer . . . no. This wouldn't even cause a tremor.

The decision made, she pictured her next move. Getting up and walking toward the back door. Then what? He'd probably grab her arm again, ask where she was going, and she could say she had to check on Indy, who was drunk and upset.

She took three more sips of beer, bigger ones, nearly finishing the can. Wiry did the same, leaning back against the wall of the van, closing his eyes like "Stairway to Heaven" was reaching his soul.

Back to the exit plan.

He'd let her go, maybe offer to help find Indy.

Or, and now this thought barreled in, the beer reaching her head. What if he didn't let her go? What if he grabbed her arm again, bone on bone, and pulled her back onto the rug?

Excitement gave way to fear as the beer impaired her judgment.

"Are you okay?" Wiry asked, his eyes open and trying to look sexy. Or maybe he was stoned.

And oh my God, what *would* happen next in the exit strategy—if he didn't let her go?

She would fight as hard as she could—scream, yell, pound on the sides of the van until someone heard it and rescued her. And then, the doors would open, and Jolene would be there and Kayla would be there, and Jean Jacket and Sporty too, and Wiry would be like, *What the fuck? We were just talking,* and she would look like a complete freaking idiot. Because—that was actually what had been happening. They'd just been drinking beer and talking.

It was the fear of not knowing. That was all this was. She should be used to it by now, having not known one single thing, the day she arrived at The Palace and Avery Hall, about the things that really mattered. Like this.

And it felt so ironic that fear was now creeping into this part of her life—*her first kiss* of all things—that she laughed out loud, and let her head fall against the side of the van.

Wiry got them more beer, and when he placed it in her hand, his bony finger lingered on hers. "You're pretty," he said.

"Thanks," she replied, feeling her cheeks blush.

She drank the beer and laughed again, this time thinking about Dawn and her dream, and *fight the fear*, and Dr. Fear's lessons, and wasn't she doing that now? With a little help from the second beer, chasing away the flight response?

Still, he hadn't leaned in for a kiss, so after the beer, and after this song, she would implement the plan to leave and find Indy. That would be long enough to have been here with him, alone. No one would think less of her.

But "Stairway to Heaven" was a freaking long song, so she chugged beer number two, her mind already at the door, then outside, and then in the car with the Orphans, heading back to Avery Hall, where they would be dying to know what happened, and she would tell them that he smelled bad, and no way was she kissing him. Jolene would bump her shoulder and Kayla would shake her head and Indy would laugh.

Suddenly she felt his bony fingers running through her hair, spreading like a claw around the back of her head, pulling it forward, twisting it to the right, toward his thin, bony face and open mouth. Which was now on hers.

Wait! she thought. But he was too fast, and she was too stunned to say it, as he thrust his tongue into her mouth. Saliva, hot breath, strange, guttural sounds, *mmmm* and *yeaahhhh* and the beer swimming in her head, overriding the fear as his hands reached inside her shirt, his mouth moving to her neck, then his teeth, and . . . wait! Was he *biting* her?

Now she wondered if every kiss she'd ever heard about had been a lie. Was this what it really was? Tongues, saliva, beer, biting. And what *now*? Then a voice in her head said: *Just let it happen. Learn.* And anyway, it was over now, the first kiss. Like a fall on a jump. You had to get through shit like this to get past it, to the other side. And what would she give to not be so ignorant of so many things?

The kiss and the biting didn't stop until the song ended, finally, and a new song began to play. Was that *Meat Loaf*? Kayla would hate this so much.

It was enough, she thought.

"I think I need to find my friend."

Wiry didn't answer. He put his empty beer can down with one hand and reached inside her shirt with the other, searching for things that were barely there, then moving down. When he reached for the button of her jeans, she stopped observing the situation so passively.

Because she'd been an Orphan for nine months, with girls who weren't ignorant. Girls who knew things and who talked about those things, constantly. About hand jobs and blow jobs and doggy style and reverse cowgirl. Jolene had demonstrated with a pretend man she made with two pillows, and Kayla rolled her eyes but then couldn't help but laugh because watching Jolene *fuck a pillow* had them all rolling on the floor in hysterics.

And, even though this knowledge was like someone telling you about the time they climbed Mount Everest—a story that leaves you totally ill equipped and unprepared to climb even a small boulder—she was able to weigh the likely outcomes and consequences of where this was going.

A new plan formed in her mind—it involved needing to pee, from all the beer, because who would want to put his hands in her jeans under those circumstances? And in her mind she was getting ready to push him away and tell him this. But in these last few moments while she'd been assessing and reflecting and making her plans of escape, she must have been frozen, still, because Wiry stopped biting her neck and reaching into her open jeans.

"Are you okay?" he asked. And she realized that he thought she'd passed out and that had made him stop.

Without her having to run for the door or make excuses about Indy or peeing. He'd just . . . stopped.

So she stayed still and quiet. An opossum playing dead. And Wiry shook her by the shoulders.

"Ana?"

And then. "What the fuck." *Annoyed.*

And then. "Oh shit." *Scared.*

And then the bony fingers slid out of her jeans, and Wiry moved away, off the beanbag. She heard metal on metal again, the back door opening.

Moments later, more voices came, so she sat up and hung her head in her hands like she was feeling sick. But she wasn't. Not at all. Still, this plan had fallen into her lap, and she was committed now, like she'd just taken off for a jump. In the air, turning, turning.

Before she knew it, Jolene and Jean Jacket were there, in the back of the van.

"What did you do to her?" Jolene yelled, with Jean Jacket yelling too. "Dude, what the fuck?"

"Nothing!" Wiry answered. "We were just making out . . ."

Jolene sat down on the beanbag where Wiry had been. One hand was on Ana's back. The other picked up the second empty beer.

"You gave her beer?"

"Yeah, man," Wiry said. "Why not?"

"Asshole!" Jolene said. "Because she's only thirteen!" Even though she'd offered Ana plenty of beer since the first week she arrived.

Collective gasps and *oh shit*s from Jean Jacket and Wiry, and then Jolene grabbed her arm and helped her up.

"Girl, what did you do?" Her voice was lighter when she looked in Ana's eyes and saw that she wasn't dead and looked at her clothes and saw that they were intact. "Let's get you out of here."

When Ana was safely returned to the car, she in the back and Jolene in the front, Indy appeared from the other side of the gray pickup. She'd managed to ditch Wavy Hair, who climbed into the black van. It started up and peeled away *like a bat out of hell*, Ana thought—the Meat Loaf song still playing in her ears.

Indy got in beside her. "What happened?"

Jolene watched the van disappear through the maze of parked cars, leaving tracks in the weeds.

"They gave her beer, and she passed out!"

Indy moved closer until her hands could reach Ana's face. With two soft palms on her cheeks, she turned it square to her own and studied Ana for damage. Then one hand slid down to her neck.

"Oh my God!"

"What?"

Jolene turned around and saw what Indy was seeing. "That little weenie."

"What?" Ana asked again.

"Tell her," Indy said to Jolene.

"You tell her," Jolene answered.

"Tell me what!" Ana demanded, now touching her own neck. Feeling a spot that was tender. Then another and another. Remembering his teeth and his tongue. His entire mouth sucking on her skin.

"He gave you hickeys," Jolene said, stifling a laugh.

"Like, huge hickeys," Indy confirmed, touching Ana's neck. Running her fingers over each one. Both girls stifled laughter, but just barely.

Ana sat up so she could see herself in the rearview mirror. "It's not funny!"

Indy wrapped her arm around Ana's waist and pulled her back into the seat.

"Sorry," Jolene said. "We're just relieved that you're okay. Jesus—how many beers did you drink?"

Ana leaned her entire body into Indy, who stroked her hair.

"I don't remember," she lied. "When will they go away?"

Jolene told her it could be a few days. Indy said her friend back home once had a hickey for over a week.

"Toothpaste will suck the blood out," Jolene said.

"That doesn't work," Indy said. And then they argued about it, but neither one had ever had a hickey, so there they all were, in another Mount Everest situation.

"We'll figure it out," Jolene promised.

"Yeah," Indy said. "It'll be fine."

And then there was Hugo, the boy from Spain who knew about some stuff that would heal Indy's bruise, walking toward them. All the boys from Avery Hall had come in a separate car.

"Hey," he said. "We're heading back. This place is lame."

Jolene turned to face him. "Same. Let's get out of here." She put the keys in the ignition, then stopped, suddenly.

"Wait—where's Kayla?" Jolene asked, looking back at Ana and Indy.

"I haven't seen her since she left with that guy—they went into the woods," Indy said.

"The short one," Ana said, remembering nothing more about him.

Jolene turned back to the front of the car and the tree line about four car rows away. "You two stay here," she said. And then she hopped out and grabbed Hugo, and the two of them marched toward the woods where Kayla and Sporty had disappeared.

Only Sporty had been in the van when it drove away. He was the one driving.

Ana and Indy sat for a few minutes, contemplating everything. A silent, subconscious recalibration taking place inside their brains and their bodies.

"What else happened?" Indy asked Ana, her eyes looking out to the woods.

And Ana told her the truth. About how she'd just pretended to pass out after she realized he thought she already had because the beer made her dizzy, and because she had somehow detached from the whole scene by making plans to escape.

Indy shook her head. "That's fucking pathetic."

Then she kissed Ana on the cheek and laughed.

Ana laughed with her, but with the laughter came a release of a million other things that had been trapped inside. Indy's fall at the show, the bruise on her hip, the marks on her own neck, and the feel of Wiry's hands up her shirt and down her pants, his tongue in her mouth when she didn't want it there, and how she could still feel all of those things like they were still happening. Maybe more so now that she was safe, here with Indy.

And then her face flushed and her eyes welled with tears, even though she was laughing so hard her stomach hurt and she actually did have to pee.

"Indy," she started to say, thinking she needed to tell her how scared she was in that van, but how the fear had disappeared. How a switch was flipped inside her, a reckless acceptance of what was happening. Maybe even wanting it to happen so she wouldn't have to fear it ever again, and how stupid was that?

But before she could begin, they saw Hugo running out of the tree line and across the weeds, weaving through the parked cars. He reached them breathless and didn't speak as he got in the front seat of Jolene's car. The keys were in the ignition, and he started the engine.

"What happened?" Indy asked.

Hugo drove through the open spaces between the cars until they got right up to the first row of evergreens.

"Stay here," he said, and they did. They stayed right there, this time frozen with a new kind of fear.

Both girls leaned forward, staring at the trees where Hugo had disappeared—until they saw them. Three figures emerging from the woods. Hugo on the left. Jolene on the right. And in between them, draped in their arms, was Kayla's listless body.

Chapter Fifteen

ANA

Now

I'm stunned when Shannon tells me about Kayla. How she attacked her mother, threatening her with the heel of her blade—the same way Emile was killed. We heard rumors about Kayla mouthing off to them, but that wasn't unusual. She never elaborated, and we didn't ask. We didn't go near any topic related to the night in the field. And then she was gone.

I tell Artis I need to see Kayla and I need to go alone. We've planned to meet with Dawn after speaking with Shannon at Avery Hall, but this feels more urgent. I don't tell him why—how Shannon's story has struck a nerve.

When that girl in the video, Tammy Theisen, told Grace to *ask Emile—he knows the truth*—we both assumed it was the truth about taking Dawn's skaters to California, breaking up the program and not bringing Grace with him. Grace was devoted to Dawn. She would never leave, from what Jolene told me.

Maybe this angered her because of what it would do to The Palace. Or, maybe, we didn't know the nature of her relationship with Emile. That thought has been with me from the start. That Grace and Emile were in a sexual relationship. But Shannon said he was paternal with her, like a father. And he was so much older than when we were here, when he was just starting as a coach. He'd been a skater right up to the year before we arrived. One of us.

Still, there is another possibility—one Artis wouldn't know about. The other things Emile knew. Things from the past.

I have to see Kayla, one of the four Orphans who shared this story.

It's just past noon. The morning is gone, and the storm has fully arrived. Half an inch of snow covers Artis's car when we leave Avery Hall.

"Let me drive you," Artis offers, as he turns on the wipers and waits for the windows to clear. "This is just the start of it."

"I'll be fine," I insist. "I'll take Jolene's car. You should see Dawn—and Westin—about Emile's plans to move the skaters. Find out what they knew and when."

"I don't see how Kayla can help," Artis says. "What could she possibly know about Grace and Emile?"

"You were there," I remind him. "Shannon brought up that story about Kayla and her mother for a reason. And the fact that Kayla lives an hour away."

Artis steadies his face and says what I've just come to suspect is in his mind.

"Do you think it's a possibility? That Kayla killed Emile?"

"No," I say, shutting this down. "That would mean she framed Grace. Put Emile's blood on her skates."

"Exactly," Artis says. "So we need to stay focused on the here and now. This new information is clutch, Ana. You know that. There must be a dozen skaters who are pissed off about Emile leaving and not taking them along. Not to mention their crazy mothers. The cops have a lot more to investigate before they can charge Grace."

I don't know how to explain it—my need to see Kayla—without telling him about the story, and the connection to Indy. So I don't try. Artis—reluctantly—drops me back at the condo, where I tell Jolene that I need her car, that I'm going to see Kayla. At first, like Artis, she doesn't understand. But then she bites her lip and nods. "She knows what's happening. I'll tell her you're coming."

This stops me in my tracks.

"You've been in touch with Kayla?"

Jolene nods. "Yes. Soon after I left here, I found her. We've kept up over the years."

I don't know why this shakes me, but it does. In my version of the story, each of us left and never wanted to think about this place again. And now Jolene and Kayla are still friends.

Jolene gives me the keys, and I walk away.

Twenty minutes later, I'm halfway to Pueblo. Headed south on the highway into the storm. A gust of wind smacks the car like it did earlier at the field, pushing it to the right, and I wonder what the hell I'm doing. I clench my hands around the wheel and keep it from moving onto the shoulder. The road's been plowed once but is again covered with snow.

I think through the arguments for tomorrow—the ones I would make if I had no connection to the case.

They start with Dawn and Dr. Westin. The two people who had the most to lose from Emile leaving. I would also raise the possibility of other skaters and parents psychotically invested in their children's skating careers.

But, then, I would point to the past.

To us—the Orphans.

I clutch the wheel, my eyes glued to the tracks on the road made by the last vehicle to pass along the highway, and I think about the way he was killed. The four strikes to his head with the heel of a blade.

Then I see Indy bouncing around the room, telling a story about a blade, about me, and Dawn.

I picture Kayla marching into the stands with her fist inside a skate, threatening Mrs. Finch.

The method of his killing—the image lived inside us. And we all had motive—each and every one of us.

I think about the way we were trained here. The push and pull, the desperate attachments Dawn created. And then Westin and the sessions in the office next to Dawn's. He frames it now like it was nothing more than cognitive behavioral therapy, learning to overcome our fears. Our instincts. Eliminate our innate response to situations that screamed out for retreat, caution.

We were trained to override it—the fear of falling—with a greater fear: of Dawn and what she might do if we didn't succeed.

"Does that make you sad?"

"Does your sadness make you angry?"

"Feel the rage."

"Fight the fear."

And what did that do to us? What did it do to Grace?

I see her face in that video. The still shot at the end, right after she attacked that girl over whatever it was she first said, the words not captured by the other girl's phone. And then the words Shannon heard when it was over—about Emile knowing the truth. Tammy would be following Emile to California. They were undermining Dawn and The Palace. That much we know. But that look on her face—it doesn't fit with the narrative we've been building around this altercation.

It's a face I recognize from Indy Cunningham but also from my clients accused of violence. *Guilty* of violence. And I think about what I've learned since leaving this place, both in my life's work and in my own recovery. What I know about fear and what happens when it's caged inside us. How it can turn to rage, all on its own. That's what I saw on the face of the girl in that video. Grace. Jolene's daughter.

This is the argument—the training, the mindfuck. I know it well, and I can sell it if I have to. If the evidence keeps pointing to Grace and only Grace.

I follow the GPS to the exit off the highway. I'm still north of Pueblo, and it feels like I'm driving toward nothing. Into empty space. Finally, I get to a mailbox and a narrow road that leads to a small rustic house at the end of a clearing. On either side are structures that look like chicken coops or barns for small animals.

Through the gusts of snow, I see a pickup truck in the driveway, and I park beside it, turn off the engine. Kayla is there, already at the door.

The woman I see is both different and familiar, and it elicits confusion as I walk toward her. Long brown hair that was once short and jet black. Soft, bare skin and gentle eyes. She smiles as she steps aside, letting me in from the storm. The wind blows snow into the small foyer and she quickly closes the door behind us to keep it out.

"My God," she says. "I can't believe it's you." And then she pulls me into her arms with strength that belies her tiny frame.

When she backs away, there are tears in her eyes. But all I can do is study her, head to toe, as I shake off the disorientation.

"How long has it been?" she asks. And I have to think for a moment before arriving at the number. It's been sixteen years since I last saw Kayla. She left a year into my stay at The Palace and Avery Hall. Her journey cut short by that night in the field and the betrayals that followed.

She takes my coat and hangs it on a hook while I stomp the snow from my boots. I follow her down a narrow hallway into a kitchen that faces the back of the property. Through the window I can see vast, open space all the way to the base of the mountain.

She's made a pot of coffee, and she pours cups for both of us.

"When Jo called to tell me you were coming, and *why* you were coming, I couldn't believe it—any of it," she says. "I heard things on the news, but I had no idea they even had a suspect, let alone Grace Montgomery. Did you know Jo had sent her daughter there? To The Palace?"

"No," I tell her. "I had no idea."

There's a small rectangular table against the far wall, and I sit in one of the chairs across from my old friend. I try to be here in this room and in this moment, but my mind has traveled back in time. Stunned by the power of the past.

When Kayla left, I was certain she would be destroyed. I realize that, just now, as I look at the grown woman before me. That's what's thrown me. This expectation I've formed.

But here she is, Kayla—not destroyed, but with kindness in her eyes and a home she's created. An entire life she's built after leaving Echo.

She lifts her coffee cup to her mouth. Her hands are delicate. Her movements, gentle. Her eyes stay glued to mine.

"So you came here to help her daughter?" she asks, hanging her head and giving it a slight shake. A mannerism I don't remember, another piece out of place.

"Yes," I answer. "This is what I do now." I explain that I'm a lawyer who specializes in juvenile criminal defense. And how Grace's lawyer, Artis Frauhn, was in my eighth-grade science class and found me on Facebook years ago when we both went to law school. Now he helps skaters get out of scrapes with the law, among other things.

"I don't remember you ever speaking of him," Kayla says. "But there's a lot about that time that I've wanted to forget."

She looks at me with round brown eyes that are so different without the makeup she once used to hide them.

"I know," I tell her. "It was the same for me. I left two years after you did, and I never looked back."

"Well," she says with a shrug. "In some ways, it saved me. The family who took me in became my parents." Kayla inhales deeply and straightens her back. "They still live in town—the family they cobbled together—me, two of their own children, another foster kid. My mother is a therapist, and she knew what kind of help I needed. It saved my life—I'm a counselor now. At the high school."

"I'm so happy you found your way out of there."

"Yeah," she whispers. Then I see her thoughts shift. "I heard about what happened with Indy. Were you still there at the time?"

"I was," I say. "And for another year after that."

"Oh." I've surprised her. "I had no idea. You had so much promise. So did Indy. The two of you." Now she smiles, remembering something. *"IndyAna."*

My hands reach down and grip my thighs, digging in until it hurts.

"I've felt so much guilt over that night in the field—bringing you with us. You had no business being there."

"None of us should have been there," I tell her. "But you couldn't have kept me away. You and Jolene and Indy—you were all I had."

Kayla nods sadly. "You also had Dawn, though, didn't you?"

I feel a jolt inside me. What does she mean by this? I wonder if she knows about the dinners, how Dawn would meet with me at her house to go over the programs. Maybe it wasn't such a secret after all.

"That's part of the reason I came to see you," I say. "In the middle of this crazy storm and with not much time before they have to decide whether to charge Grace with Emile's murder. Did Jolene tell you about the evidence they have?"

"Yes," she says. "It's so strange. She said Grace would have had to kill Emile in the field, then clean her skates, put them back in her locker, and get home to Avery as if nothing happened."

"Right," I agree. "Not many girls could do something like that."

"And motive?" she asks. "Why would this girl want to kill him?"

I tell her about Shannon, and what she revealed about Emile's plan to leave Dawn, pulling out some of her best skaters.

"Grace wasn't one of them, apparently."

Kayla echoes the same doubts I have about this as a motive. So then I tell her about the video and pull it up on my phone. As it plays, I watch her expression change as she sees the transformation on Grace's face.

"Holy shit—now I get it, why she's a suspect."

"Right," I tell her. "And if they show this to a jury, it'll be hard to get them off the judgments they'll make about her."

Kayla hands back the phone and places her palms on the table. She pauses for a moment. And when she looks away, I fix my eyes on her like this might anchor me in the present.

"Why, though, are you here?" Kayla asks. "Like you said—in the middle of a storm and with so little time?"

I open my mouth to speak, then realize I don't have an answer. Not one I want to say out loud.

"No one else understands that place," I tell her. "The way we were on our own. The things that happened to us. And Dawn . . ."

Kayla looks confused. "Okay . . ."

"But Jolene doesn't remember it the same way," I continue. "She saw it as a great opportunity for Grace. To train at The Palace."

Kayla boards her shoulders. "We all came to it differently," she says. "I never expected to make the Olympics. Or even get close. I was just grateful to have a place to be where I could skate. And then, really, to be away from home."

"And it didn't bother you the way Dawn treated us? And the mothers in the stands? It didn't make you angry?"

"It was a long time ago, Ana. Shit happens to people," she says.

I think about Kayla and Jolene, friends all these years. And how I've seen this place as a black hole I could never go near again.

Kayla searches for something to give me. "It was totally fucked up," she says. "That fucking doctor. And Dawn, trying to make us afraid of her. I wish I'd killed her that day."

Now I look at her curiously. "What day?"

"The day—after what we tried to do to her."

"Kay—I have no idea what you're talking about."

"We never told you?" she asks.

"Told me what?"

She pauses, searching for memories.

"Jesus—we never told you."

"What?" I ask again, my mind scanning images from those first few days after I arrived. There was so much to learn, but I always assumed it was all there. Laid out for me. Like a textbook I just needed to read.

"Fuuuuuck," she says, shaking her head. "Something happened, Ana. Before we ever knew you. Do you remember how angry I always was?"

I nod. "I thought it was because of your childhood—in New York."

She laughs in one short burst. "Well, that did cut some rough edges. My grandmother—no wonder my mother ended up in jail. Never got her shit together. But it wasn't that."

I see her that night in the field. And then the aftermath. The anger that followed. But she's right—it was there from the day I arrived.

"What then?" I ask. "What happened before I got there?"

She draws a long breath. Then tells me a part of the story I never knew.

Chapter Sixteen

Excerpt from Testimony of Hugo Aguilar

ADA OLSON: Mr. Aguilar—you were a skater at Avery Hall on and off during the time Ana Robbins was there.

HUGO AGUILAR: Yes.

ADA OLSON: Do you know why they were called Orphans?

HUGO AGUILAR: Well, no one else that young came for that long without a parent or a coach from their other rink. So I guess they were alone. Like orphans. And that was how they acted—like they couldn't trust anyone for anything.

ADA OLSON: Is that how they felt that night in the field? And what happened after . . .

HUGO AGUILAR: I guess so. We tried to help. We tried to do what we thought was best for them.

ADA OLSON: And who is "we," Mr. Aguilar?

HUGO AGUILAR: Me and Emile.

ADA OLSON: Emile Dresiér?

HUGO AGUILAR: Yeah.

ADA OLSON: And given everything that followed, leading right up to this moment, do you still believe that you did what was best for them?

HUGO AGUILAR: Hey, we were young too.

ADA OLSON: You were twenty-one. Mr. Dresiér was twenty-three. And Mr. Dresiér was a coach. He had a lot to lose. Did you ever think about that?

HUGO AGUILAR: No. I didn't.

ADA OLSON: You just trusted him? Or maybe you let him take over so you wouldn't have to take responsibility?

HUGO AGUILAR: Like I said—I was young.

Chapter Seventeen

ANA

Before—Eight Months at The Palace

"Help us!" Jolene yelled. She and Hugo carried Kayla out of the woods, one holding each arm. Kayla's legs were dragging and her head was hanging, eyes closed, swinging from side to side with each step.

Ana felt a rush of panic that paralyzed her body. Until Indy gave her a shove.

"Come on!" she said, her voice trembling.

They jumped out to help Jolene and Hugo get Kayla inside, laying her on the back seat.

"Kayla?" Ana's voice barely rose above a whisper.

She climbed back in and cradled Kayla's head in her lap. Indy got in from the other side and slipped her legs beneath Kayla's like a pillow.

Hugo and Jolene got into the front, with Hugo driving.

"Go!" Jolene screamed before she'd even closed her door.

Hugo stepped on the gas, maneuvering out of the field between the rows of parked cars, bonfires, clusters of kids. Ana and Indy stared at Kayla, taking in the damage. The swollen eye, already black and blue. Bleeding lip. Her shirt torn open, exposing a red bra, shiny like a candied apple.

Jolene turned to face them, her eyes growing wide as the car jerked forward, then stopped.

"What should we do?" Indy cried out. She and Ana looked to Jolene for answers, but Jolene didn't have any. None of them did. They were helpless. The four Orphans.

Finally, they reached the access road. Hugo turned left, away from the base of the mountain, and stepped on the gas.

"What are you doing?" Jolene snapped.

"I'm taking her to the hospital!"

Ana caught Indy's eye. Then they both stared at Jolene.

"No—we can't go there," she said.

"What are you talking about?" Hugo pulled to the shoulder and stopped the car. "Look at her! She's unconscious!"

Ana was crying. *Please know what to do. Please!* Jolene followed Hugo's gaze to the back seat, where Kayla lay still, draped over Ana and Indy, Ana stroking her hair and Indy holding her hands.

And then Jolene told him what they were all thinking. About how they were kids, and they shouldn't have been in the field. Shouldn't have been drinking. Shouldn't have been hooking up with strange guys in a black van.

That the bleacher bees, the teachers, even Edie—their dorm mother—were just waiting for a reason to send Kayla home. The girl with the piercings and dark eyeliner, the Orphan who smelled of cigarettes and skated so recklessly, like she was trying to hurt herself. Like she wanted to feel the pain of falling.

And the hospital was just the kind of place where things could go very wrong for a girl like her.

"She'll get kicked out of the program," Jolene said.

Hugo stared at her. "That's what you're thinking about? The program?"

"Kayla has nothing else," Jolene started to say. "She's got no home to go back to."

Hugo didn't understand.

But then a deep groan silenced them. Kayla was waking up.

"Kay! Kay!" Jolene said. And she leaned her body all the way over the seat to touch Kayla's arm.

"I'm taking you to the hospital, okay?" Hugo said, in spite of what Jolene had just told him.

"No!" She tried to open her eyes, but one was swollen shut and the other was crusted over with eyeliner and mascara. Still, she shook her head, back and forth. "No!"

Jolene yelled at Hugo. "I told you! No hospitals! No Dawn! No Edie! She can't get kicked out of the program."

Hugo slammed his palms against the steering wheel. "This is fucked," he said. He looked back to Kayla, bruised and bleeding, her shirt torn open.

"Here," he said in a soft voice. He took off his T-shirt and passed it back to Indy, who laid it across Kayla. Then he started to drive the other way—up the mountain. And they all sighed with relief thinking they were headed home to Avery Hall.

The access road was dark, the entire outside world dead quiet, even as the wind rushed past Ana's ears. Ana used the corner of Hugo's shirt to wipe the makeup from Kayla's eye, the black gooey paste making streaks on the white cotton. When it was clear, Kayla looked up at them—Ana and Indy.

Ana didn't know what she was seeing, but it wasn't her friend in there. Not even when she was pissed at Jolene and giving her the silent treatment, or at the bleacher bees, flipping them off the second she cleared the entry to the snack bar, or even Dawn when she left a lesson and called her a c-u-n-t in the locker room.

They drove farther into the silence, until they passed The Palace, and then the dorm.

"You missed it!" Jolene said. But Hugo kept driving, up the mountain, across the switchback.

"Where are we going?" Kayla asked.

"Shhh, it's okay," Ana said. She looked at Indy, who knew she didn't mean it.

They locked eyes for a moment longer. *Why are we going up the mountain?* The question sat between them. Surely they couldn't be going to Dawn's house. But then there it was, up ahead. The fifth house along the access road.

Eyes wide, Ana tried to smile as she wiped more of the tears and dirt from Kayla's face. Why were they coming here? It felt like a trap. Kayla hated Dawn. This would be worse than the hospital.

"Hugo!" Jolene grabbed the steering wheel.

"Stop it!" Hugo yelled, pushing her away. "I know what I'm doing." And he continued down her driveway to the fork, where he turned right onto the dirt road. The one that led to the guest cottage where Coach Emile lived.

It was hidden from the access road and also from the main house. Surrounded by evergreens and woods, it had no outside lights. Like it didn't want to be found.

Kayla felt the car slow down and lifted her head.

"No!" she shouted again.

But Hugo pulled to a stop and turned off the ignition.

"Let me talk to him first." He reached over and placed his hand on the side of her face. "Just trust me, okay? He's my friend."

Jolene glanced back at Kayla, then at Hugo.

"Give me the keys," she said. "If you're not out in five minutes, we're leaving."

Which he did, with a disappointed sigh, like he was trying to take care of them and why wouldn't she believe him? He would talk to Emile and Emile would just—what? Help them with no questions asked, and not tell Dawn or anyone at The Palace?

They would give him five minutes because that wasn't enough time for anything bad to happen, even if Emile called the police or Dawn—they could still drive away and get Kayla somewhere safe, miles and miles from here.

Hugo had sacrificed his shirt to cover up Kayla's wounded body, but so what? Ana thought. That didn't mean they could trust him.

Hugo walked down the path to the entrance of the guest cottage, and Jolene pulled out her phone and checked the time.

"Five minutes," she said, like she was asking for their approval. "That's it."

Kayla nodded and said, "Okay." Ana and Indy did the same.

And when the seconds turned to minutes, Kayla started to sit up, the one eye open and now looking at her red bra. She reached for the sides of her torn shirt and pulled them together, her knuckles scraped and blackened with sap from a pine tree, and Ana sat closer so she could feel her body on one side and Indy's on the other. The protector now in need of protecting.

"Just go back to Avery," Kayla said, giving up on Hugo, but then her eyes shifted to the figure coming down the path, the distinct limp of their coach, which they all knew in an instant.

With Hugo following right behind.

Coach Emile stopped at the side of the car and looked at Kayla.

"Jesus," he said, his face steeped in concern. "You poor thing. Come on. Come inside."

He opened the door, and Indy got out, making room for him to reach in and take Kayla into his arms. Even with his damaged knee, he carried her like a small child all the way up the stone path and inside the house. Hugo and Jolene slipped ahead to open the front door, leaving Indy and Ana to follow behind.

This vision of Kayla in Coach Emile's arms, broken and helpless, stirred something rebellious inside Ana. They didn't need him. They didn't need anyone. They could help Kayla all on their own.

But then came a burst of something else. A feeling so primal it made her vision blur: that she should run to Dawn, who was right down the driveway. Run there, right now, and fall inside her blue puffer coat and beg for help, plead for her to make all of this stop.

"Ana . . ." Indy's voice pulled her back. "What if he tells?"

Ana shook her head. She had no idea what they would do then. Maybe they would all get kicked out. Maybe this was the end for all of them. Their punishment for going to the field. Mio's warning coming back to her now. *"Nothing good is happening there."*

But it was too late to heed her warning.

They went inside to a room with a couch against the wall. A round table with two chairs in front of a refrigerator that buzzed, and a wood cabinet with a stove on top.

But it was the bed that Ana's eyes returned to, a plaid duvet twisted up with white sheets, two pillows piled on top of each other. Unmade. Emile, their coach. A grown man. And why did this send a shiver through her body—being this close to the bed where Coach Emile slept, where he had just been sleeping?

He carried Kayla to it and laid her down on the pillows.

"Get me a towel from the bathroom," he said to Jolene, who followed where he was pointing. She came back with the towel, and Hugo brought a glass of water from the sink while Indy and Ana stood side by side, staring at their friend in their coach's bed.

As if this wasn't completely messed up.

Emile took the towel and began to clean her. Wiping away the blood from her mouth and the rest of the makeup from the one eye. Jolene brought ice from the freezer, and Emile gently placed it over the other eye. He drew a bath so she could clean the rest of her. Then he gave her a button-down flannel and a pair of gym shorts to wear.

He took her clothes, said she didn't need to see them again. He would get rid of them for her.

When they were all ready to leave, Hugo said to Emile, as if the girls weren't even there, as if it was up to the two of them to decide, "Should we call the police?"

And even though Kayla reacted, saying *"No—no way,"* Emile said something that made everything clearer.

"No—they could trace the call back here, to Dawn's house. And besides, think about it."

"But she has to report it, right?" Hugo asked.

"She doesn't have to do anything," Emile said. "If she reports it, and no one believes her—then what? Her life will be over." His voice was infused with certainty. Which was exactly what they all needed. Even Hugo.

So that was that.

Hugo stayed at Emile's to "have a drink" he said, like this had been so difficult for him. That left the Orphans to drive back alone. Kayla smoked a cigarette and finished the Jack Daniel's, the wind blowing her hair across her face. She didn't speak until they'd sneaked through the open window at Avery Hall. Back to being four girls afraid of getting in trouble for breaking curfew. Afraid to trust anyone else in their lives. And this became clearer as they huddled in their room, Kayla changed into pajamas and sitting on her bed, clutching a pillow to her chest, Ana and Indy flanking her on either side.

Jolene stood at the foot of the bed, worry on her face.

"Are you sure you don't want to go to the police?" she asked.

"I remember part of the license plate," Indy said.

But Kayla shut it down. "It wasn't the guy from the van," she said.

Their eyes all widened at the same time, their heads turning to face their friend even though it was painful to look at her while she told the story.

"That guy—the short one—after we were in the woods, he saw some friends smoking a joint through the trees. He asked if I wanted to come, but I said I'd wait. And when he'd been gone for a while, I figured he'd decided to hang out with them, so I headed back to the car."

Kayla continued with her story, each word a twist, another turn inside Ana's head.

"I don't know where he came from," she said, her face devoid of expression. "I felt a hand grab my wrist. He spun me around, and then he punched me on the side of my head. I don't know how many times. It was so fast. He hit me so hard. Then I was on the ground and he was over me and then I saw his hand raised and that's all I remember before I was in the car."

Jolene cleared her throat, the words catching. "Did he . . . could you tell?"

And then Ana felt another twist, but she held a steady gaze, everything inside, not outside. Expressionless. Motionless. Following Kayla's lead.

Kayla closed her eyes. "When I was in the bath, at Emile's house . . . I think so, but I don't remember it happening."

Jolene understood more than they did. She was the only one of them who'd been with a boy. "You would know," she said.

Kayla hung her head and closed her eyes. "Then, yes," she said, the words taking on shape and meaning inside her. Turning her face, red and contorted, shoulders rising and elbows pinching her sides like she was trying to keep it in, and then she lifted her hand in the air and made a fist and pounded it into a pillow, again and again.

She said, finally, "I'll fucking kill him!"

Jolene swallowed Kayla in her arms until her fists unclenched and she cried, her entire face nestled into the crease between Jolene's neck and shoulder.

And what now? Ana watched the older two Orphans exchanging something unspoken, like, okay, he did that to you while you were passed out, after he punched you in the head and you fell to the ground. And we didn't go to the hospital, or the police, because Emile raised the question—who would believe you? And then what? Your life would be over, he said. And then Emile drew you a bath, told you to wash, took your clothes, the only evidence of this heinous crime.

Emile was the adult. They'd agreed to trust him. But nothing about this felt right.

So now, after she knew all the facts, whatever part of her wanted to reach out to the adult universe, with the parents who had sent them here and the bleacher bees who wanted to slit their throats, and now Dawn who couldn't have something like this touch The Palace, vanished.

This was how it would be. Some man in the woods who, Kayla told them, was not a kid, and who smelled like one of those pine-scented trees that hang from rearview mirrors, and who had a necklace of black and white beads.

And now that man would get to drive to wherever he was from. He would get away with something so horrible, and they would never tell a soul.

Because—well—who was there to tell?

Later that night, when Ana still wasn't asleep but lying in her bed, her insides churning—listening to Mio breathe with her insides perfectly still—she thought about where this had all started. Jolene's giant smile, her words saying *"there's four of them and four of us"* like somehow this meant they were destined to be together.

Everything she'd fantasized about first kisses and falling in love was buried in the pile of rubble that her world had become, along with the road map to making the Olympics one day, neither of which had accounted for boys in black vans and men who smelled of car fresheners.

And there was nothing to do but dig through it all and see what was left to save.

Chapter Eighteen

ANA

Now

My mind is reeling with the question as Kayla sits back in her chair.

"What happened before I got there?"

It doesn't seem possible that anything could have impacted her life more than the night in the field. I can still feel Indy's hand on my neck, then grabbing my arm as we watched Kayla being dragged out of the woods.

"You started to train there the winter after Indy arrived, right? After Nationals?" Kayla asks, her eyes looking to the window and the storm outside.

I nod. "Yes. The year Indy got fifth."

"I remember meeting you that first time. You were with your mother. Jo and I were in the hallway."

I feel a swell of emotions as I think back to that day. When the world was light. Not even a shadow, except the one I chose to ignore. How tired my mother had grown. The sudden urge to send me away. The scarves she once wore around her neck now tied over thinning hair.

"Indy came a few months before you—at the start of that season," Kayla says.

My heart aches as I remember the moment when I first saw her.

"She was hiding in the room, texting Bobby Stark."

Kayla turns her gaze back from the window.

"Dawn was brutal to all of us in her own way. But there was something about Indy. We all thought it was because of her mother, Patrice—that she harbored resentment over her life-altering loss when they were rivals. And I still think that was true. But Indy didn't help her cause."

I meet her eyes. Now I'm the one who's curious.

"But Indy did everything Dawn told her," I recall. "She had that bruise—from falling on the triple Axel." The bruise that took my breath away the first time I saw it. The night we went to the field.

Kayla lifts a shoulder. Tilts her head. "Yeah, well. Indy made that choice. That's how I always saw it. But it's not about that. Things happened—and not just to Indy but to all of us."

"Okay," I tell her, trying to be patient, though my mind is screaming for this piece of information, the same way it used to when I was with them. The Orphans. How I craved knowledge about everything in my new world. About them most of all. It felt imperative to my survival.

Kayla continues. "Indy arrived at the end of the summer—right before school started. Jo and I had been in our room for sixteen, seventeen months maybe."

I think back again to their stories. How Jolene had come because her parents were traveling. She called them Mr. M. and Mrs. M., like they were characters in a sitcom. They'd given her a choice—The Palace or boarding school. She came here because she still wanted to skate. And Kayla—she got a scholarship from a nonprofit organization. They sponsored underserved girls in sports.

"We knew we didn't have what it took to make it," she says. "But we loved to skate." Now a pause and a slight smile. "Do you remember that feeling? When you just loved it for what it was? Before it became about winning?"

I stare at her, wondering if I do. It's hard to love something that set your life on fire.

"I fucking loved it." Kayla smiles broadly. "The speed, and the power . . ." Now she holds her hand in front of her, making the shape of a blade.

"That one edge, carving into the ice, holding your entire body in any position you wanted—anything. It was a kind of . . ." She thinks now about how to describe it. "Freedom," she says finally.

For a brief moment, we stay there, remembering that part, before she continues.

"She was there for maybe three weeks before the tears started."

"Because she missed her coach back home—Bobby," I say, picturing Indy on her bed the day I arrived, crying into her phone.

"I think she believed she could come and try it out, then convince her mother to let her go home. But there was some reason Patrice wouldn't allow it—even after Indy fell at the ice show. That night we went to the field. The night I was assaulted."

"I remember," I tell her. I reach for her hand across the table and grab hold. She doesn't stop me but pulls away after giving my fingers a quick squeeze.

"That night—I always see it as two separate stories. The show, the fall, the bruise—that belongs to Indy. The field, the man in the woods—that belongs to me."

Kayla looks into her coffee.

"Oh God—Kay. I'm sorry." I don't know what else to say.

A moment passes, both of us reflecting on that night, how it started. Where it ended. Even though that night was not the start. Not the ending.

"Indy used to call home every day," Kayla says. "At first with tears and pleading. But when that didn't work, she started making threats to her mother. Calls and text messages. Like a little kid. How she was going to run away and they'd never find her. Or how she would single all her jumps that season, blow her chances to even make it to Nationals. And still, she got the same reply. Patrice didn't believe her. Called her bluff."

Kayla gets up from the table, pours more coffee, even though her cup is only half empty. And I can see that she, too, is strangled by these memories.

"We told her it wasn't that bad—she would land the triple Axel soon enough, and then she could go home. No big deal. On and on. None of it helped."

Indy was stubborn. I felt it the first time I saw her sitting on that bed, crying but somehow still determined. Defiant.

"It was never about Bobby," I offer now. "I've thought about her over the years, of course, and I think he became a test in a way. For her mother."

Kayla nods. "Yeah—she just kept pushing it and pushing it to see if Patrice loved *her*—or just her skating. Living out the dream she never came to realize for herself."

And then she adds, "Those mothers. They were all the same, weren't they?"

"The bleacher bees."

"Indy wouldn't let it go, and Patrice wouldn't budge," Kayla continues. "So she came up with a different plan. One that involved us. Me and Jo."

My hands are on my thighs again, digging in as Kayla describes their lives before I drove 289 miles with my sick mother, a silver trunk, and two duffel bags.

"It involved a letter to the skating association." She pauses, takes a beat. "A letter about Dawn."

Electricity runs down my arms. Somehow I can feel where this is going, this story she starts to tell, my eyes glued to her face. Lips as they move to form words, and cheeks as they rise and fall with the cadence. My entire history shifting with this new information.

The letter was anonymous, she explains. Disclosing dangerous training schedules, cruelty, and neglect at Avery Hall—Dawn Sumner had promised a safe, supervised environment, but what existed was anything but.

"We wrote how we walked or biked to the rink at five in the morning, in the dark, because there was no car service—as she'd promised—and because the roads got too icy for a bike. And how Edie was never there, always hiding in her apartment watching soap operas and reality shows, unless she was cooking food—and how that food was sometimes recycled for days. How we had no access to doctors when we got sick. And then the jumps and the falls—Dr. Westin and his Fear Training—and that was before Indy got that bruise."

I think about this, all of it true—but how ill-conceived this plan was. In my mind, Kayla and Jolene were wise. But this was anything but. Mio had warned me from the start. How they were just kids themselves.

She smiles. "We thought it was so official, you know? We organized it into paragraphs with headers all in bold, underlined. Like a legal document. We referred to ourselves as 'the Skaters.'"

Now she recites the letter as though it's sitting right there on the table.

"The Skaters are not provided adequate transportation. The Skaters are not provided adequate nutrition. The Skaters are required to meet with a psychiatrist against their will. The Skaters are trained in a dangerous manner. My God—we thought we were so smart."

"Did you send it?"

Kayla laughs like she still can't believe what they did. "Oh yeah. Straight to US Figure Skating. The USFS."

"And Dawn got ahold of it."

"Of course. Because that's how the world works. We just didn't know it yet."

My heart races as if Dawn is standing right behind me, her blue puffer coat unzipped, ready to fold me into it. To swallow me whole for even listening to this story.

"Indy thought if they investigated the program, her mother wouldn't be able to keep her there." Her tone turns to sarcasm. "Because *of course* the association would look out for us, and not Dawn and The Palace—the most important training facility in the world. And *of course* Patrice would then let Indy come home. And *of course* Dawn wouldn't figure out who wrote the letter."

They spent hours drafting it, she says. Typing it at school, sending it with no return address.

But *of course* Dawn knew exactly who'd sent it—and why, though they never got an official reply. They could tell by the sudden shift in her demeanor.

And just when I think I've got my head around this secret they never told me, she tells the rest of it.

"Dawn called me to her office on a Sunday. There was no training—just public skating sessions. So it was only me. I was anxious, you know. But I was always anxious. Always waiting for bad shit to happen. I convinced myself it was about my scholarship, or—and this is hilarious—that maybe she had news about one of the fall exhibitions—someone dropping out and me finally getting a spot. I needed to get in front of the judges. Make some headway before Regionals."

Her words swim inside me, looking for a place to settle in. Searching for the memories attached to the knowledge of these things. The ISU exhibitions. The pressure to get from Regionals to Sectionals, Sectionals to Nationals. But I've buried them so deep the words have nowhere to go. They swirl in my gut.

And then I picture Kayla in Dawn's office. On a Sunday.

"It's strange how I remember every detail about that day. What I was wearing. How I got to the rink. Even what the air smelled like with the leaves falling. Do you remember how the pine needles started to cover the roads?"

She glances at me, and I give her a nod.

"The rink was so different on Sundays," she says. And I get a quick flash because I can see it and feel it as she draws it all out.

"Dawn asked me to come at four o'clock. That's after the last public session, so it was empty. The rink, the locker rooms. The snack bar was closed, but it still smelled of stale coffee and grease from the fryer. The cleaners hadn't come yet, so there was ketchup and other shit on the floor. Soaking into those black rubber mats."

Yes. It's all right there.

"I walked around the boards by the lockers to the other side. Up the steps to that hallway, then the first door on the left."

Dawn's office. The long hallway that was dark and smelled of mildew.

"It was open, so I walked in. Dawn was always at her desk, but on that day she was standing in front of it. She told me to come closer. She told me to close the door behind me."

Kayla's voice grows unsteady, her mouth beginning to quiver. And suddenly I'm back to that night in the field, when she lay in the back seat of Jolene's car. When she cried for the first time, at least that I'd seen. How it rocked my world as much as anything else that night.

"She had that look on her face," Kayla says. "The one she gets when she has the upper hand." Now a pause and another bitter laugh.

"This may be hard to believe, Ana, but I was a lot like you back then. Dawn was the only grown-up in my life. And not just because I was at Avery Hall. But because I was an orphan in *every* sense of the word. There was a time when I longed for her approval—the same way you did."

With each piece of this story, each disclosure, the landscape of the past is ripped from the ground. Like a tornado that's pulled up all the trees and flower beds. I have no idea where it will all land.

"So she walked up to me and put her hands on my shoulders with that smile. I was still thinking about good news—or maybe just *something* good—when I felt her hands move from my shoulders toward my collarbones on either side. The same smile on her face, but her eyes growing—I don't know. Smaller? Darker? She didn't say a single word, but instead . . ."

Kayla draws her hands to her throat. "She started to close her fingers around my neck. Her thumbs pressing—here." She traces her hands over her trachea as she says the words.

"And then the other fingers wrapped around the back, here . . ."

Again, she places her hands where Dawn's were over seventeen years ago.

"I can't believe I'm saying this out loud because it's so surreal. But she started to squeeze my neck. And at first, I thought it was a joke. I think I may have even smiled and tried to laugh. Because she was smiling, and her eyes were narrow, like the way eyes get when someone's just being mischievous. But she kept squeezing and squeezing, and I lifted my hands and placed them on hers and tried to get my fingers between my skin and her skin, but there was no room and then I couldn't breathe . . ."

I sit, frozen, arms buzzing, heat building in every cell. Because I can see this, I can see Dawn, her face, her narrow eyes, as if I was right there in the room with them.

"She pushed me step by step until my back was against the wall, and I could feel my head growing dizzy, and my arms flailing against her."

Kayla pauses to draw a new breath, while my mind spins wildly. Picturing Dawn with her hands around Kayla's throat.

"Just when I thought I was going to die, and I did think that—she let go and stepped away, leaving me buckled over, coughing and holding my neck where her hands had just been."

She strokes her skin, softly, with the delicate fingers I never noticed before.

"She said—and I remember her exact words—'I am what you should fear. Don't forget that.'"

I gasp, seeing the words from her book. "That's what she wrote about," I tell her. "Creating a fear that surpassed anything we faced on the ice. Like a gun to our heads. Kay—I'm so sorry . . ." Dawn became the bigger fear. Westin taught us to channel fear to rage. To fight for her approval. To land the jumps and perform for her.

Kayla wipes her face with the backs of her hands.

"Well, I suppose it worked. She told me to leave, and I did—I ran out of there as fast as I could. I went back to Avery Hall and told Jo and Indy what happened. And they did what you would think. They hugged me and told me all the ways they would get revenge—but I told them to stop. Because where would I go if Dawn made me leave?"

Her face steadies, and she regains control. This is not the end of the story.

"Later that week I had a session with Dr. Westin. I didn't tell him what happened, but he knew. He kept asking if I wanted to talk about something. And I kept saying no, that I was fine. And then he said the strangest thing to me, which didn't make sense until hours later. Something like 'Your friends will follow where you lead them.' And how that power came with 'great responsibility.' And about Indy—how I had a friend who was 'poised to see her dreams come true, but she can't seem to get out of her own way. Can she?' He said it was important that I help her. 'It's important,' he said—and this I remember, his exact words—'that all of you are devoted to the program.'"

Jesus Christ. I think about Westin, who was just in the condo with me. His wool sweater and gray socks bunched up by his ankles. The boots by the door. His name on that book.

There's so much I want to say to her. But I can't contain the questions that take on a force inside me.

"Do you really think he knew what Dawn did to you in her office? That she put her hands around your neck? Threatened you?"

She doesn't hesitate with an answer.

"Of course he knew. And I don't think I'm the only one, though Jo swore Dawn never touched her. But she didn't care about Jo. And the thing is, I don't think she cared about me either," she says, spinning the coffee cup in circles on the table. "It was about Indy. That was who she cared about, and that was who needed to fall in line. Westin's message was pretty damned clear."

Yes, I think. Dawn was always sending messages behind her fake smile and that one crooked tooth. Indy was her prized skater. And Patrice's daughter. It was an irreconcilable conflict inside her.

"And it was received," Kayla continues. "Indy fell in line as best she could, crying to us and Bobby Stark behind Dawn's back. Begging her mother to let her come home, but never telling her the truth about Dawn. And we—me. Well . . ."

"You became reckless," I interject. The pieces land in a new place, but one that makes sense. "And Jo—she did what she always did."

Kayla lets go of the cup and leans back. "She pretended it never happened."

When I met them that first day, all of this had come and gone. I'd stepped into the aftermath.

"I told you that story to explain. So you would understand . . . if I wanted anyone dead, it would be Dawn. What happened at the field was horrible. But it's that day in Dawn's office that haunts me."

I consider this in light of my work. My experience. How abuse by someone trusted leaves a different kind of wound.

"Do I wonder what shape my life would have taken if Emile hadn't told me not to report the rape—that no one would believe me, and then my life would be over? All the fucking time." And now her face reveals the scar that hasn't fully healed, and I think there are layers upon layers of faces hiding behind this one.

"And how he took my clothes and gave me a bath? Like I was a child. He stayed in the bathroom while I washed myself."

Her body recoils as this all plays back.

"I mean—was he really looking out for me? Not knowing any better? Or was he protecting The Palace?"

I don't have an answer. Emile was only twenty-three. But trying to erase Kayla's rape wasn't the only time he changed the course of our lives.

Kayla leans forward, elbows on the table, and shakes her head. Then she gets up, and retrieves a piece of paper from a small desk in the corner next to the pantry. She slides it across the table in front of me.

"The thing is," she says as she sits back down, "about six years ago, someone sent this to me."

I look at the paper. It's a clipping from *The Denver Post*—an article about a man who was killed in the woods off Route 27—a mountain road north of Denver. A picture shows the man when he was still alive. He's wearing the necklace that Kayla told us about that night. The one with the black and white beads. It says he drove semis. That it was a robbery gone wrong. His truck was stolen.

I feel my back straighten, and the air cling to my lungs. I don't move a single muscle in my body as I stare at the article.

"It's so strange," I manage to say.

"I always thought it was Emile who sent it," she says. "I thought it was his way of, I don't know, apologizing maybe. Like he saw it and thought it would make me feel better knowing this guy was dead."

"Did it?" I ask, thinking about the text I got at the conference in Aspen, as I slide the article away from me. The emoji of a blade. It was the day Emile disappeared.

She smiles a little. "Yeah. It did actually. And I don't care if that makes me a bad person. What I do know is that I felt differently about Emile after that. It took me a while to sort it out. It took the therapist and the stability of my new family."

Kayla picks up the paper and stares at the man who raped her.

"I heard things after I left. About Indy, of course. But also about you," she says. "We all knew about your dinner parties with Dawn."

My heart stops. I thought this was the part of my story I lived alone. In secret. Even from the Orphans. When Dawn would pick me up from down the street. *Don't tell the others."*

And then the night when there were three place settings, and the light came on from the path to the guest cottage. It was after everyone had left but me. Kayla, Jolene, Indy. I was the last Orphan. I thought no one knew.

"Coach Emile is joining us for dinner."

My God, how many hours I've spent deconstructing the time I spent at the house on the mountain. The fifth light along the access road. And that one night—when Emile joined us.

And right then, as this memory flashes, Kayla looks me dead in the eye.

"I know you came here to see if I could have killed him."

And then:

"The truth is, Ana—the only person I know who might want Emile dead—is you."

Chapter Nineteen

ADA OLSON: When did you learn about Indy's injury?

DR. WESTIN: The bruise?

ADA OLSON: Yes. You were seeing her twice a week, correct? For the Fear Training?

DR. WESTIN: Ha! I always found that amusing—a term of endearment really. It was just sports conditioning. And yes, I knew about the bruise.

ADA OLSON: What did you do to help, if anything?

DR. WESTIN: I told her to get the rotation. If she could get the rotation, she could land the jump.

ADA OLSON: So you told her to keep injuring herself?

DR. WESTIN: No—that's not what I said. You don't understand how it works. Athletes fall down, and it hurts, but they get back up. It's a valuable life lesson. And with Indy, the psychology was even more complicated. I believed she was holding back on purpose. That as much as she said she wanted to go home, she didn't want Dawn to claim a victory—or her mother for that matter. It was a deep inner conflict.

ADA OLSON: You believed that she was falling on purpose? To be defiant?

DR. WESTIN: Oh yes. I think her subconscious defiance toward Dawn and her mother was holding her back from getting the height she needed.

ADA OLSON: Are you saying her falling was a form of self-harm?

DR. WESTIN: In a way, yes.

ADA OLSON: You didn't see it as Dawn purposefully hurting her?

DR. WESTIN: No.

ADA OLSON: And the other girls? What about the things Dawn did to them?

Chapter Twenty

ANA

Before—Ten Months at The Palace

Ana kept waiting, but none of the Orphans spoke about it again. That night in the field. The black van. The four boys. The man with the beaded necklace. Not even the bite marks on her neck. She'd hidden them at the rink beneath a black sleeveless turtleneck Indy loaned her, and the rest of the time by wearing her hair down.

Kayla stayed in her room until the bruise around her eye was faded enough to cover with makeup. She had a stomach bug. She had a headache. She'd twisted her ankle on the stairs.

No one checked on Kayla. Not Edie or Dawn or Emile. Not even the school when she didn't show up for the first day of junior year. She had the Orphans, but they were just teenagers, like her. To the rest of the world, she was irrelevant.

Ana watched the other Orphans for signs about how she should be now. Like nothing had happened? Or like their lives had all been set on a new course? Kayla's had shattered. Or maybe not. Maybe the pieces had glued themselves back together the way her bruises and cuts had healed.

Somehow, Jolene became bigger and brighter. Her smile, her laugh. Glitter nail polish and bright-blue eye shadow. Pink dresses and white sweaters. Nothing but talk of movies and the new bleacher bee who'd arrived from California with her daughter, who couldn't even land a double Axel.

And Indy—she became one-dimensional, like she'd gone deeper inside herself, focused only on the training. On landing the triple Axel, hoping this would mean she could finally go home to Bobby Stark. Dawn barked her orders—"*Stay on your feet! Higher! Faster!*" And Indy tried, stroking the length of the rink, crossovers at the corners, then cutting into the center, turning backward, shifting to an outside edge, then forward onto the left blade into the takeoff. And then the fall, every time flipping off the right blade and landing on her hip.

She couldn't get the rotation no matter how many times Dawn commanded her to "*fight the fear!*" Or how many sessions she had with the doctor, the one who was supposed to teach her how to override her brain in that last split second. There was no way a girl as strong and powerful as Indy, who could also spin so fast in the air, couldn't get the height she needed. It had to be in her head, he told her.

Then came the rumors about an altercation Kayla had with one of the bleacher bees, but she never said a word about it and neither did anyone else. Eight weeks after that night in the field, she was gone. A car from Pueblo parked outside Avery Hall. Edie helping carry the bags, ordering the rest of them to "*grab a duffel, a suitcase, a box.*" Kayla had been kicked out of the program and was going into foster care because her grandmother was dead and a family had been found for her about an hour south, in Pueblo.

There was a quick goodbye at the front door, where only Jolene cried and hugged her for more than a second, saying "*I love you Kay—always.*" For Ana and Indy, it was too short for tears to come, or for words to form, other than stupid things like "*I'll miss you*" and "*good luck.*" That night, Ana lay awake and stared at Mio's cat poster. *Good luck?* Seriously? Was that all she could come up with? It happened fast and without warning. The changes kept coming.

Hugo and Jolene sat together at dinner and right next to each other when they were all watching TV, and even when they weren't. They would sit and talk, so close their entire sides would be touching, from shoulders to hips, thighs to calves. Their feet would intertwine on the floor, like a pile of unsorted socks.

On Saturday nights, when there was no training the next day, Ana and Indy would look for Jolene to ask what they were doing. Cruising the strip near the downtown? Going for ice cream? A movie?

But Jolene would be gone, her red Jeep not in the parking lot, the smell of her perfume lingering in her room, where she'd gotten dressed and slipped out for the night.

Hugo would also be gone, his friends asking for him later in the TV room, or by the Ping-Pong table, or on the front lawn where Ana and Indy would sometimes sit and stare at the sky, waiting for Jolene to come home.

Mio returned to Japan for the season, and their room was given to a pair of girls from Norway, here for just a month. Ana was moved to a room across the hall with a girl from Holland, and later, a girl from Poland. And then no one.

Change and more change and more change—the air growing cold, the first gusts of snow, and a new competition season underway.

She sometimes thought about her brother, who was now in college, across the country in Ithaca, and her father and mother 289 miles away. None of them would tell her about Connie's condition, just that she was in a new trial or on a new drug, and wasn't that exciting? Wasn't modern medicine something? Only it wasn't excitement she heard in her mother's voice.

Her family was slipping to the back of her mind. She noticed it one morning in the dining room, making a peanut butter sandwich. That was what her mother had always packed for her in the car. Peanut butter sandwiches in plastic baggies. Oranges cut into quarters. The smell of either of these had choked her up for months after she'd arrived at The Palace. Sometimes even sending her to the closet with the Pine-Sol. But then that one morning came when she opened the jar and smelled the smell and thought, not about her mother, but about Dawn and her lesson later that day. And whether she would be folded into the blue puffer coat, or left sprawled out on the ice after a fall, alone.

Just the smell of Dawn's cosmetics became a hit of dopamine, and the need for her approval a gigantic weed inside her. The kind her mother had to pull from the garden using all her might. She wondered how she would stop it now, without Kayla. She was the only one with arms that were strong enough.

But then came a reprieve—the Midwestern Sectionals being held in Denver that November. Even though the sky was gray, and the city was coated in a brown blanket of dirty snow that sprayed up from the road and down from the exhausts of passing cars, it felt like a burst of sunshine. The three remaining Orphans were there together, sharing a room in the hotel. Indy and Ana in one bed. Jolene in her own across a small nightstand. A little cocoon.

Dawn had ten skaters competing and insisted everyone who wasn't commuting from Echo stay at the same hotel near the rink so they could walk to the practices. None of the Orphans' parents made the trip.

Ana's father was tending to her mother.

Patrice told Indy this was just a formality. Everyone knew she would make Nationals, and she had just been here for the show three months ago.

Mr. M. and Mrs. M. were on a trip to Asia. Another continent checked off the list.

So here they were. Together and alone. When Ana walked into the room on the first day, she hopped onto the bed near the window and jumped up and down like a little kid. Indy joined her, taking her hands, the two of them jumping together.

"For fuck's sake, *IndyAna*!" Jolene said. "Grow up!"

But she was laughing when she said it.

She sat down on the other bed and picked up a small folder by the phone.

"Shhh," she told them. She flipped the pages, then grabbed the receiver and dialed a number.

"Hello. I'd like to order room service, please."

Indy and Ana sat on the edge of the bed, eyes wide as Jolene ordered two pizzas, french fries, three ice cream sundaes. And while it made no sense because Ana had been in plenty of hotels before, this felt like the best day of her entire life.

That morning, Ana had a perfect run-through of her free skate. Four triples (two toe loops and two Salchows), one in combination, a double Axel, and six more doubles. The spiral sequence, footwork, and four spins, including the final flying camel spin into a whirring scratch. Dawn waited at the boards and pulled Ana into her arms like there had never been any doubt.

But all eyes would be on Indy tomorrow during the senior ladies' free skate. She still hadn't landed the triple Axel clean. Sometimes she stayed on her feet with a quarter-turn cheat. Other times, she fell—just like she had at the show, landing on that same hip so hard you could feel her bone crack the ice.

Then came the knock on the door. Ana got up, thinking it was room service. But Jolene held her arm.

"I'll get it," she said.

"What's going on?" Ana asked Indy. But she didn't answer.

Jolene looked through the peephole, then opened the door.

It was Hugo—Hugo, who skated for Spain and should have been back in Echo.

And yet Indy wasn't surprised to see him. "Do you have it?" she asked.

Hugo glanced around the room to make sure they were alone.

"It's fine," Jolene told him, planting a kiss on his cheek.

"I've got it." He had a backpack that he set on the ground. He unzipped it and pulled out the contents.

"What's happening?" Ana asked again.

"It's for the bruise," Jolene said.

Ana felt a quick breath fill her lungs. A little gasp of surprise she tried to swallow because Indy and Jolene had made these arrangements behind her back. At least, that was how it felt. The sunshine beginning to fade.

Hugo pulled out a plastic container with a screw top. It was clear with no label, like a giant water bottle.

"What is that?" Ana asked.

"It's DMSO," he said. "A chemical compound that speeds up healing."

Indy asked to see it. But Hugo told her, "There's nothing to see—it's not labeled or anything."

"Is it safe?" Indy was worried.

Ana froze, just like she'd done that night in the field, and back at Emile's house when Kayla lay in his bed with her busted lip and bruised eye. It was still in her—this instinct. In spite of her sessions with the doctor.

"Yes," Hugo insisted. "We use it all the time back home."

"What do I do with it?" Indy asked.

Ana listened to the conversation about how the liquid chemical worked. How it passed easily through membranes in the skin and reduced inflammation. Jolene read things from her laptop—dimethyl sulfoxide, a colorless liquid, a by-product of papermaking, a solvent but also now used for wound care.

Ana's head was spinning with each new piece of data. Hugo was so brazen, so certain. Jolene so trusting of everything he said, blinded by love.

"There's a vet who mixes it with something that numbs the pain while it's healing," Hugo said. "It's totally safe if you just put it on your skin."

Hugo went on about how it was used to treat animals here but hadn't been approved by the "backward government" and "political bullshit," even though everyone knew it was safe, but they were all so paranoid about painkillers.

"Indy . . . I don't know about this," Ana said, tugging at her arm.

"What else am I supposed to do?" Indy's eyes welled with tears, which she quickly brushed away. "I need that stupid jump."

Dawn was never going to send her home, and her mother was never going to let her, not until she had the triple Axel.

Ana saw a flash of Patrice when she'd been here for the show. The way she'd been practically skating Indy's program herself from the boards, her face like that of a young girl, on the ice, jumping and spinning.

She searched her brain, but nothing came forward to answer the question. What else could Indy do?

So Indy went into the bathroom with Hugo and Jolene, the door cracked open enough for Ana to see inside to the mirror and the reflection of Indy in her underpants—in front of Hugo—who was now dripping the liquid into the palm of his hand, covered by a latex glove, and rubbing it into her leg, and Jolene's hands on Indy's shoulders and Indy's face getting red.

And Hugo: "This bruise is fucked up."

"Will it really help?" Indy asked.

"Yes," he promised.

And there she was, in her underpants, with Hugo's hands on her hip and butt cheek now, rubbing DMSO into her skin while Jolene looked on, holding her so she wouldn't cry.

Because Indy knew the morphine in the DMSO might kill the pain, but it couldn't make her jump higher and make the rotation. And it couldn't fix her mother and Dawn, and their rivalry, which was more *fucked up* than the bruise, and so was the fact that neither one could see past it to the beautiful girl they were using to serve their ends. Patrice's own daughter.

Three words formed in Ana's head, surprising her as she thought about her best friend, the person she would fight for and sacrifice for, almost anything. No, not almost—she would do *anything* for Indy. She let the words burn inside her.

Fight the fear. She thought about that moment in the black van and watching Kayla in Emile's bed, both times frozen. The impulse taking over. And now here she was, watching this scene unfold. All because of Dawn. Indy was desperate to get home. She would never give in. And Patrice—neither would she.

It's easy to say you'd do something. Like leaving Dawn's side to try the triple flip, promising not to slow down this time. Ana was all talk. When it came time to fight, she froze. She was a coward.

The doctor said the fear needed to become rage to change the impulse.

So she closed her eyes and began to search for it.

The rage that would help her fight for her best friend.

Chapter
Twenty-One

ANA

Now

I'm driving back to Echo faster than I should, my head filled with the image of Dawn's hands around Kayla's throat, when I feel the car skid, glide, drift from the snow-covered highway onto the shoulder. Then a jolt of adrenaline, foot off the gas. My mind returns to the road, and the wheel, until the car is stopped, but then it goes where it wants—to these images from the past.

From Dawn's hands around her throat, and Westin reinforcing the message, to the field, the trucker who attacked her. And then to Indy's fantasy about killing Dawn with the heel of her blade. What Shannon had told me about Kayla, threatening her mother the exact same way. With her skate, her blade.

And the message I got in Aspen. The one that jolted me into the past, so hard I missed an entire session of the conference. Westin was right—I wasn't there on the second day.

Kayla said she didn't have any anger left toward Emile. She believed he'd sent her that article from a print newspaper, no return address so it could remain anonymous, letting her know that the man who'd assaulted her was dead. I left her house convinced of this truth. That she didn't hate Emile.

Then she'd asked about me. Me and Emile. And I'd done what I've been doing for fourteen years.

I lied.

Shhhh. I can see Grace in the shadows. Now I can see myself when I was her age. In that dress. Keeping secrets.

I shouldn't have allowed myself to deviate from my work. My mission. *Focus, Ana. Shhhh.*

The evidence is strong, and we need a story by tomorrow. Something to tell the ADA.

This has to be about Grace, and nothing more. I sketch out the arguments again, looking for ways to refine them with the new information I have from Kayla.

First—Grace is innocent. Someone framed her. Not someone from the past—but an angry skater or parent. Dawn or Westin even. They had the most to lose. Someone found her skates where she'd forgotten them in Dr. Westin's office after a session. And the dress—maybe another skater thought it was hers. They all had one. Blue with yellow butterflies. And we don't know where Emile went after he picked up Grace. He lived alone in a condo at the edge of town. His neighbors couldn't remember when they'd seen him last. Not exactly—leaving a three-day window for the murder.

It's not our job to find the killer. But telling them this story about Dawn's violence with Kayla will help. I can spin it so it's Dawn, not Kayla, included among the suspects.

Second—there's no motive for Grace to want Emile dead. Grace was angry at Tammy. She cried in Shannon's arms, then asked for Emile. Maybe she wanted an explanation for what she'd heard—about his departure. His betrayal of Dawn. It's weak.

Third—they could have something we don't know about. A piece of evidence they haven't disclosed. They have no obligation until she's officially charged. So—I consider again the other line of defense. The so-called excuses.

Most of my clients are guilty. It doesn't change my commitment. My compassion for them. They are children—damaged children—and we owe them a better path forward. A chance to heal. This is what I'm known for. I can hear the argument inside my head. Grace was traumatized. Not responsible for her actions.

A thought emerges as I sit in the car, parked against the wall of snow covering the shoulder.

I grab the file on the passenger seat—Grace's records. From doctors and her schools. The ones Jolene had to submit to apply to board at Avery Hall. I look through them and see what I expected. Straight A's. Glowing comments from her teachers. Routine checkups and some physical therapy for a strained hamstring. All normal.

I get to the older ones—the records from Grace's home in Oklahoma—and see more of the same. I hear the words I'll need to say. *This perfect child was terrorized by Dawn Sumner. Taught to channel that fear to rage. Her young brain conditioned to fight.* Dawn and Dr. Westin. The mindfucker.

My phone sits on the console, and I hear the familiar ringtone from my office.

"Jill?" I ask, picking it up, putting it on speaker. I can barely hear her with the whipping wind whistling through the seams of the windows.

"Are you okay?"

I answer, "Yeah—there's a huge storm. I'm on the road."

"Goddamned Colorado," she says. Jill hates the cold—and she knows my history here. At least the parts I've been willing to share.

Her sigh is loud and distinct, and the familiarity of it reaches inside and makes me shudder.

"No luck with the girl's story?" she asks.

"I'm working on it," I tell her. "Anything on your end?"

I asked Jill to look into The Palace, Dawn, Emile, Avery Hall. Even Jolene. I can't presume to still know her, especially when she sent her daughter here to train. Our memories are so different.

"It's true about Emile Dresiér's position in California," Jill says matter-of-factly. "I had the intern call the rink in San Diego and ask about trying out for him. They told her he was supposed to start this summer, but—didn't she know? That he'd been murdered?"

Jill lets out a little laugh, like she's pleased with her resourcefulness.

"There's something else."

I clutch the file, bracing myself as Jill tells me about the calls she made to her news sources.

"Emile was shopping a story—insider stuff about the training methods at The Palace."

I feel my pulse quicken. "What kind of stuff?"

"Something called Fear Training. I mean—what the fuck goes on in that place?"

"Christ."

"What?" Jill asks, her voice growing concerned.

"That's what we called it," I tell her. "When I was a skater."

Suddenly, I don't like where this is going.

"Well," she says. "My source wasn't the one he approached, so her intel was spotty. But she said it wasn't just now—it went back to an injury he had, the one that ended his career or something."

The quad toe. The twisted knee.

"Okay, yeah . . ." I say. All that is true. I feel a burst of relief—maybe Emile was telling *his* story. Not ours. But then, Jill continues.

"And something about a girl—with a terrible bruise."

No, I think. *Indy Cunningham.*

"Does that ring any bells?"

A moment passes before I answer.

"She was a skater—when I was here."

If he was talking to them about Indy, what else has he told them? About Jolene and Hugo? About Kayla and the trucker? The one who turned up dead years later?

About me?

Jill continues, unaware of the panic coursing through my body. I hold a hand over my mouth so she can't hear the breath that heaves in and out.

"My source said Emile wasn't just giving them a fluff piece to justify why he was leaving The Palace. He was trying to burn it to the ground. Apparently with things that happened a long time ago," she says.

Things that happened to us. The Orphans.

"The list of suspects besides Grace is spectacular!" Jill says, excited now about the case. "Anyone from the past with a secret they didn't want told—and anyone with something to lose if Emile's exposé ran. That should buy you some time until the girl sorts out her bullshit story. My gut says she's covering for someone."

I think about Grace waiting for me back at the condo. Her words last night.

It's not safe here.

It's all your fault.

"Ana?"

"I'm here. Sorry—yeah," I tell her. "I'll talk to her again—tell her about the article."

Jill's voice grows concerned. "Hey—listen—I know this can't be easy. I know you hated it there."

She has no idea. I've shared little of my past with her. With anyone in my life.

"I'm okay."

"Take care of yourself—right? Focus on the client. That always helps you."

"I will," I promise her, though I feel like a different version of myself. Not the one she knows, but the one who never really left Colorado.

No—that can't be true. I did leave. I moved on. All of this is behind me.

The call ends, but I stay right here, staring over the headlights.

My instincts feel disorganized, triggered by the past and the thought of what Emile has disclosed.

A wave of heat flushes my body, and I roll down the window, desperate for cold air. The snow pricks my skin, and my eyes water, but I don't care.

We all heard Indy tell that story. And now Emile has been killed with the heel of a blade.

And now—*oh God*. A memory rushes in, and I wonder—did Dawn know about that story? About Kayla and the way she raised her skate in the air when she was lashing out at the mothers in the stands?

Yes—God, yes. Dawn knew, I realize as the memory plays.

I was so desperate to help Indy. She couldn't stop falling. Everyone had failed her. Her mother. Dr. Westin, who told her it was all in her head. Self-sabotage. He told her to fight the fear and get the height, the rotation, the landing. Once she retrained her brain, she would stop hesitating on the takeoff. He told her to read the book.

Yes, yes.

And then what?

It comes back now in one flood, one punch to the gut. Dinners at her house. She would pick me up on the corner so no one would see us. Her car smelled of leather and perfume. She played classical music. She hummed along to it. And then the table—always set with linen place mats and fine crystal. She said it was important to appreciate the finer things in life.

And that one night, when I was quiet, searching for courage.

"*What's wrong?*" Dawn asked me. "*I can always tell with you.*"

I felt my mouth go dry and my lips tremble, but I got the words out. About Indy's bruise from the falls and "*I think she needs help.*"

She smiled, rose from her chair. Left the room. And I followed her.

Into the front hall where she kept her bag. Inside was a notebook where she recorded her lessons. Good girl. Bad girl. Her beige skates with the gold blades.

I see her now as the cold air stings my face.

"*Don't tell me what Indy needs*," she said.

Then she took one skate from the bag and shoved it into my chest.

"*Take it!*" she commanded. So I did. I took her skate and held it.

She reached for me quickly, grabbing my other hand and shoving it into the boot.

She pushed me, one step at a time, until my back was against the wall. She raised my hand over my head, the one that was inside the boot of the skate, and turned the blade to face her.

"*Is this how it goes?*" she asked then.

"*Is this how you imagined it?*" She pressed the end of the blade to her throat. Then she went on, about Indy's story, her fantasy about me with blades for hands. She did know!

"*Or like this?*" she asked, moving my hand and the blade to her temple.

"*Do it! Come on! Do it!*"

And I started to cry as she pulled the skate from my hand, gripping its heel with her own. She turned the blade to face me. Pressing it first to my neck. And then to my head, while tears streamed down my cheeks and my knees began to buckle.

I could feel her breath on my face when she said—"*I am what you should fear.*" The same words she'd said to Kayla after she closed her hands around her throat.

She told me to never speak of Indy again. Not to her. Not to anyone.

"*I'm the coach. I know what's best for her.*"

Then she told me to leave, to walk home through the woods, down the mountain. And I did—I ran as fast as I could away from her.

But I would be back two days later as if nothing had ever happened. Except for one thing. I never spoke to her about Indy or the bruise ever again.

I see a truck's headlights barreling from behind. I'm blocking its path. It swerves to the left—barely missing me. I hang my head, which is suddenly light from the rush of adrenaline.

My God.

Pressing gently on the gas, hands back on the wheel, I talk myself through it as I resume my return to Echo. Realizing for the first time.

Dawn knew about Indy's story. How? It could have been a million different ways. We didn't think anything about it, except me with my guilt. Indy probably told half the rink. Jolene would have told Hugo. And from there to Emile, maybe. He would have loved telling her that story. Watching her face twitch with humiliation, however fleeting it might have been.

Dawn knew. Emile knew. The method of the murder is too distinct to be a coincidence.

I drive past the condo where Grace and Jolene are waiting for me, all the way to the stop sign and intersection with the access road.

I turn left and pass The Palace, then Avery Hall. Around a bend, a straightaway, another sharp curve along the switchback until I come to the entrance of the long driveway. The one that splits at a fork, with the dirt road on the right. The path to the guest cottage where Emile used to live.

The left one, heading to Dawn Sumner.

It's all coming together. Dawn had so much to lose if Emile left, if he finished that exposé about the things that happened back then. And she knew about the dream. The blade used as a weapon. And three of us were here when Emile was murdered. All three of us with reason to want him dead.

Maybe Grace isn't the one being framed for his murder. Maybe she's just a breadcrumb for a trail that leads right back to us. The Orphans.

I let the car move, slowly, toward her house and stop by the steps that form a path to the front door. Her lights are on. I can smell the wood burning in her fireplace.

My hands stay on the wheel as I chase away the fear that rises. This woman wields no power in my life. I have been through the exorcism to rid her from my mind. My heart. To kill the giant weed.

I place my hand on the car door handle, skipping ahead to the look of shock, maybe even fear, when she sees me. I have the power now. The skills, the knowledge, the facts about what Emile was doing.

I'm not a child. I'm the protector of children.

I march through the snow to the front door, coat undone, and make a fist to pound on the wood.

I hear footsteps inside. Feel a rush of adrenaline.

"I am what you should fear."

But she's wrong, I tell myself as I struggle to swallow with a mouth that's bone dry.

Then the turn of the knob and the pull of the door.

It opens to expose a small older woman in loose joggers and a sweatshirt. Pale skin that pulls from her bones, painted with red stripes. Lips and cheeks. Her fake eyelashes, thick black spider legs on top of small black pupils. And that smile, exposing yellowed teeth, the crooked one at the bottom.

I'm shocked by this unfamiliar image, but then my mind adjusts as the scent of her enters my nose and my brain identifies the things that are the same. *It's her. It's Dawn.*

Her expression gives nothing away, and I think how good she is at this. Fighting her own fear. Because that's what she should be now. Afraid.

She speaks through slightly parted lips. "Can I help you?"

As if she doesn't know who I am. But she must. The same way that I still know her.

"It's me, Dawn," I say, my voice finding strength. Because fuck her, pretending she doesn't remember. "It's Ana Robbins."

She studies me, head to toe, with that same blank expression.

Which now appears genuine, and it pulls from every cell in my body the same sense of panic I felt when she would skate away. *"Bad girl. No more lessons this week."*

"I'm sorry," she says after a moment. "I don't know who you are."

Chapter
Twenty-Two

Excerpt from Testimony of Dawn Sumner

ADA OLSON: Were you aware of the relationship Emile had with the skaters sixteen years ago—the skaters called the Orphans?

DAWN SUMNER: Well, back then, Emile was still one of them. He'd just stopped skating himself.

ADA OLSON: Did you know how he intervened after Kayla Johnson was assaulted in the field?

DAWN SUMNER: Of course not.

ADA OLSON: And the other girls—

DAWN SUMNER: I only saw them on the ice.

ADA OLSON: Except the time he joined you for dinner—you and Ana Robbins.

DAWN SUMNER: Yes. He came to dinner sometimes. He lived on my property. Like I said—he had just stopped skating.

ADA OLSON: Were you aware that he blamed you for that?

DAWN SUMNER: Emile and I coached together for over seventeen years. If he blamed me, he must have gotten over it.

ADA OLSON: Or maybe he was just biding his time until he could leave and be head coach at his own facility. Until he could finally discredit The Palace and the training practices you employed.

DAWN SUMNER: And how could he possibly do that? My record speaks for itself.

ADA OLSON: Come on, Ms. Sumner. You know the answer. By disclosing what happened to the four Orphans of Avery Hall.

Chapter Twenty-Three

ANA

Before—One Year at The Palace

Ana and Indy stood beside her bed, assessing the situation. There were three neat stacks of clothing and costumes but just one suitcase. The limit imposed by the airline. But that wasn't the biggest problem.

"I wish you were coming with me," Indy said.

She was headed to Phoenix for Nationals—without Ana.

Ana had placed sixth in the junior division at Midwesterns, one spot short of making it to the last and most important of the domestic competitions. With few exceptions, Nationals would determine which skaters would compete on the international stage.

It wasn't a bad outcome for her first year at The Palace. In fact, it set her up nicely for the next season if she could get the remaining triples in the coming months. That was the only thing holding her back. It was right there in the scoring. She just needed the triples to get into the higher range of awarded points.

"Indy—we have to figure this out," Ana said.

Ana held the bottle of DMSO in her hand, examining it for labels, instructions, anything that would indicate what was inside.

"Look," Indy said. "There's nothing on it."

"But that's even worse," Ana replied. "If they search your bag, they'll wonder what it is, and then they might confiscate it. And then test it. And then . . ."

Indy grabbed it back. "Well, it has to come with me to Nationals."

The bruise on Indy's hip had turned a yellow brown over the late fall and then the holidays—better, but still not gone by mid-January.

It was a battle now, between the falls and the liquid in that bottle. Each fall caused a new injury. Indy would rub the liquid into her skin at night, and the DMSO would speed up the healing, and the morphine would kill the pain. It never healed and never got worse. None of them wondered what this might be doing to the rest of her.

Hugo told them the morphine made it illegal, so now they were freaking out over the security at the airport.

Indy started to wrap the bottle in a warm-up jacket.

"This will hide it," she said. But Ana shook her head.

"That's not how the screening machines work. They'll see it's a bottle of liquid."

"I'll tell them it's shampoo."

"Wait!" Ana had an idea. She walked over to Jolene's closet, where she kept a basket of toiletries, and grabbed a bottle.

"If we put it in here, they'll think it really is shampoo!"

Indy smiled, her eyes lighting up. "You are a genius!"

They set the DMSO and shampoo aside and got to work on the clothing. *This can go, this can stay,* every decision another step closer to Indy leaving, her bed empty. This *entire room* empty except for Jolene, but she'd spent every night sneaking off to be with Hugo until he'd gone back to Spain for the holidays. And now she moped around because he hadn't returned.

"How many of these do you need?" Ana asked, holding up a practice dress from The Palace. The light blue with yellow butterflies.

Dawn made them wear the dress on the practice sessions so everyone would see her prowess. A sea of blue dresses. An army of skaters at Nationals.

But out of nowhere, Indy snatched the dress from her hands. She held it up by the sleeves and looked it over. Top to bottom. Disgust creeping over her face.

"I hate these stupid dresses," she said.

Indy threw the dress on the floor, then dug through the pile for the others like it. She had three in total, each of them landing on the beige carpet by her feet.

"What are you doing?" Ana asked.

"I'm not bringing them."

"But it's Nationals. Dawn will be so mad." Ana felt the words stick in her throat as she thought about Dawn and her anger. And, in particular, that night at her house when Ana had tried to tell her about Indy's bruise. The way she'd pressed the heel of her blade against Ana's throat. Then her head.

The message had been clear. Indy was Dawn's business, not hers, and this had created an impossible tug-of-war inside her. Every day, Ana prayed that Indy would land the triple Axel so she would stop falling. But every day she fell, over and over, then rubbed the DMSO into her skin. She was so close.

Indy had become resigned to the training. She'd stopped believing she could go home if she landed it. Which meant she'd stopped believing her mother cared more about her than her skating. Just like those bleacher bees. This made Bobby Stark grow even more important, the one grown-up she could trust. But she was stuck here, with Dawn and these small rebellions.

"I'll tell her I forgot them," Indy said with a smile. "What can she do to me?"

"Indy . . . don't," Ana pleaded, feeling that blade against her skin. What could Dawn do? What *would* Dawn do? The truth was, Ana had no idea. And she didn't want to find out.

Ana saw Indy off on that Saturday afternoon, the DMSO hidden in Jolene's shampoo bottle. She had her gray dress for the free skate, the emerald dress for the short program, and a dozen practice outfits—including the three blue ones with the yellow butterflies. Ana had shoved them into her suitcase when Indy was in the shower.

An hour later, Ana went to the rink, dead quiet now that Dawn was on her way to Phoenix with Indy and the other skaters who'd made it to Nationals. The Palace felt deflated. Like a balloon after a party. For the first time since she'd been here, there were no bleacher bees. No coaches. No international skaters. Everyone was slacking off, licking their wounds from the last round of competitions.

And in this quiet, dead space, Ana felt lost.

She didn't finish her last session. She skated off the ice and went to the locker room as if it didn't matter what she did or didn't do. Because it didn't, actually, matter. No one even tried to stop her or ask her why she was giving up for the day.

Sitting on the bench, unlacing her skates, her hands began to tremble, and her fingers grew stiff as they pulled the nylon loose. She could have cried right then and there. And how was that possible? Indy had only been gone for a few hours, but this was how it seemed to go. The year divided into comings and goings, not just people, but feelings too. Adrenaline in the fall, longing in the spring. The summer a blur of excitement. Nothing was ever here to stay.

Her heart was in her throat, the ground shifting beneath her with a tremor that threatened to bring down the world she had begun to rebuild after that night in the field, and Kayla leaving, and her mother being in bed most of the time she was home for Christmas, saying she was getting better. That she was just resting. Like Ana couldn't see what was happening. Not even Tim would tell her the truth. They'd talked again about treatments and trials. Carl said it would all be fine, even though Connie was forgetting words and looking right through her.

They both told her she should focus on her skating, and Tim should focus on school, and they all needed to live their lives.

Still, before she'd left, she'd crawled into bed next to her mother and buried her face against her shoulder while she slept, a blue scarf around her head and dark, hollow circles under her eyes. And it was a horrible feeling because she knew they were all lying and there was nothing she could do. No one wanted her there. Not even her mother. *"Go live your life."*

As if that life was no longer there, with them.

The silence of the locker room buzzed in her ears as these thoughts filled the space between them.

But before the tears could come, she heard someone around the corner, in the bathroom. Coughing. Or, puking, maybe.

She pulled off the skates and left them on the rubber mat.

"Hello?" she asked, walking to the partition. Then she peeked her head around.

No one answered. Then another cough. A gag. And then a cry.

She recognized the phone with the pink sequined case on the sink counter, then saw the closed door, then Jolene's black leggings tucked into her white sneakers under the stall. She'd wondered why Jolene hadn't been on the session, and why she hadn't come back to Avery Hall to say goodbye to Indy.

Ana knocked. "Jo?"

"Ana," she said, her voice trembling. "I couldn't make it to the ice."

"What's wrong with you?" Ana's blood surged with worry.

"Can you find Hugo?"

"I thought he wasn't back." As far as Ana knew, Hugo was still in Spain.

Jolene had been spinning fantasies about their romantic reunion since he'd left five weeks ago for the holidays. It cheered her up when she missed him, and that was pretty much all day, every day.

"He was supposed to get back last night," Jo said. "But no one knows where he is, and he won't answer his phone."

Ana pushed on the door, and it swung open, revealing her friend on her knees, leaning over the toilet, hands holding on to either side as she puked again into the bowl.

Ana kneeled behind her and grabbed her shoulder as Jolene slid to one side, then slumped down with her knees to her chest. Her face was bright red. Her eyes filled with tears.

"Are you sick?" Ana asked, even as facts began to creep from the back of her mind to the front. Like the way Jolene had stopped coming to breakfast. Stopped making the morning sessions. How she went to bed early now, curled up in a little ball. Ana had thought she was lovesick, missing Hugo. But this wasn't that.

"I know you've heard the bleacher bees talking," Jolene said. "Everybody has."

And that was also true. The bleacher bees had been buzzing about "*Jolene having sex*" and "*does her mother know*" and "*maybe someone should tell Dawn*" and "*it's none of our business*" and "*she needs to be on the pill,*" and then, in a chorus, "*she's such a little slut.*"

All the pieces suddenly formed a picture.

"Jo," Ana began, afraid to say it out loud. "Are you . . ."

Jolene nodded, then lurched back to her knees, grabbing the bowl. Vomiting this time with nothing but a dry heave.

Ana raced to the sink, pulled a wad of paper towels from the metal holder, ran them under the water.

"It's so bad, Ana," she said. "This can't be happening."

No—it can't, Ana thought. *It can't!*

Ana handed her the paper towels, then stroked the side of her face with one hand, and held her ponytail with the other.

"What can I do?" she asked. But it was a stupid question. Ana felt useless. Just like with Indy and Kayla.

"I need Hugo!" she said. "I know he's back. He said he would be . . . He booked his return flight before he even left, and why would he change it?"

Jolene sat back down and stared at Ana with eyes so weary they looked like they wanted to die.

"I need to know what the fuck is going on!" Jolene pleaded.

"I can't leave you here," Ana said. Not with eyes that wanted to be dead.

Jolene took a deep breath and calmed herself.

"Please—this is what I need."

So Ana agreed and hurried out of the bathroom, slipped on her boots, and wiped her skates and shoved them into the locker, her heart racing in her chest.

How had she not seen this earlier? It had been going on for weeks, but she'd been so preoccupied with Indy and the bruise and her family back home.

Poor Jo!

Outside the locker room, Ana stopped a new girl from Miami walking toward her, the girl who looked like she belonged on a beach, long blond hair, tan skin, Barbie body. They'd decided to call her Florida because she was only here for the season, staying in the first floor wing with another short-term skater, so what would be the point of learning her name?

"Have you seen Ivan?" Ana asked.

Florida pointed toward the snack bar. "He was on his way out."

"Thanks." Ana started to walk away, but then turned around. "What about Hugo?"

Florida looked confused now. "Hugo? That dickwad from Spain?"

"Yes," Ana answered, stepping closer. "Why?"

"He's not coming back," Florida said.

"What? How do you know that?"

Florida shrugged. "I heard he decided to quit and go to college—Ivan knows the whole story. He just left."

Ana took off around the boards, inhaling the smell of ammonia and Zamboni exhaust and rubber mats and then the shitty coffee as she rounded the corner to the snack bar.

Hugo was never coming back, Ana suddenly understood, and he didn't tell Jolene because he was a dickwad, or because Jolene never meant anything to him. They'd been having sex and she needed the pill and now she was puking and crying. And what would Ana do? Without Indy. Without Kayla. The bleacher bees dying to see another one of them go because they were *little sluts*.

She ran outside, where the sleet had turned to snow and was now falling hard and fast, a frozen film covering the pavement. She had to find Ivan. Find out if this was true—about Hugo. And then what?

What did she think she could do?

The doctor would tell her to channel the fear that was now pulsing through her blood. Turn it to rage. Then fight. She'd tried to fight for Indy, and look what had happened.

Suddenly, she was slipping, her feet out from under her, body in the air, then crashing down. Onto her elbow and wrist, smacking her head.

She lay there, perfectly still, absorbing the shock of the fall, and the shock of what was happening to her friend, on top of everything else. Indy on the plane with the DMSO and hidden dresses she probably wouldn't wear. Kayla gone forever. And Ana's mother in that bed.

She started to cry from all of this, but also because she should be on the ice, circling the rink close to the boards, practicing the triple flip, just being a promising skater with a sixth-place junior finish at Sectionals. Or maybe the girl back home with Connie and Carl and Tim, whatever was left of her.

She felt like leaving right now, walking through the front door of her old house, marching up the stairs to Connie's room, climbing into her bed, and curling up next to her and never leaving. Telling her—*This is still my home. My life is here. My life is with you.*

She saw herself doing it—packing up her skates and dresses and medals and trophies and shoving them in the attic. She would forget about skating and never look back.

Because she was drowning here. They all were. In the middle of a lake, holding on to one another as they slowly sank, their heads tilting back to gasp in one last breath of air before the black water covered their mouths and noses and filled their lungs.

Fight the fear. But it was too big.

They were not enough. They were children playing grown-up, just like Mio had told her that day before they went to the field, and the game had taken a turn right off a cliff. Just like that, two months after Sectionals when she felt like this dream was slowly becoming real.

She lay there for a long time, until the tears started to freeze on her skin and the pain in her elbow and the back of her head demanded her attention. She began to gather herself, rolling to her side. Propping herself up on her forearm. That's when she heard someone approaching.

Boots crunching snow, then two legs standing before her. And a hand reaching down.

"Are you all right?"

Ana wiped the tears and the snow from her eyes.

"Ana?" Coach Emile said. He was on his way inside, crossing the parking lot from his car. But now he was here, standing over her. Throwing her a lifeline.

"Take my hand," he said.

Like hell. Emile couldn't be trusted after what he did to Kayla.

Fight, Ana! she screamed at herself.

But her hand was already there, reaching for his.

Chapter
Twenty-Four

ANA

Now

Dawn steps aside and politely welcomes me in. Like I'm a stranger. Like we have no history between us.

I follow robotically. Accepting her invitation to take my coat. To remove my boots. Shake off the snow on the doormat. I walk behind her in my wool socks and say nothing as she tells me which way to go.

"The living room is through there," she says. Like I haven't been here before. "I made a fire."

Dawn sits down on a love seat and motions for me to take the sofa. The furniture looks new, with rounded arms and straight backs. Large square cushions made of linen. Light gray. Four decorative pillows sit in the corners. Off white. Gone are the deep reds and blues. The soft velvet. And the television that once hung over the fireplace—the one that would play my programs—has been replaced with a framed print of Monet's *Haystacks*.

She sits up straight on the edge of the love seat. Legs crossed. Both hands folded around her knee. My mind lags, steps behind, fighting to make sense of things. I mirror her movements on the sofa. Fold one leg over the other. Interlace my hands on my knee. My back is perfectly straight, just like hers.

I hear her speaking, but I'm disoriented by this room, new and different, scrambling my memory. And by this woman who has loomed so large for my entire adult life, and most of my childhood, but who now looks at me without recollection.

"Ms. Robbins?" She's been speaking, and I've said nothing. A deer in headlights of my own making. "How can I help you?"

I close my eyes and search for knowledge, drawing from my years in the courtroom, being thrown curveballs by prosecutors and judges. My clients. Questions in the air. Needing to find an answer. Scrambling. Everything at stake. And I whisper to myself the same words I do then.

Do your fucking job, Ana. I open my eyes.

"Anything you can tell me about Grace would be helpful," I say, my mouth bone dry, voice trembling. But I get the words out. "And her relationship with Emile."

Dawn clears her throat and tilts her head. "I really wish I had something useful to tell you," she says with a shrug. "I've thought about nothing else since I heard the news. And after they found the blood on her skate . . . Well, you can imagine it came as quite a shock. What is she saying?"

"That she didn't do it," I tell her. My voice is steady, though it feels like it belongs to someone else. Like I've been divided into two people. The girl crying in the closet at Avery Hall. The lawyer saving a child in a courtroom somewhere back home. "I'd like to understand the history."

"Well," Dawn says, more quickly than before. "There was nothing out of the ordinary. Grace has had a spectacular year. Her training has been flawless. As for the rest of her life, it's not really my business."

Her eyes are wide, like she's trying to hold an expression. I recognize this body language from my work. She's defensive, and knowing how to read her feels like a lethal weapon I can use.

"Whose business would it be?" I ask. The lawyer kicking into gear, calming the child in the closet. "Grace lived here year-round. We used to call girls like that Orphans." I speak of my past like it has no power over me. I speak of it like it was nothing out of the ordinary.

Dawn sinks back against the square cushion. She pulls a throw pillow under her right arm. She appears casual. Nonchalant. But it's stiff. Orchestrated. She's having to think about it.

"Have you spoken to Shannon Finch? She's the dorm mother," Dawn asks. "From what I understand, she takes a very close interest in the girls' lives. And Grace's mother. Jolene Montgomery. She was a skater. I imagine she was very involved, even from afar."

I think now of what I would do if Dawn was on the stand. Or in an interrogation room. A stenographer taking down every word. A device recording our voices. Maybe even a video, capturing every inch of her face. The wrinkles growing deeper when she pretends to be surprised. The corners of her mouth curling as she fakes a smile.

"Yes," I say. "I have." I don't tell her what I've learned. Instead, I press forward. "What do you know about her relationship with Emile?"

"I can only speak to what I observed at the rink," she says, this time with a little shimmy of her shoulders like she's shaking off the question. "Emile has a wonderful rapport with the skaters. He's very casual with them."

"Casual?" I ask.

"He jokes around with them. Makes them laugh." She says this as if he hasn't been murdered right down the mountain outside her house. In the woods by the side of the field. "We make a good team that way."

"Good cop, bad cop?" I ask, remembering the first thing Jolene said to me about Emile Dresiér. *"He dries the tears Dawn makes you cry."* I picture Kayla mocking her. *"That's so poetic."* And the anger begins to rise.

"Well—I don't like to think of myself as a bad cop. But I am stricter, and I don't joke around," she says. "You said you skated here years ago. Was Emile here then? You must know what I'm talking about."

She's lying now. I know she remembers me. And Jolene, and Kayla and Indy. I whisper again, to myself. *Do your job, Ana.*

"So nothing more than that?" I ask.

She shakes her head. "I have a lot of students, Ms. Robbins. I can't be their coach and their mother. There's no time, and it would be inappropriate."

I want to scream now, at the top of my lungs, into this room where we watched my videos. This house where she had me for secret dinners. Picked me up on the corner so no one would see. I wonder if she really believes this. That she did her job as a coach and left it there. That what happened when we left the ice was none of her business. None of her making.

"But you must hear things," I say, finding the right words as I consider the possibility that she believes this. That she had no idea what damage her training methods caused. "From the mothers in the stands. The other coaches."

"What things?" she asks.

Fight, Ana. Throw the punch.

"Things like Emile planning to leave The Palace and take some of your best skaters with him?"

She reaches her hand to the back of her neck and gently squeezes a small, tight bun of bleached blond hair. I have a flash to another time I saw her do this. It was at a competition in Minneapolis. The year I made Nationals. It was Indy's turn to skate, and she was by the boards. I remember every detail from that day.

I train my eyes on her face, my heart in my chest with thoughts of Indy. I picture me and Dawn in the foyer, which I can see from the corner of my eye. On the day I told her about the bruise and begged her to help. She shoved that skate into my hands, mocking me. Knowing I could never do anything to hurt her. The desire was there. For Indy, but also for myself. I could feel what she was doing to me. The weed growing inside. I wanted to take that skate and press it against her throat. Press the heel of the blade into her skull. But I froze.

I move in for the kill now, the way I wanted to then.

"Emile was going to leave and take your skaters with him, and I think you knew. But more than that," I say. "You knew about the information he was giving to a reporter. The exposé about The Palace."

She stares at me, her face steeled. But I can feel her blood pulsing through her veins as if it were my own.

"It's okay," I say. "You don't have to answer." I hold my hand in the air and trace her outline with my finger. "I can see it," I tell her. "On your face."

Dawn leans forward again, her arms crossed at her chest. "And I can see that you think you're clever. All grown up. Some big lawyer," she says. "You think you're somehow better than this place. Better than these girls who are making it to Nationals and the Olympics. Because it's just skating, right? It doesn't mean anything to you, does it?"

She says this to drag me back to the time in my life when skating was everything. When I lived and breathed it. When I lived and breathed *her*. But she's wrong. I don't know if I realized that until just now.

"This isn't about me," I say. "I'm a lawyer now—and Grace is my client. And tomorrow I'm going to tell the assistant district attorney that she needs to widen the investigation. There's a three-day window for Emile's murder. I imagine there's some time in there that you can't account for. Living alone the way you do. You had access to Grace's locker. And she was such an easy target, wasn't she? You knew exactly how to do it. You showed me, right here in this room."

I look directly into Dawn's eyes. I hear the question inside my head. *Are you really doing this? Do you really have no fear?* How many times have I sat in this room, desperate for her affection? Hanging on her every word?

I look at her now, saggy skin hanging over frail bones. The smell of cheap cosmetics. But something else. A rotting from the inside. Maybe that's just the anger coming out, any way it can. Through petty, juvenile cruelty. But I swear I can smell the weakness.

Then Dawn tilts her head to the side like she's having a pleasant recollection. "*Rhapsody in Blue*," she says. "I remember now. It was a free skate, wasn't it?"

And I think, *yes,* the free skate my last year at The Palace. The one Jolene was playing on her computer earlier that morning.

"You had the most beautiful layback," she says. "We put it at the start of the program, didn't we?"

I make split-second calculations about where this is going. Whether I should respond, let her lead us down this road, diffusing my accusations.

"Yes," I answer. There's no point in denying it. I haven't forgotten one moment with this woman.

"I remember," she says. "We did that so you would get more points for the jumps."

"Yes," I say again. Everything was about the points. We put the hardest jumps after the halfway mark.

She smiles now, and I know—I just know—I've made a tactical error opening this door to the past. Behind the armor plates of my accomplishments, my knowledge, is the girl crying in the closet, and she knows it.

"The truth is," she says. "It was really the only thing you were any good at."

The words worm their way inside and start to rewrite the past. I was never a promising skater. It was all a lie. Dawn was just doing her job. She wasn't trying to hurt me, hurt us. We were just weak, alone. The Orphans. She did nothing wrong. We just couldn't handle it.

I look to the entrance of the foyer where she held that blade to my temple. Then the dining room where she served me dinner with linen place mats and crystal glasses. And I think of the night when there were three settings.

I try to shrug her off.

"I've thought over the years," I tell her, "that if I'd been a better jumper, I could have made it to the podium at Nationals. Maybe even to the Olympics. And then what?" I ask. "I would have wound up right back here. Or some other rink. Never anything more. I suppose it was a stroke of luck that my jumps were for shit."

Dawn lets out a guttural sound from deep inside her. And then she says, "Not like your friend Indy. She was a fabulous jumper."

Heat rises inside me. I want to grab Indy's name from the air and shove it down her throat until she chokes on it. I want to see her gasp for air. I want to see nothing but fear in her eyes. But I stop myself, because that's what she wants. And I won't give it to her.

"I should get going," I say. "My office is following leads on that exposé. I have a lot of work to do before tomorrow. And the storm is getting bad." I stand up as if we've just had a pleasant cup of tea. I know how to do this. Still, I'm hanging by a thread.

She stands as well, now mirroring my actions. I follow her out of the room, into the foyer, and to the front door. She places her hand on the knob. Then she stops and turns to face me.

"Have you considered," she begins. "All the things Emile might know? From the time when you girls were here? If there is a story, might *you* not be the headline?"

I hold her stare and keep the blood from rushing into my cheeks.

"Thank you for your time, Dawn," I say. Then I put on the boots that sit by the door. And the coat that hangs on the hook on the wall. I zip up the coat and pull the hood over my head.

She opens the door, and I walk past her without saying another word. Into the storm. To Jolene's car, which has gathered an inch of snow.

And then I hold my breath until Dawn disappears in the rearview mirror and I reach the end of the driveway, past the fork that led to the guest cottage where Emile lived. Her last words still swimming in my head. About all of the things Emile might know.

The girl inside me flies from the closet, tears streaming down my cheeks. Another lesson I've learned from my work. Revisiting a source of trauma outside a therapeutic setting is not cathartic—it just inflicts a new wound. But there's no time for that. I think about the things Emile might know—not just about her but also about us. The Orphans. Three of us, all nearby the night he disappeared.

One of us, at least, wanting him dead.

Chapter
Twenty-Five

Excerpt from Testimony of Hugo Aguilar

ADA OLSON: Looking back now, Mr. Aguilar, do you have any regrets about your relationship with Ms. Montgomery?

HUGO AGUILAR: I loved Jolene.

ADA OLSON: But you left and never looked back. Without saying goodbye. You went on and lived your life—went to college, got married. Had two children . . .

HUGO AGUILAR: That's not true.

ADA OLSON: What do you mean?

HUGO AGUILAR: I wrote her a letter explaining everything. How I lost my funding to train at The Palace. I found out when I went home for the holidays. I couldn't afford to come back. And then, I just—I just quit while I still had time to go to college. It wasn't what I wanted. But I didn't have a choice.

ADA OLSON: That's not what you told everyone at The Palace.

HUGO AGUILAR: No—I didn't tell anyone but Jolene about the money. I wanted to leave with my head held high.

ADA OLSON: But Jolene never got the letter. She never heard from you after you left.

HUGO AGUILAR: But—no. I wrote her a letter. I sent it to Emile and asked him to give it to her.

ADA OLSON: You sent a letter to Emile Dresiér? To give to Jolene?

HUGO AGUILAR: Yes.

ADA OLSON: Are you aware that Emile never gave it to her?

HUGO AGUILAR: I had no idea. My God . . . Jolene.

Chapter Twenty-Six

ANA

Before—One Year at The Palace

The story unfolded as Emile walked Ana back inside, through the snack bar, around the boards to the ice, where the session was about to end—the session Ana was supposed to be on—and finally into the girls' locker room, where Jolene was still hugging the toilet.

Emile said Hugo was going to start college and get married to a girl named Isabella—the girl he'd left behind in Spain. They'd been together for eight years, having met when she was a mediocre skater at his rink, and he was the almighty Hugo who'd placed third at Europeans one year. His claim to fame that meant nothing outside the skating world.

At twenty-one, and without a World medal, he decided to move on—from skating, and from Jolene. Another skater from Spain was coming to The Palace in the spring, taking Hugo's room and the government sponsorship money. Emile had scouted him, and Dawn was thrilled.

"What did you expect?" Emile asked that day when it was snowing and Ana had fallen outside The Palace. "That they would live happily ever after?"

Still, it was Emile, once again, who came to the rescue. Just as he'd done with Kayla. Like he was one of them. Still a skater. A friend. He protected Jolene's secret. Told the school she was sick with the flu, and convinced Edie of the same. *"It's going around, very contagious"*—so it was best if she left her alone.

Ana stayed with her whenever she could. Sneaking ginger ale and crackers from the kitchen, cleaning puke from the trash can, wet towels, dry towels. Stroking Jolene's hair while she cried. *"He said he loved me."* And Ana's reply, the only thing she could think of. *"I know."*

Emile came to check on them every day at four o'clock. And every day, she found herself watching the time, checking it every half hour, every fifteen minutes, until she heard his footsteps on the hard floor outside their room. She came to know them because they were uneven from his limp, like the distinct rhythm of a song. Boom-*boom*, boom-*boom*. And sometimes they made her think of her mother's feet on that floor just over a year ago. Down the hall. Down the stairs. And away. Clip-clop, clip-clop.

Emile made an appointment for Jolene at a clinic in Colorado Springs. The same place he'd brought Kayla after she was raped in the woods.

On Friday, Ana got behind the wheel of Jolene's car and drove to the clinic, where they met with a woman named Marta who made Jolene listen to the heartbeat of Hugo's baby growing inside her. *"It's our policy,"* Marta said. There were also several pages of information Marta said she had to read, word for word, as Jolene pleaded with her.

"You don't understand! My father will kill me."

Marta's voice began to tremble with discomfort.

"There are other options, such as adoption . . ."

"You don't understand! He left me alone!"

She whispered, "*I'm sorry, sweetheart.*" But then, "*The baby might feel pain.*"

"*Ana! Make her stop!*"

Marta told them they could come back "*with proper ID, or a signed parental consent form. Or they could notify her parents and wait forty-eight hours . . .*"

Her eyes glanced at the Palace logo on Jolene's sweatshirt.

"*We helped your friend, but that was different. We have to follow the law and notify your parents,*" she said. "*And don't wait longer than a week—you're too far along.*"

They rushed out of the clinic, back to the car. Ana was already spinning solutions, about getting another ID or going to a clinic somewhere else. But Jolene was shaking her head, like she knew it was useless.

Finally, she looked at Ana.

"Stop, okay. It's over."

Jolene cried while Ana drove, eyes fixed on the road, hands gripping the wheel.

In between her giant sobs, Jolene said these words—"*He's going to kill me.*" Until she finally fell asleep with her head against the window.

Now Ana was alone with her thoughts, and they weren't good ones.

One whole year, and where was she in this dream that had brought her to The Palace? One whole year she could have spent with her mother, and maybe she should have. But that was not what Connie wanted. What Connie wanted for her was this, the dream Ana had come here for. The one she could no longer help her daughter achieve.

Eyes on the road. Hands on the wheel. Listening to tires on the asphalt, the wind wisping past the windows. Jolene's soft exhales, fogging up the glass.

Thoughts turning to Emile.

Emile. Emile. Emile.

Carrying Kayla up those steps, and into his house, and into his bed. *Emile.*

His hand reaching for Ana as she lay in the snow.

Ana blinked, hard. Because what the hell were these thoughts? And why was all this happening? Why couldn't she stay focused? On the skating and just the skating. Fight the fear. Land the triple flip, and then the Lutz and the loop?

Eyes on the road. Hands on the wheel. Ana started breathing like Dr. Westin had taught her to. She examined the fear and talked to it, telling it how strong she was. How smart and capable. But most of all, how angry it made her feel. Being afraid.

And for the first time since she'd been having her sessions in the room next to Dawn's office, she felt it talk back. She felt her mind asking her questions. Asking for proof about this strength and knowledge she was claiming to have. Proof that she could keep herself—or any of them—safe, in this place.

Eyes on the road. Hands on the wheel. She searched for something soothing. One anecdote. One story that would convince the fear to loosen its grip around her throat. She thought about Indy's fantasy, where her hands became blades that made Dawn run away. This brought a smile and one quick burst of laughter.

But her brain was left unconvinced. Indy's story wasn't real, of course, and Dawn had shown her that. How quickly she would yield to her longing for that monster. The giant weed.

They got home after dark, and Jolene felt sick the moment she opened her eyes. Ana followed her down the hall, away from the skaters who had gathered to watch the Nationals on TV, even the transplants and locals—the room was packed. Shannon Finch called after them.

"Hey—where have you been? You missed Indy's skate."

Indy! Her free skate had been that night.

Florida chimed in, her voice gleeful. "She crashed on the triple Axel and fell apart. She popped her second triple Lutz. She dropped to ninth place! Don't you want to see?"

No. Ana didn't want to see. Not any of it.

When they got to the top of the stairs, Jolene puked in the bathroom, then sat on the floor next to the toilet, just like she'd done at The Palace.

She looked at Ana, her face no longer despairing. It was something else—determined, maybe.

"I'll never get a better ID in time," Jolene said.

Ana's heart was pounding. "Will you go home?" she asked, the thought already breaking her heart.

But Jolene shook her head.

"I have a credit card and a passport. I can go to Spain, Ana."

"What?" Jolene had lost her mind. Hugo was gone—she didn't even know where he lived.

"I'll find him, and he'll help me. I know he will. I know he loves me."

Ana didn't know what to say. Hugo had left without a word. And what was she supposed to do now? Jolene was smiling, the life returning to her eyes. Ana couldn't take that away.

"I have to try," Jolene said.

She stood up, the smile growing wider. Ana followed her to the Orphans' room, where Jolene pulled a duffel bag from her closet and started to pack. Going on and on about how Ana could drive her to the airport in Denver and she could take the next flight to Madrid. She knew where Hugo skated. They would know where to find him. She would use her credit card and get a cash advance. She would be long gone before her father saw what she'd done. And then, even if he came after her, Hugo would be there.

"I know he loves me," she said again. "He never even mentioned that girl from Madrid."

Ana stood, speechless, listening to the plan. It was absurd. Jolene was sixteen. What would she do if Hugo turned her away? And why was she so afraid to go home?

It was then that they heard footsteps coming down the hall. The familiar boom-*boom*, boom-*boom*. They stopped. Listened as a second set trailed behind them. And then the knock at the door, the door opening, and the shadowy figure of Emile standing in the darkness. Not alone, but with another man. An older man.

Jolene whispered, but it sounded like a scream. "Daddy!"

As the man charged toward them, his face bright red, his belly heaving, Ana felt a rush inside her like never before. She stepped in front of Jolene and spread her arms wide.

"Get out of the way!" he commanded, and Ana struggled to make sense of what she was seeing. In those mere seconds, the picture forming.

Mr. M., the jovial globe-trotter Jolene had described, was a lie. The fear in her voice at the clinic. The words she'd said, pleading with the woman. *My father will kill me.*

Ana didn't move away, though she couldn't speak. Part of her frozen. The other part knowing what to do, her arm bracing over her face as Jolene's father reached them.

Then a blow to the side of her head. Her body on the ground. Jolene's scream, louder now, a piercing shrill. "Daddy, stop!"

She heard his palm smack Jolene's face, and now they were both on the ground. Ana started to move, to stand. Jolene held her back with both arms.

"Don't," she said to Ana, then braced herself as Mr. M. grabbed her by the hair and pulled her back toward the closet.

"Pack!" he screamed. But Jolene curled herself into a little ball.

"Do it!" Mr. M. ordered, louder this time, and then he lifted his foot and swung it back. He was about to kick Jolene.

But then another voice was inside the room. It was a woman.

"I'll help her. Go back to the car."

And then:

"There's a baby in there."

And with that, Mr. M. drew a giant breath into his giant belly. He turned from both of them, Ana standing now, her face beginning to swell. Jolene on the floor holding the duffel bag.

Her mother took his place as he stormed out of the room. She reached for clothes hanging in the closet, pulled them down and shoved them into the bag.

"Get up," she ordered. And Jolene obeyed, walking meekly to her dresser, opening drawers. Taking out her skating dresses.

When Mrs. M. saw what was in her hands, she grabbed the dresses and tossed them to the floor.

"You don't need these anymore. Stupid girl. You've just ruined everything I did for you."

Ana stared at the woman, new pieces to Jolene's story falling into place. The reason she was here. Her mother had sent her away, but not so they could travel.

Mrs. M. walked to the door. "I'll get more bags from the car," she said. And then she, too, was gone.

Ana rushed to Jolene, wrapped her in her arms.

"I'm sorry, Ana. I'm so sorry," Jolene whispered.

Chest to chest, cheek to cheek. They stayed there for a long time, sorrow pulsing between them. Ana had never seen violence like this. She'd never felt it, never been hit by anyone. Jolene, she imagined, had lived with it her whole life, until she came to The Palace. And now she was facing her return to the place where that violence lived.

Jolene let go. Wiped her eyes.

"I have to finish packing," she said. "It'll be worse if I don't."

Ana sat back, resigned to helping her friend leave. And just then, it occurred to her—where was Emile? Her eyes scanned every corner of the room, confirming what she already knew.

Emile—the traitor, the coward—had vanished.

Chapter Twenty-Seven

ANA

Now

I hated Emile Dresiér.

This thought consumes me as I stop the car, put it in reverse. I feel the four tires dig into the snow, skid, and then steady. I follow my tracks until I can see the path to the guest cottage where Emile used to live, nothing more than a break in the trees now, lit up by the headlights and the traces of the moon that make it through the storm.

And now Emile is dead, and here I am. In Dawn's driveway. In front of his old house. I know I shouldn't be here, but that doesn't stop me. The memories have come alive and yearn for a stage.

I step outside and feel my feet sink into the powder, the wet, the cold, sneaking inside my boots. I pull my coat around me as I walk the path to the front door.

Smoke comes from the chimney, the smell reaching my face. The lights are on. I can see in the window as I approach the entrance.

I knock, once and again, but there's no reply. No voice or footsteps, and I wonder if Dawn has been here. If maybe she uses this cottage now, in the winter months. She's all alone in that big house.

I reach for the doorknob and turn it until I feel the release, and then the warmth and light spill into the night from inside.

"Hello?" I call out as my eyes scan the room and my memories tangle. This place is different.

The table that had been small and round is now a rectangle, with eight chairs around it. A couch and two plush chairs face a coffee table and a fireplace with embers still burning.

Against the back wall where Emile's bed once was, the sheets always strewn about, never straightened or tucked in, are an Eames chair and reading lamp. Another small table where a book is laid open. The light is on. I see a door to another room that wasn't here before. It's closed, concealing the bedroom, I imagine.

Then I see a flash of Emile's bed and Kayla lying upon it.

I see the round table with two chairs where I sat across from Emile after he joined us for dinner.

The night when there were three settings at Dawn's table, and my program playing on the TV. Orange soda and stir-fry. The linen place mats and crystal glasses.

"Emile is joining us for dinner."

I remember thinking the same thought. That I hated Emile after what he'd done to Kayla. How he'd made us feel that night—like we were worthless. Like no one would believe us because we'd been in the field. The Jack Daniel's and boys in the black van.

And then Jolene—*my God*—I see him standing in the doorway of the Orphans' room at Avery Hall. I feel the explosion on the side of my head and the pain that radiated into my skull, and the rough carpet beneath my body as I lay there, helpless, listening to the sound of a hand striking Jolene's soft face.

Emile had done that. He'd called Jolene's parents, then sent us to the clinic, knowing we would be turned away. He *must* have known. He was buying time for Jolene's father to come and get her.

I look at the place where that table once was. I can see Emile clear as day.

"Want a beer?"

He'd brought me here after dinner, instead of taking me back to Avery Hall. He'd offered me a beer, and then brushed my shoulder with his arm as he walked past me to the refrigerator.

"Or do you want to go home?"

I didn't have a home anymore.

I hated him. But I hear the word in my head. My answer that night.

"No."

And then, *"What do you need?"* he asked. I didn't know the answer. But he did.

A burst of cold air hits me from behind. Then the voice explodes in my head, just like the fist that struck me the night Jolene left.

"Ana!" Dr. Westin says with enthusiastic surprise. I turn to see him in his boots and parka, a bundle of wood in his arms. "What are you doing here?"

I stumble with an explanation. "I went to see Dawn, and then . . ."

He walks to the fireplace and sets the wood in a metal stand. There's a smile on his face as he pulls off his parka and hangs it on a hook by a back door.

"Ah," he says. "Of course. This place holds your history. Or part of it, anyway."

I don't answer. He was a part of that history. He still is—not only working with Dawn but also living on her property.

"How long have you lived here?" I ask. Emile moved into a condo complex soon after I left. I wonder if Westin has been here since then, but he says it's more recent.

"I scaled back last year—and this place was renovated, no one using it," he explains, walking to the stove, turning on a kettle. "I don't need much. And I love the view, being on the mountain."

He gets two mugs from a cupboard and sets them on the counter. Reaches for tea bags like all of this is perfectly normal.

Like he always did. And I suddenly remember what Kayla told me not two hours ago.

"I saw her," I tell him.

He turns, curious. "Dawn? Yes—you've said."

"No," I continue. "Kayla Johnson."

His arms cross, and his head bobs like he finds this of interest, but not alarming.

"Was she helpful?"

"Very."

The kettle whistles, and he pours the water into the cups, then brings them to the table.

"Do you want to sit down? You left so abruptly this morning—I was hoping to get an answer to my question."

Yes—his question. The one about Jolene and what happened to her. The question Grace didn't want me to answer.

I walk to the table and sit, leaving my coat and boots on. I watch the steam rise from the tea and think about the night before. The questions about Grace and that video. The rage I saw on her face.

"I think you may know more about Jolene's history here than I do," I say. "You've been working with Grace for two years. I'm sure she spoke about her childhood. If I recall, you were always quite interested in our lives back home."

I take a beat, and then add—"Especially the things that made us vulnerable."

Westin sits and blows on the hot water.

"You know how important the past is. How it shapes young minds."

"Yes," I say. "So what did you learn about Grace that I might not know—from Jolene and Artis? I think I have a rough draft."

"Well," he tells me before bringing the cup to his lips, then setting it back down to cool some more. "She and Jolene lived with her parents until she met her ex-husband. Eventually, she and Grace moved in with him. He was older. He had other kids who came around on weekends and such."

I know all of this. "And then he left—for another woman. Moved to California."

"Right," Westin says. "Jolene had enough money from the settlement to get her own place and send Grace here. But I'm more interested in how it all came about—Grace, I mean."

This place—I begin to smell it as the air settles. Something familiar. Just like Avery Hall. The odors living in the floorboards and the walls. I feel the hard wood of the chair against my back and my feet planted on the ground as my eyes move to the reading chair and table. The lamp. The corner where the bed used to be.

And I remember why I came here.

"Well," I say, "I'm interested in something else. Something I learned when I was driving back from Pueblo. About Emile leaving to run a rink in California. And a story he was giving to a reporter—about The Palace. The training."

This gets more of a reaction, though it appears to be genuine surprise. "What kind of story?" he asks.

"My source said he was trying to 'burn the place to the ground.'"

"Really?"

I nod. "Before, when we were talking about Emile and his conflicted relationship with Dawn—we never got to finish. But I think this new information answers that question."

"It certainly gives you leverage for tomorrow's meeting with the prosecutor. Ample suspects now, right?" he asks.

"Yes. And we're both on that list," I confess.

He dives into the hot tea, slurping it into his mouth. Swallowing as it burns his tongue.

"Ah," he says when he's done, and the tea is back on the table. "Because of the exposé—he was talking about the past, wasn't he? When you were here?"

I feel this sink into my gut. The past that is now front and center in my mind. The smell seeping from the floor and walls. The ghost whispering in the room.

"What do you need?"

"Because you were in Aspen. At the conference."

Yes—and I was gone the second day. Spooked by that text message, the emoji of the blade.

"You knew I was there before it even started," I tell him. "Who else?"

Westin shrugs. "You were on the website—as the keynote speaker."

"For a conference on childhood trauma. Not exactly a rock concert."

"True," he says.

I pull out my phone and find the message. I hold it up so he can see, squinting his eyes to focus.

He leans back, and I place it face down on the table.

"You think Emile sent that? The day before he died?"

"I don't know. I'm asking you."

Now a long pause. A deep breath. "Maybe. Emile was . . ."

"Damaged."

Westin nods. "And this exposé . . ."

"It was about this place—now, but also fourteen years ago. It was about Indy."

"Well," Westin says. "I didn't know anything about it. Not the exposé, not the text message."

I study his face. I can't decide if he's lying, which is unlike me. I can read my clients, a judge, a juror—like the back of my hand.

"But I do know something you may not," he says. "That's what I was trying to get to earlier, when I asked you about Jolene and her experience here."

"Why don't you go first," I tell him. Grace didn't want me to tell him about Jolene. She must have known why he was asking. The dots he was trying to connect.

Finally, he tells me.

"Have you read her file? The one that came from her school back home? From her doctors?"

I think about the papers sitting on the passenger seat of Jolene's car. How I was reading them by the side of the road when Jill called.

"I got through most of it," I tell him.

"Well—you might want to start from the beginning."

That night—that's the piece to the puzzle I didn't see until just now. Jolene went home, pregnant with Grace. A home that was filled with violence.

Violence begets violence. It was the first thing I learned when I started to work with child offenders.

Westin has been wondering the same thing. Trying to understand Grace's behavior—he must have seen it before that video. The rage that was inside her.

I get up from the table, pushing out the chair. And do what I should have done that night fifteen years ago.

"I have to go," I tell Westin.

And then I leave this place like it's the black van in the field that night. Like a bat out of hell.

Chapter Twenty-Eight

Excerpt from Testimony of Jolene Montgomery

ADA OLSON: Isn't it true that you were concerned about Grace before she was a suspect in Emile Dresiér's murder?

JOLENE MONTGOMERY: In what way?

ADA OLSON: You sought a psychological evaluation of your daughter when she was five years old. Isn't that right?

JOLENE MONTGOMERY: Yes, but . . .

ADA OLSON: And what did that evaluation say?

JOLENE MONTGOMERY: That she had an extremely high IQ. That she had some impulse issues . . .

ADA OLSON: I have the report here. It says more than that.

JOLENE MONTGOMERY: Okay.

ADA OLSON: It says that she demonstrated signs of conduct disorder—a precursor to antisocial personality disorder in adults.

JOLENE MONTGOMERY: Yes, but that all went away after I got her on the ice. There's been no sign of it since she was six or seven.

ADA OLSON: Until the day Emile Dresiér disappeared. It's right here—captured in this video.

Chapter
Twenty-Nine

ANA

Before—One Year and Nine Months at The Palace

Jolene was gone, just like Kayla, except with a shorter goodbye and a much bigger heartache.

And Indy grew even more defiant after her disastrous finish at Nationals, her trajectory flattened, her promise fading. Dawn pawned her off on Coach Emile that whole spring and throughout the summer.

But when the fall rushed in and The Palace began gearing up for the start of the competition season, Indy's reprieve from practicing the triple Axel appeared to be over. And the bruise that had receded came back with each new failed attempt, each crash, hip onto ice.

Mio didn't understand any of this when they told her. It was Monday at ten o'clock, and they should have been asleep because of the early training and school the next day. But they needed help.

"Why didn't you tell me about this sooner?" Mio asked, looking at the bruise on Indy's leg, holding the near-empty bottle of DMSO.

"It's not legal," Ana answered.

"I didn't want you to get in trouble," Indy added.

But, they both explained, taking turns as Mio absorbed the information with great alarm, her supply was low and she needed a ride to the vet where Hugo used to go . . . and *please just drive us there tomorrow.*

Mio leaned in closer, gently touching Indy's damaged hip.

"You need a doctor," she told her. "This stuff from the vet—how do you even know what it really does?"

Indy started to explain about Hugo, and how he said it was legal except for the morphine that was added, but Mio cut her off.

"This has to stop, Indy," she said.

"It will—when I land it. And I will. I know I will. I'm getting closer. I just have a mental block."

Mio shook her head. "No, Indy. That's not why."

Indy explained about Dr. Westin. "He said my mind is making my body hold back, not get the speed, not use all my strength on the takeoff . . . because I'm afraid."

Mio cut her off again. "That is all bullshit," she said.

She climbed out of bed and straightened her pajamas. "It's not your body holding back, Indy. It's not about fear. It's your technique. The takeoff is wrong, and Dawn knows it."

Indy was stunned. "What do you mean?"

Mio sighed. "I told her last year, when you fell even harder. I told Dawn what I saw. She even nodded, because *she knows.* I thought she told you, but that maybe you didn't listen."

Ana watched as Indy turned bright red.

"Why would she do that?" Ana asked. Her grudge against Patrice couldn't be so strong she would sabotage herself—Indy was her ticket to having a skater in the next Olympic cycle.

"Nothing Dawn does makes sense," Mio said. "She uses the jumps—and her ridiculous training methods—to make all of you worship her, and only her. Isn't that what she says in that dumb book? She is crazy."

Indy shook her head defiantly. "Well, I don't worship her."

"And that's why she's been hurting you."

Indy stood up, straight as a giant tree.

"I don't care about Dawn Sumner—show me how to land the Axel."

The rink was locked, but Mio knew a way in through a bathroom window off the lobby.

"I leave it open so I can come here alone," she said. "I only train in Echo to see my competition. Not for Dawn."

Ana looked at Indy, surprised, though now so many things made sense. The way Mio always brought her own coach. And why she never stayed for more than a couple of months at a time.

They followed her past the ticket counter to the rink, using their phones to light the way. Then around the boards to the back corner where the Zamboni sat idle, smelling of gasoline and oil. On the wall was a panel of switches.

Mio flipped three of them, bringing light to the empty arena.

Ana stared up at the rafters. "It's so quiet," she whispered.

Mio smiled. "Yes. Exactly."

They put on their skates, opened the boards, and stepped onto the rink, taking the first strokes.

"It sounds different," Indy said.

"It feels different," Ana said.

"Without Dawn, it's just ice," Mio said. "Magical ice."

Like baby ducks, Ana and Indy followed Mio, building speed, strokes and crossovers, front and then back, until she eased them all into the center and came to a stop.

Except for their breath, in and out, and a soft buzz from the lights far above their heads, the rink was suffused with a profound sense of ease.

"These are the problem," Mio said, taking Indy's arms by each wrist. Swinging them back by her hips, then up into the air.

"The takeoff?" Indy asked.

Mio shook her head, up and down. "I told Dawn. And she knows. She is a good coach. But not to you, Indy. She is not good to you."

Indy held a hand to her mouth. "So she's been letting me fall all this time? Knowing how to make it stop?"

"I don't know what is in that woman's heart," Mio said. "But let's make her not matter to you anymore."

"Show me," Indy said. "What am I doing wrong with my arms?"

Mio let go of her, then took off, stroking around the edge again, building speed, cutting into the center, making a three turn onto her back-right outside edge.

"Watch my right arm," she called out, then stepped forward onto her left blade, both arms swinging behind her, right leg extended parallel beneath them. She shot up into the air, arms and free leg now in front, then tucking in. Two and a half rotations, then the release onto the right toe pick, then the back outside edge. A perfect double Axel.

"Did you see it?" Mio asked when she skated back to Indy and Ana.

They were still confused, until Mio went again with the same instructions—to watch her right arm. She took off—the same double Axel, only this one higher.

"Did you see what I did that time?" she asked.

Indy's eyes lit up. "You swept it *up*, not around."

Mio nodded. "Yes!"

And from there she gave them both a lesson about physics and propulsion, and how Indy needed that right arm, the one on the outside, to drive straight up past her hip and her chest right up to the sky.

Indy was sweeping that arm from right to left—the direction of the rotation but not the height.

"Punch it," she said. "Punch the sky," because that would bring more height, and it was the height she needed more than a faster rotation in the air.

They used Mio's phone to film Indy as she practiced the double Axel, focusing on that one arm, punching the sky, not sweeping to the side, until she made the correction. Only then was it time to try the triple.

Which she did, and not just once or twice but three times because her right arm was stubborn. She skated back to Mio and Ana, tears in her eyes, rubbing her hip.

"I can't stop it," she cried. "It keeps swinging around."

Mio took off her mittens, which were padded with down.

"You do have fear," she said. "Your brain is hijacking the instruction because it doesn't understand. It doesn't believe you must get higher to stop falling."

It was just like Dawn said, Ana thought. Just like Dr. Fear. But then Mio seemed to read her mind.

"It's not a fight," Mio said. "You don't fight the fear. It's so stupid, these things Dawn says. And that old man."

Then Mio took the mittens and slipped them inside Indy's leggings, right on top of the bruise, like a crash pad.

"You have to be kind to the fear. Thank it for protecting you. You have to show it that you've heeded its warning and have made adjustments to keep yourself safe."

Indy looked confused. "Will these really help?"

Ana waited for Mio to tell her the truth—a pair of mittens would do little good against the weight of Indy's body crashing down on the ice.

But instead, she made a fist and tapped it against the mittens and Indy's hip.

"See?" she said. "Of course it will help."

Then she held Indy's face in her hands and pulled it down so they were eye to eye.

"Your arm is like a broken wing that stops you from flying. And you have to fly."

"Okay," Indy said. And Ana watched, desperate for Indy to fix her arm, her broken wing, but also terrified that Indy would crash again and the mittens would do little to help and Mio would be out of tricks.

"Go," Mio said. "Go and fly."

Indy skated away, slower this time, until she reached the edge of the ice. She circled the rink, but didn't cut into the center to set up the jump, and Ana thought maybe she was going to give up, to skate to the doors and then walk to the locker room, take off her skates and never put them on again.

The thought felt like a rebellion, like freedom, until Indy passed the doors and went around another time, her eyes focused on the ice, her expression changing with each shift of the blades, right, left, right, left. Then she picked up speed, cut into the center.

A three turn. Backward, on the right outside edge. Hips square before she stepped forward. Left outside edge, both arms back. Free leg beneath them. Ana heard Mio pull in a gasp as Indy's arms began to move, the left arm sweeping up and the right arm—there it was—her right arm punching a hole right through the sky.

One, two, three and a half rotations, then the right toe pick sticking the ice just as her arms opened and her left leg unraveled and pulled her down from the pick and onto the blade—a split-second transition.

Like a miracle—a landing.

Chapter Thirty

ANA

Now

Jolene and I stand side by side as images of that night emerge and begin to play. It's all right there. Her father in the doorway, hitting me. Slapping her. Then her mother. Packing her clothes.

I can't believe it didn't occur to me sooner. This thread about Grace. I read the rest of the papers in her file—the reports from her first year of school. There are cycles of abuse within families. Violence can spread like a virus from one generation to the next.

She sees the questions on my face.

Did it spread to Grace? And is she now capable of murder?

"I did the best I could after that night," Jolene says.

I don't doubt this. Every parent I've seen—they all had good intentions.

"What happened after that night, Jo? I need to know—it could help Grace."

I want to grab her by the shoulders and shake the story loose. Was Grace raised in the shadow of abuse? Was she abused herself, by her grandfather? Is that what I saw on her face in that video?

Jolene turns from me and walks to the window. There's nothing to see but complete whiteout as she places both of her palms against the glass. Like she's looking into a snow globe. Or maybe looking out, trapped inside.

"I did what my mother did," she continues. "I saved her with skating, Ana. I know I did!"

Maybe it was already too late.

"What happened in kindergarten—the evaluation—do you think it could still be inside her? Enough rage to kill someone?"

These words sound crazy as they now sit between us. The child conceived sixteen years ago now a part of that story. *Our* story. Emile's murder a new chapter.

Her face quivers. She wants to say no, but she can't. I've been here before. It's devastating to see what your own child might be capable of.

She looks at me with pleading eyes. "Do you?" she asks.

Yes.

The answer is part of my bible as a lawyer for violent children. Years of exposure to unpredictable rage can damage a child. Wire their brains to be hypervigilant. To always anticipate danger. Be prepared to fight at any moment. It can interrupt the development of empathy—and lack of empathy is the defining trait of sociopathic illness. There is so much controversy over the ability to rehabilitate. To fix the wires that were laid down in the early years.

Yes, I think. It could still be inside her.

But what matters now is that we keep Grace from getting charged with this crime.

"We have to explain why she asked to see Emile after that fight with Tammy Theisen," I tell her. "That's the missing piece to this puzzle."

Jolene shakes her head. "Fucking Emile. He sent me to that clinic knowing they would turn me away. Giving my father enough time to get here."

"Oh my God!" I say, having a sudden thought sparked by the memories of the day we went to the clinic.

"Shannon Finch told me that she heard Tammy say something to Grace after the fight. When the video had stopped. She told Grace to ask Emile. That he knew the truth." I try to explain where this thought has taken me. "We've been assuming it was about Emile's move to California—but what if it wasn't?"

Jolene's eyes light up. "The clinic!" she says. "Tammy knew—that's what she must have told Grace. That I tried to terminate the pregnancy . . . oh God!"

"How would Tammy Theisen know about that?" I ask. "I never told anyone."

Jolene rises from the couch and begins to pace the room. "Neither did I," she says. "It was just you, me, and Emile."

Then, suddenly, I have the answer.

"Shannon Finch," I tell her. "It was Mrs. Finch who knew about Kayla—when we took her to the clinic after the rape. That's why she attacked her in the bleachers that day—Shannon told me and Artis the whole story. If Shannon and her mother knew about Kayla, she could have known that you went there too. I don't know how, but that has to be it."

Jolene stops walking. Her face streaks red, and her eyes become wide and dark.

"How could she do that? She's a grown woman now—and Grace has been living with her all this time!"

"Don't think about that," I say, taking her hand. "This is it! This is why Grace isn't talking to you. We can use this to get through to her . . ."

I'm about to tell Jolene the things we can say to get Grace to trust her, to trust me.

But then we feel a gust of cold air sweep through the room. And hear the front door slam shut.

Jolene and I run from the living room to the foyer, where the air lingers, spilling specks of fresh snow on the carpet.

"Grace?" Jolene calls out. She leads the way upstairs to the two bedrooms. Both doors are open now. Both rooms are empty.

Jolene is already back in the hallway, yelling her name louder. "Grace!"

"She wouldn't go out in this storm," I say.

But Jolene looks through the coats that hang on the wall.

"It's gone," she says. "Her coat is missing."

I open the door, and we both look outside.

"There!" I point to deep footprints on the landing, leading down the three steps to the parking lot.

Grace is gone.

Jolene reaches for her boots, about to run out into the storm. I grab her arm and pull her back.

"Wait," I plead with her. "The ankle bracelet will set off a chain of calls—to the DA's office first, to Artis next. He'll be able to track her."

I pull out my phone and dial Artis's number. Jolene watches with wide eyes that dart from me to the footprints in the snow.

Artis answers. It sounds like he's in the car. "Where are you?" I ask him. He said he was going to see Dawn, then head home. That was hours ago.

"Tracking down loose ends," he says. "What's going on?"

I tell him what's happened—Grace has left the condo. Gone out into the storm.

"I'll call the monitoring station," he says. "I'll get her as soon as I have the location."

I assure Jolene that Artis will find her, but she shakes her head. "I need to go!"

She's exhausted from lack of sleep and worry. Not thinking straight. I grab hold of her shoulders.

"Jo—please. Stay here in case she comes back," I plead with her, but I can see this isn't enough.

"I'll go look for her, okay? I'll go."

I slip on my boots and coat while Jolene watches.

I take her in my arms and squeeze with all my might.

"Find her, Ana. Promise me . . ."

So I do. I promise her and rush off, wondering why Grace is running.

When I step outside, the wind rushes, pushing against me. I lean into it, headfirst, thinking about where she might go. Her words filling my head.

"It's not safe here . . ."

I find the footprints, one set, quickly disappearing. They head through an opening between two condo units, and I follow them, walking where she's walked before I lose her trail. The snow rises from the ground and covers everything now, the parking lot, the cars, the pavement. It flies through the air on swirls of shifting wind, and I stop to zip my coat and lace my boots. I can't see more than a few yards in any direction.

I follow the steps, lifting each foot from the imprint, the deep holes they've carved, then into the next one. Left, then right. Left, then right. Following her tracks as the cold whips across my face, burning my skin.

The footprints lead to the access road, the one that snakes up the mountain. A plow has just come through. It's carved a tunnel, which I step into and continue walking, following the trail.

My phone pings, and I take it out, pull off a glove to touch the screen, but my fingers are too cold. I lift it to my face, and it opens, revealing a message from Westin.

I just heard about Grace—let me know when you find her . . . be careful. It's not safe in the storm.

Artis must have called him, and I remind myself that Artis knows nothing about the exposé. Or the report about Grace from years ago.

The air is cold when it hits my lungs. I let it out slowly, slipping the phone into my pocket.

The wind quiets to near silence, the kind that comes after a storm leaves, when the ground is covered, and there's not a car or truck for miles. And in this strange silence I hear my body, heart beating, blood flowing. I hear Jolene crying in my arms, begging me to find Grace. I see her on the floor of the Orphans' room at Avery Hall. Cowering beneath her father. Her mother yelling about the baby inside her.

Kayla in the woods. In Emile's bed. In his bathtub while he washes her. The memories are wired. A string of lights, like the cars that move along the highway at night.

I shake off the snow, pulse pounding in my ears, as I walk this familiar road. Step by step.

Left, then right. Left, then right.

I walk this road I know by heart, even in the blinding snow, up the incline, the hill that becomes the mountain.

Then I reach the entrance to the place I swore I would never return to. That I'd put behind me.

The Palace logo, with the circle and the pine trees, the stencil of a skater in a layback spin. The parking lot toward the side door, the one that opens to the snack bar.

Get inside, I hear myself think. I hurry across the lot, reach for the handle, and pull, the same way I've done hundreds of times, but so long ago. The door sticks and releases, just like it used to. My body remembers. My fingers know exactly how hard to grip the metal.

I walk in, let the door slam behind me, closing out the storm.

The place is empty and dark, but it smells of fried food, so I think they must have been open. Neon lights buzz from behind the counter, a sign that says **SMOOTHIE**, which wasn't here fourteen years ago but now provides enough light to see the shape of things. The benches in the back. The wooden tables. The rubber mats beneath my feet. I shake off the snow and search for the opening to the rink on the other side of the counter.

Images appear now, of walking through that opening, the mothers sitting in the stands to the right, the doors to the boards that gave access to the ice, here and again around the corner, at the south end where the locker rooms were, and my locker in the third row, and the bench where I would sit and lace my skates, the nylon cutting into my fingers.

And farther around to the other side, the hallway and the offices in the back. Dawn's, and the room where Dr. Westin met with the skaters. With us.

These images provoke visceral reactions that explode inside me, the same way they did last night when I looked out the window and saw the four lights on each corner of this place. And when I sat with Grace and studied her. When I looked at the photos of blood pooling in the snow, the four gashes in Emile's head.

And today when I walked inside Dawn's house.

Don't think. Just move.

I pass through the opening to the rink, where the smell hits me hard. Ammonia, minerals, gasoline, rubber. The sweat of the skaters that leaves their bodies and hangs in the air.

I close my eyes and inhale three long breaths and focus on conscious thoughts to remind myself that I'm me, Ana, now, at thirty. Not thirteen. Not fourteen, fifteen, sixteen. Not a child. My heart slows. Then a door slams from the other side of the ice, and I open my eyes to a brighter light, coming from across the rink to the hallway that leads to the offices.

Cautiously, I move toward the light, along the edge of the boards to the hallway that leads to the locker rooms, then up two levels, crossing through the seats to the opening on the other side.

Don't think. Just move.

I walk down the passageway that leads to Dawn's office, and I stop at the open door and look inside. I can smell her from where I am, the perfume and cheap cosmetics that linger in the dark, empty room. It pulls me like a siren, just like it did earlier at her house, and more memories flood in.

"Emile is joining us for dinner."

"I am what you should fear."

"What do you need, Ana?"

My cheek pressed against her body and that fucking blue puffer coat.

Her desk is meticulously organized. Stacks of papers in black wire organizers. Matching cups to hold pens. Slowly, I walk around the desk to her chair and the sweater that's folded over the back. She always wore one when she worked here. When she called us in to tell us something good. Something bad. We never knew.

And then I see her skates resting against the far wall. The beige leather with the gold blades. I remember—the edge pressed against my neck, my temple.

I walk toward them, these relics from my past, but just as I reach the wall, I hear a whimper coming from the office next door. From Dr. Westin's room.

"Grace?"

I step into the hall, then to the room next door.

Where I find Grace, standing in the shadows.

"Grace," I whisper. Her body shakes as she sobs, and I move toward her, slowly, not making a sound, until I'm there and reach out to take her in my arms. But she shoves me, hard, and I fall to the ground.

"Stay away from me!" she screams.

Soaking wet from melted snow, shivering in the clothes she was wearing before, beneath an open coat and unlaced boots, she braces for a fight.

On her face is the same rage I saw in that video.

Chapter
Thirty-One

Excerpt from Testimony of Marta Lyons

ADA OLSON: Ms. Lyons, you were working at the women's clinic in Colorado Springs when Jolene Montgomery came in for a termination procedure, correct?

MARTA LYONS: Yes. I was a nurse practitioner there for seven years.

ADA OLSON: Do you remember Ms. Montgomery?

MARTA LYONS: Yes. After reviewing her file, I remember.

ADA OLSON: She asked to terminate the pregnancy, correct?

MARTA LYONS: Yes.

ADA OLSON: But on the first visit, she had to comply with the law at the time, correct? Which required parental notification for minors forty-eight hours before the procedure?

MARTA LYONS: Yes, that's right. And our clinic had its own guidelines to ensure the well-being of our patients—the ultrasound and informed consent information.

ADA OLSON: Right—their well-being. And did Ms. Montgomery say why she wanted the termination?

MARTA LYONS: She said she was afraid of her father.

ADA OLSON: And did you ask her to elaborate?

MARTA LYONS: No. It wasn't unusual for a teenage girl to say that.

ADA OLSON: How did you know she was underage?

MARTA LYONS: Her ID was clearly a fake. And she was a skater.

ADA OLSON: How did you know about the skaters?

MARTA LYONS: Because my sister lived in Echo. In a condo unit where a lot of the skating families stayed. She was friends with a skating mother. She used to tell me stories about that place. Some of the skaters were in the Olympics.

ADA OLSON: Yes, they were. Ms. Lyons—was your sister's friend named Mrs. Finch?

MARTA LYONS: Yes. That was the name I remember. Finch.

ADA OLSON: Did you ever tell your sister things about your patients at the clinic?

MARTA LYONS: Only in general. I never used names.

ADA OLSON: But descriptions, perhaps? Like telling her if they were skaters?

MARTA LYONS: Yes, perhaps.

ADA OLSON: Skaters like Kayla Johnson, who'd come in for emergency contraception and STD testing after an assault?

MARTA LYONS: She didn't say it was an assault.

ADA OLSON: And Jolene Montgomery, who sought medical care to terminate her pregnancy?

MARTA LYONS: I was concerned about them. They were living away from home, and these things were happening to them. They were making decisions without any parental guidance.

ADA OLSON: And your response to that concern was to tell your sister? Who was friends with Mrs. Finch?

MARTA LYONS: I thought maybe someone would step in and take care of them, if they knew what was happening. It wasn't right—those girls on their own . . . I never said their names . . . I was within my ethical boundaries . . . I didn't know about Jolene's father . . .

ADA OLSON: Thank you, Ms. Lyons. That's more than enough.

Chapter
Thirty-Two

ANA

Before—One Year and Ten Months at The Palace

Ana glanced across bowls of pasta and bread laid out on the Cunninghams' dining room table. Patrice was at one end. Indy's father, Paul, at the other. Next to Ana was Indy's little sister, Sally. None of them were talking. Not one word. Just forks and knives scraping plates, chewing, swallowing, shifting in seats.

Indy gave her a quick wink before looking into her plate of food. She wasn't really eating, Ana noticed. Just twirling strings of spaghetti round and round with her fork.

Earlier that day, Ana had skated her free skate at the Midwestern Sectionals, held in Minneapolis that year, at the rink where Indy had trained before coming to The Palace. The same rink where Bobby Stark coached. Ana had been invited to stay at Indy's house, with the Cunninghams, so she didn't have to be alone at the hotel.

She'd landed two triple-triple combinations, earning a silver medal in the junior division—which meant she was going to Nationals for the first time. Dawn had pulled her into the puffer coat so hard she thought she might actually break some bones, causing a euphoric swell of emotion, tears of relief that felt distinct from the joy of her success. She could feel the need for Dawn, right alongside the hatred for herself for having it.

But that was only part of the ache she now felt at the Cunninghams' table in mid-November of her second year at The Palace.

It was also about Indy—who was in first place after the short program. The free skate was tomorrow, and Indy could now land the triple Axel! Mio had fixed it, showing Indy how to punch the sky with her right arm. She'd landed three more before they went home that night. And the next day, Indy landed it again for everyone to see on the seven a.m. session—including Dawn, who was giving a lesson to Ivan.

Mio had made Indy promise not to tell Dawn how this miracle had happened. "*She won't like it,*" Mio said. "*She'll find a way to punish you.*" Indy had protested the whole way home, and again as they brushed their teeth.

"*Please!*" Ana begged her. For once, she said, they needed to do what Mio told them. Indy said she wanted to "*shove this down Dawn's scrawny old throat and watch her choke on it.*"

But in the morning, Indy kept her promise. She landed the triple Axel like it was nothing. Emile let out a holler and skated over to her. He was joined by a handful of skaters pretending to celebrate her accomplishment, but Ana had felt their stomachs sink. Like someone had just pulled the plug from a drain, and now they were all going down it. The ones at Indy's level would never stand a chance against her now. The ones below knew what Ana did—the bar had just been raised.

Ana stood at the boards, watching the bleacher bees shrivel, finding glee in their misery. She didn't care what it said about her.

Her eyes turned to Dawn, standing at the far end by the entrance to the lockers, beside Ivan. She pretended not to see any of it—the triple Axel, the celebration. But when the session was over, she remained by the boards where everyone had to exit the ice. Ana skated over to Indy and was there when Dawn stopped her.

"*You see?*" she said. "*I told you it would come.*"

Ana shot Indy a look, another plea for her to keep their secret. Indy complied, pursing her lips into a tiny, rigid smile. And as she skated away, Dawn raised the hand holding her guards, and swung them down. Right across Indy's right hip. Into the bruise.

Anyone else seeing this might have thought it was an affectionate gesture, like a pat on the shoulder. When Indy looked back at her, shocked by the sudden pain, Dawn winked and said, "*I knew I'd get you there!*"

Indy held herself together until they reached the locker room. But then she raced into a bathroom stall with her bottle of DMSO and rubbed it into her hip. She didn't cry, though Ana knew she wanted to. Maybe needed to.

But that was the end of it. Five weeks later, here they all were. Back at Sectionals. Indy poised to win and ride into Nationals that January as the favorite—likely to win there too. Certain to place, making the Olympic team. It was an incredible journey back after last season, when she'd placed ninth.

Ana knew how happy this would make Indy. Not just because of the Olympic team. Patrice had promised her two years ago that she could return home if she landed the triple Axel in competition. Which meant after tomorrow, Indy might leave The Palace for good. Ana refused to be sad about this, even though it meant she would be alone.

So she sat quietly as the Cunninghams scraped their plates and chewed their pasta—until, finally, Paul broke the silence with talk about Indy's little sister, Sally.

It was directed to Ana, this information about their family, because she was the only one who didn't already know that Sally had quit skating after just a year of lessons when she was five, and that she now played lacrosse because that could "*buy her a ticket to college*" if she practiced and played all year on her middle school travel teams and summer leagues.

He told Ana other things the rest of them knew, but that he apparently wanted to say out loud. Things about their home. It was *modest*, he explained. And the guest bathroom needed updating. And that they couldn't put in a swimming pool, apparently.

"Skating is expensive," Patrice said. "It's a sacrifice the whole family has to make. Everyone has to be committed. Indy started skating as soon as she could walk," Patrice laughed. She said this as if Indy had discovered the sport on her own. As if it had nothing to do with Patrice being a former Olympian.

"It's important to start young."

Ana could picture Patrice shoving Indy's little feet into doll-size skates, then dragging her around in circles at a public session. She looked at Indy across the table, wondering if she had cried because it was cold and her feet hurt. That was what they said had happened when they tried to get Sally on the ice. But Indy didn't look up from her plate. Spinning the pasta around and around with her fork.

"Sadly, she wouldn't have any part of it," Patrice said, glancing briefly in Sally's direction. "But we already had our skater."

Patrice was the only one left talking, like she had started down a road they all knew not to travel—but once on it, Patrice couldn't steer away and was now pedal to the metal.

"My parents didn't know any of this—about starting young, finding the best coaches. I'll always wonder what might have been. But not you, sweetheart."

And with this, Paul picked up his fork and speared a meatball so hard it split into pieces.

Then Patrice passed the bowl of pasta and the plate of bread, suddenly quiet. Maybe she was thinking about Indy's free skate tomorrow. Her first attempt at the Axel in competition.

Or maybe she was having memories of the year she made the Olympic team, beating Dawn Sumner, but then didn't make the podium. The photo of her with Team USA hung on the wall above the stairs with the worn carpet, next to the family portrait taken by a lake, and then Sally and Indy when they were little girls.

When he'd swallowed the meatball, Paul said, "It's a shame you outgrew Bobby. We miss having you around."

Indy looked up from her plate at the mention of her old coach. She smiled at her father. "I'll be back soon enough."

And then Patrice cleared her throat and looked in a disapproving way at Paul, who seemed confused, like maybe he had no idea about anything that was happening between his wife and daughter. Promises made. Maybe about to be broken.

It left Ana totally confused. And she thought, as terrible as life was for Indy being an Orphan at The Palace, maybe things would be worse here, even with Bobby as her coach again. In this modest house with an outdated bathroom and no swimming pool, and where they couldn't send their kids to college—all because of Indy, and the dream she had to finish for her mother.

The senior ladies' free skate began in the afternoon. Indy was third to skate and now circled the ice near the door while they announced the score of the girl who'd just finished, having fallen on one triple, but landed the rest, three in combination.

Indy seemed focused, her mouth reciting the mantra she'd chosen with Dr. Westin, the repetition meant to *stimulate her vagus nerve*, calming her fight-or-flight response, which was clamoring to take over, and for good reason. Because it all came down to this: four and a half minutes in a yellow sequined dress.

Ana prayed Indy was better at the Fear Training than she was; she'd skated with a surge of adrenaline she hadn't been able to contain. She'd somehow landed the jumps anyway, but two had been shaky and one had felt stiff. Indy couldn't afford one disconnection between mind and body. The triple Axel was too new for her to rely on muscle memory. Every cell in her body had to follow orders.

"Punch the sky."

Ana was in the stands with three skaters from The Palace who'd made it to Sectionals in the novice and junior divisions. Patrice, Paul, and Sally were down several rows to the right, close to the boards and behind the row of judges. Dawn stood by the door, now closed, in her blue coat and thick makeup, her hair sprayed into a tight bun at the back of her neck.

And what was going through her mind? She'd been neutral toward Indy these past few weeks, impossible to read. Before Mio had gone home to Japan for the season, she'd told Indy to be careful, but neither of them knew for sure what she meant.

Whatever Dawn felt about Indy and her path to the Olympic team, and possibly a medal, part of her had to be pleased now. Everyone knew Indy had the triple Axel, including the judges, who were waiting with great anticipation for her to skate. And Dawn was the one standing by the boards, an even greater coach than before—taking credit for the jump even though she had tried to sabotage it by not showing Indy how to fix her arm.

The announcement came over the speaker. "From The Palace Skating Club, please welcome Indy Cunningham."

Then applause, hoots, and hollers from Ana's row. "Let's go, Indy!" Paul and Sally shouted. Patrice, jaw clenched, grabbed the back of the seat in front of her like she was in the first car of a roller coaster.

The opening notes from her music—*Phantom of the Opera*—bled from the speakers, and Indy pushed off onto her right blade, arms by her side, fingers extended, free leg pointed, before reaching down to the ice, sending herself into motion.

The program was simple, focused on the jumps, and the first one came. The double Axel, which Indy could land in her sleep, was flawless. More applause, but muted this time because everyone knew, as she rounded the boards at the far end, then cut into the middle, that this was the moment. History in the making if another American woman landed the triple Axel in competition.

Ana chewed her lip, her heart in her throat, as Indy stepped onto her left blade, the forward outside edge. Both arms peeling back behind her hips, then sweeping forward, punching the sky, the way Mio had showed her.

She flew into the air, then began to spin, making the rotations. One, two, three and a half turns, and then catching the right toe pick, the back edge.

"Perfect," Ana said with a gasp, wiping a tear as everyone jumped to their feet. Years of falling, injuring her body, longing to go home—and now she'd done it!

Patrice buried her face in Paul's shoulder and wept, actual tears, while Sally bounced up and down. Ana held a hand to her mouth, the relief about to explode out of her.

Indy skated as the buzz quieted, people taking their seats. Holding their collective breath. Waiting to see if she could pull off the rest of the program.

Dawn crossed her arms and tilted her head, a slight smile pulling at the corners of her mouth, and this time not a smile that took great effort to make. This one seemed to come in spite of efforts to contain it.

Ana followed Dawn's gaze across the ice, where two women in the judges' row stood and walked away from their seats and then down the stairs to the boards. They wore officials' badges around their necks and jackets from the USFS. What were they doing here?

The music played on, blending "The Music of the Night" and "All I Ask of You" and "The Phantom of the Opera," until Indy had landed all but one of her jumps. She doubled out of the last triple toe after a triple flip, but it was still a completed combination, and at the end of her program, giving her more points. And then her final pose, a big smile, and a wave to the far end of the arena, where Bobby Stark had been watching the program with some of his students.

Ana saw her face tremble because now that it was over, and she'd landed the Axel, and no doubt won the senior division, paving her way to Nationals, and from there a chance at the Olympic team, an Olympic medal, her family's sacrifice and commitment not going to waste, her mind gave way. Calm, focused concentration melted into a flood of emotions that caused her to collapse into Dawn's arms, because those were the only arms available. Ana knew Indy would hate herself for it later. But Ana also knew how powerful Dawn's embrace could feel. The giant weed with all its roots and branches.

But their embrace was interrupted by the two women with the badges, who led Dawn to the side, speaking gravely with lowered eyes, causing Dawn to listen intently, a mask on her face.

But then she turned toward Indy with a look of—what? Shock? Disgust? Betrayal? Indy, eyes wide, face almost melting, shook her head in disbelief.

And then Dawn turned her back away from Indy and the women. Ana stared at her face as it changed again to a smile, the same kind she had seen just that one time, when Dawn had smacked Indy's bruise with her skate guards. Only this one was even bigger. More pronounced. More definitive.

With the unmistakable look of revenge.

Chapter Thirty-Three

ANA

Now

Slowly, I get up off the ground. Rise to my feet. Take a few steps back from Grace.

"It's okay," I tell her. "I know—you must be pretty scared." I look behind me and see the two chairs that face each other in the center of the room. It's still the same, all these years later. The place Westin used to have us sit for our sessions. He always took the chair facing the door. We would sit in the other one, facing his desk.

"I'm going to sit down now," I tell her. I walk to the chairs and take the one for the skaters. Grace stays pinned against the wall to the left of Westin's desk.

"I came here alone," I tell her. "I walked from the condo. I followed your footsteps. But we don't have long." I point to her unlaced boots. "That bracelet around your ankle. They know where you are. Attorney Frauhn—and the police."

Grace looks at her boots. I can see that she didn't realize the implications of it when she ran away.

"Please," I ask her. "Just sit down. Tell me why you don't trust me. Why you don't think it's safe. I want to understand what I've done."

Grace looks around the room, thinking about what to do. I've seen this before. She feels trapped. Alone. Like there's no way out. And yet she didn't run away. She came here, to The Palace. There has to be a reason.

"You don't have to sit," I tell her when she doesn't move away from the wall. "We can just talk. You stay where you are, and I'll stay here. Okay?" And then I begin, building a bridge the way I've been trained to do.

"Can you consider the possibility that there are things you don't know? Or that there's more to the things that you do know? More facts. More circumstances. With me, but also with your mother," I ask. "Whatever it is that has made you not trust her, that can be true—right alongside the fact that she loves you."

I give this a moment as her face softens.

"All of these things can be true. All at the same time," I say again.

She pushes away from the wall and takes one step forward.

"You must be tired. Just sit down. Take Dr. Westin's seat. You know how much he would hate that."

I see the acknowledgment on her face. We've both been in this room for sessions with Westin. It's one small thread connecting us. But it's enough to make her take the short walk to the chair. She sits across from me on the edge. Ready to bolt if she needs to.

"Let's talk about the day Emile was killed. Can we do that?"

She nods. *Yes.*

"Okay. So you got back from training in the afternoon. You were in the TV room at Avery Hall when you had the fight with Tammy. Right?"

Another nod, affirming these facts.

"Where were your skates?"

Her eyes move to the corner—of this room.

"Your skates were here? In Dr. Westin's office?"

"I had a session after practice," she begins quietly. "I can't land the quad toe, and Dawn says I have to get more speed. But something is holding me back."

Anger rises inside me. Fourteen years later and she's still at this. They both are.

"So you had your session, and then you walked home?"

"But I forgot my skates. I had them with me because they needed to be sharpened."

Finally, she's talking. And in full sentences that make sense—that are part of the story. I've broken through but now tread carefully so she won't shut down again.

"You were going to take your skates to the pro shop—but then you forgot them because the session with Dr. Westin distracted you. Is that right?"

"I hate coming here," she says.

"Okay," I say, remembering the same feeling about these sessions. How Westin was so calm when he listened to our despair, always circling back to why Dawn was right and why we needed to stop being afraid. "So you forgot your skates." I repeat what she's said to anchor us in the story.

"What happened next?"

"I walked back to Avery and saw the other girls on the couch, talking," she says. "We'd all heard about Emile and his California plan that day. I thought that's what they were whispering about, but . . ."

She stops as a new wave of emotions comes. So I press forward, hoping to bring her with me.

"What were they talking about?" I ask. "When Tammy told you to ask Emile?"

"I thought they were lying. But they weren't. Emile told me."

"What did he tell you, Grace?" I ask. Luring her closer.

She tightens her face and stares at me. I feel a chill run down my spine.

"About my mother," she says. "And about you."

215

"Okay." My heart races as I imagine what is going through her mind. This secret her mother kept all these years. A secret so difficult to comprehend. A girl not much older than Grace, the child who sits across from me. Her mother's cheeks. Her father's dark hair and eyes. A child unable to comprehend the decision another child faced fifteen years ago. The violence she feared. There are so many missing pieces Grace doesn't know.

But there's no time for this now.

"What exactly did Tammy say?" I ask.

A switch flips inside her. She tilts her head with indifference as if none of this matters. But her eyes sharpen like two daggers, pointed right at me.

"She said my mother didn't want me. That you drove her to a clinic to have an abortion."

And there it is. Finally spoken out loud. I can see the expectation on her face. For an apology. A plea for forgiveness. But I don't give her any of that. "How did Tammy know?" I ask instead. I have to find out what happened the night Emile disappeared.

She looks at me with a blank stare. She doesn't know, but I have my suspicions.

"Shannon talks to all of you, doesn't she?" I ask. "Like you're her friends."

"Yeah," Grace admits. "I asked her if it was true, and she wouldn't tell me. She just tried to hug me, saying all that matters is that I'm here. I told her if she wouldn't tell me the truth, I wanted to see Emile. Tammy said he knew the truth."

"So he came and picked you up."

"Yes."

"And then what happened, Grace? Where did you go?"

She takes a long breath, closes her eyes. Silently mouthing words to herself. *Fight the fear.* As much as she hates Dr. Westin, she's internalized the training she learned right here in this room.

"He didn't deny it when I asked him. He said it was complicated and we should go to his office to talk, and then I remembered that I'd left my skates. We drove to the rink, and we went inside. The sessions were over. The snack bar was closed. I was gonna grab my skates and leave them outside the pro shop so they could be sharpened in the morning."

"And where did Emile go?" I picture the scene. The pro shop was in the back of the snack bar. I get a flash—the spinning wheels of the sharpener, the high-pitched squeal when the blades were pressed between them. The smell of burning metal and polished leather.

The rink would have been dark by then, maybe just the emergency lights glowing in the hallways. I think back to the night Mio took us there, me and Indy.

"He said he was going to his office to wait for me."

"His office?" I ask her. Emile never had his own office when I was here.

But she points at the wall to the right. "In there."

"So you were both coming to this hallway—to the offices. You to get your skates from this office, and Emile to wait for you in his?"

"Yeah," she says. "But he went ahead of me because I had to use the bathroom. So I went to the locker room first. When I was done, I walked up through the bleachers and down the hall, and that's when I heard them yelling."

"Who?"

"Dawn and Emile. They were in his office, and the door was closed."

"What were they yelling about?"

Now her face grows more distant. Cautious.

"Emile was saying 'I know everything' over and over. And Dawn was saying stuff like 'How could you do this to me?' and about how she'd given him a life. After he'd failed as a skater."

"What did Emile say he knew?" I ask, though I'm not sure I want the answer.

"He said he knew about Indy Cunningham, and how Dawn ruined her career."

I know what that was about. The drugs Indy had to use. The report made to the officials at Sectionals the Olympic year, after she'd landed the triple Axel.

Two weeks later, Indy came back to The Palace. Her mother was with her. Patrice. *Fucking Patrice.* She begged Dawn to help her appeal the decision of the USFS and ISU to not let her compete at Nationals. To help them reverse the disqualification.

Dawn swore she was doing what she could. She said she didn't know who'd reported her. Dawn told her there was always next year, and too bad she would miss the Olympics. Four years wasn't that long to wait.

It washes through me, the sequence of events, electrifying my arms.

Indy had just wanted to go home to train again with Bobby Stark. She had no idea why she'd really been sent away. None of us did.

But then Grace has more to tell me, about the other things Emile said the night he disappeared.

"He said he knew things about other girls who skated with her. And how this place would be ruined if people found out."

"What about them?" I ask, my voice trembling.

But she doesn't answer. Instead she says, "They weren't alone."

"What do you mean?"

"Someone else was in the office when they were fighting. I think it was Dr. Westin," she says. "It was a man, and he wasn't yelling. And Dr. Westin's door was wide open, and the lights were on, so I think he left here and went with Dawn to confront Emile. And then I heard someone coming from the back hallway, the one that leads to the small rink. I didn't want anyone to see me, so I came in here to hide. And then I heard more yelling. Emile knew things, and he said he'd held on to the secrets for too long."

"What things?" I ask again, Dawn's words ringing in my ears. About what Emile knew. About the Orphans. About me.

"I heard my mother's name. And her friend—Kayla," Grace says. "But then I heard your name. *Ana Robbins.* That's when it got quiet. All of them just stopped."

"When he said my name?" I ask. "Is that why you told me last night that this was all my fault?"

Grace nods. "You did something they're all afraid of—didn't you?"

"What did they say I did?"

Grace looks away. She doesn't want to tell me.

"Grace—what do they know?"

She looks at me with a new kind of fear. Like she's afraid of me.

"I . . . I couldn't hear them when they stopped yelling. But when Emile said 'I know everything,' Dawn said something like 'No one will believe you,' and then he laughed at them. That's when I heard her door open, and I thought Dr. Westin might be coming back, so I sneaked out through there." She points to the wall behind Westin's desk.

Okay, I whisper to myself. *It's okay.*

Then Grace gets up from the chair.

"I have to show you something," she says.

She walks across the room to the other side, then behind Westin's desk. There's a break in the wall where she was pointing, a panel that opens to a closet with office supplies. But Grace slides the panel to the right and walks inside, and I follow, turning on the phone light when she shuts the door behind us.

"Look." She points to a spot on the floor, under one of the shelves. I take my phone and shine the flashlight.

There's a semicircle extending out from the wall. Dark red.

I bend down to touch it. The pool is thick, the center still sticky. I know the smell. *Blood.*

"Jesus," I whisper. "How did you know this was here?"

"I came back the next day, before they found Emile's body. I wanted to look for my skates, but they were gone. I thought maybe someone had moved them into the closet. This is what I saw when I opened the door."

I study the scene. The wall where the blood seeps through—it separates this room from the office next door. "Emile's office," I say. And Grace nods.

"Is there blood there too?" I ask her. But I know the answer. If they'd found blood anywhere in The Palace, the investigation would have taken a sharp turn.

"I think they killed him," Grace says. "In his office after that fight they had."

"But the field . . . that's where his body was found," I remind her.

She starts to panic. I can see the shaking run through her body.

"I . . . I don't know—they must have moved it!" she says. "And then cleaned it up—the blood in his office. They didn't know about this closet—that it had seeped under the wall."

And now her behavior begins to make sense.

Grace did know something. Just not enough to come forward.

"I think they used my skate to kill him," she says, tears beginning to stream down her face. "Then they cleaned them and put them in my locker."

My head is spinning with the implications of this. Was it a setup? Or did they try to protect Grace by cleaning her skates?

"So you think Emile got your skates from in here, in Westin's office, then went back to his office, where Dawn found him. And Westin was there too."

"Yes," she says. "I didn't see my skates in here when I came to look."

"And then they had that fight. And Emile . . ."

"Died."

She's detached again when she says this, and I understand. This is where her mind needs to go to say these words and be in this place where it happened.

"But I have to tell you something else."

"Okay . . ."

"When I ran outside, there were four cars in the lot that I recognized."

Suddenly there's a clanging of metal. A door opening down by the ice. Grace looks at me, terrified.

"Someone's coming!" she says. And then she moves to the back of the closet, not into the office. She reaches the end of the shelves. They almost touch the wall, but there's a small gap.

"This way!" she says, and then she slips into the gap and disappears.

I try to follow, but the space is too narrow. The shelves don't move, even when I lean my body into them. They're flush against the front wall and bolted in place.

I shine the light into the gap, press my back against the wall, and turn my head and see another door that's behind the shelves, in the gap. Grace has managed to open it enough to get through.

"Grace!" I whisper, but she's already gone, and I try to piece together the layout of the room and the hallway outside and where this escape has taken her.

Because I can't get through. And then I hear another door open. And a voice.

"Ana? Grace? Are you in here?"

Chapter Thirty-Four

Excerpt from Testimony of Bobby Stark

ADA OLSON: After Indy was suspended from competition for the Olympic year, did you worry about her emotional state?

BOBBY STARK: Yes. I was there at the competition when it happened. I couldn't believe it. I called Patrice the next day and told her I would take Indy back. No questions asked. I knew this had to be some kind of mistake, and if it wasn't, she had a good reason for using the drugs. And it turned out, I was right.

ADA OLSON: What did she say?

BOBBY STARK: What she always said when Indy asked to come home.

ADA OLSON: Which was what?

BOBBY STARK: Over her dead body.

ADA OLSON: And why was that?

BOBBY STARK: I don't know.

ADA OLSON: Was it the rivalry with Dawn Sumner?

BOBBY STARK: Maybe. That's what Indy thought. Did you know that Dawn let her fall on that jump—knowing what was wrong with the takeoff? Indy told me how she learned to fix it. She said she told Dawn to her face when they were alone in her office—she told her that she was a shitty coach, and she was right.

ADA OLSON: That might explain why Dawn did what she did—but I was asking you about Patrice. Indy's own mother. Why didn't she let her come home? It wasn't a decades-old rivalry, was it?

BOBBY STARK: No.

ADA OLSON: So—what was the reason Patrice wouldn't let Indy train with you?

BOBBY STARK: It was personal.

ADA OLSON: How so?

BOBBY STARK: Does it matter now?

ADA OLSON: Just answer the question, please.

BOBBY STARK: But it's not relevant to any of this.

ADA OLSON: Mr. Stark . . .

BOBBY STARK: Okay. Okay. Look—the year before Indy was sent to The Palace . . . Patrice—she tried to initiate a relationship.

ADA OLSON: A sexual relationship?

BOBBY STARK: Yes.

ADA OLSON: Did you refuse her? Turn her away?

BOBBY STARK: Of course. I'm married—so is she. And I didn't share those feelings.

ADA OLSON: And how did she react?

BOBBY STARK: She was furious—she accused me of leading her on—and then she . . .

ADA OLSON: What, Mr. Stark? What did she tell you?

BOBBY STARK: She said I must be in love with Indy—her daughter. That must explain my interest in her—and their family. I think it made her feel better to believe that I was some kind of pedophile.

ADA OLSON: What happened after that?

BOBBY STARK: Two months later, Indy was sent away. And her mother never let her come back.

Chapter Thirty-Five

ANA

Before—One Year and Eleven Months at The Palace

After Sectionals, rumors swirled everywhere about Indy's disqualification from competition that season—including Nationals and the Olympics. Someone had reported her to the USFS for using unauthorized drugs. The morphine in the DMSO. Dawn was appealing it but told Indy she couldn't train at The Palace until it was sorted out.

Indy came to collect her things. Patrice was with her. Indy was crying so hard she could barely breathe as she carried her duffel bag down the stairs.

Ana tried to comfort her, whispering in her ear that this was all going to be okay—she would be able to train with Bobby Stark again, and they'd reverse the ruling in time for Nationals. Maybe it was a blessing in disguise.

Indy tried to smile when they held each other in the driveway, a last goodbye. Just like Jolene, chest to chest and cheek to cheek. When the car drove off, Ana ran to the basement closet, squeezed inside, and cried until she had no more tears.

Dawn seemed to know the extent of her loss. The dinners became more frequent. Ana had earned a spot at Nationals, and Dawn said they needed to evaluate her programs very carefully. "*Meticulously,*" she said. Make sure they were placing everything just right so she could get the most points.

"*Come for dinner,*" she would say, after a lesson. Then she'd pick her up along the access road. Put out the linen place mats and the fine crystal, and they'd eat stir-fry and drink orange soda.

They watched videos of her programs on the big blue sofa, and Dawn crept under her skin like never before. The weed growing bigger, around every bone and ligament. Every vital organ. Bigger and tighter, squeezing out Ana's loneliness for her mother, and Indy. Kayla and Jolene. And each day Ana would wonder if Dawn would invite her to dinner, praying she would, fearing she wouldn't.

Day after day with the Orphans all gone, their dreams all dead, Ana tried to convince herself that sadness was just a feeling, like fear. She wondered if that, too, could be turned to rage.

Because the alternative was incomprehensible. The feeling unbearable.

At Thanksgiving, Ana went home for a visit.

And what was she thinking would happen there? That her family, together for the first time since last Christmas, could turn back time? Make her feel the way she did when her mother wafted through the door after showing a house? Calling out, *I'm home!* The afternoon light streaming through her bedroom window somehow brighter when she heard her mother's voice? She would start cooking, her father setting the table. Tim blaring his music. Then—*Time for dinner!*

The smallest things that—she now realized—had filled half of her up. A baseline of happiness that she could add to with her skating and her other dreams. Like a smile from the hockey player with the steady gaze. Her first kiss.

The things she needed were laid out before her—now that they were gone.

She crawled into her mother's bed on the last night and sat close to her. Connie was too tired to watch a movie, so Ana made up stories about The Palace, all of her wonderful friends there and the silly things they did. She told Connie about Dawn's praise for her, and how her triples were coming along. How excited she was to compete at Nationals for the first time. The lies just flew from her mouth.

Then Connie started to cry. She took Ana's hand and held it to her lips, and Ana looked at her mouth to see what words she might hear next. *I love you,* maybe. *I'm so proud of you.*

But that was not what she said, or tried to say.

"Who are you?" she demanded. Angry and scared. She pushed Ana off the bed.

"Mom?" Ana said—not just afraid. *Terrified.*

Her father raced into the room, past Ana, who was on the floor, and onto the bed, where he held his wife.

"Shhh," he whispered. "It's okay. You know her, Connie. She's a lovely girl. You're perfectly safe."

Ana stared at her father's back, while her mother glared at her from over his shoulder as he held her tight. Her arms were listless by her sides. Like those of a rag doll.

Carl let her go. He laid her back down and turned on the TV.

"Watch your show, honey," he said. "I'll be right back."

He walked to Ana and led her out of the room. He explained that the tumor in her mother's brain had grown, in spite of all the trials and treatments. It had grown like a different kind of weed, stealing her memories. Taking her life before she was even dead.

Ana cried, and Carl cried. Holding her the way he'd held her mother.

"I'm going to take you back to Echo tomorrow," he said. "You have to go live your life, Ana. That's what she wanted. Not for you to see her like this."

He pulled away just far enough for her to see his eyes.

"Promise me, okay."

The following Saturday, she went to the rink for the eight a.m. session like she always did. She didn't have a lesson, but Dawn wanted her to run through her long program. She said she'd be watching from the corner of her eye as soon as the music started. *Rhapsody in Blue*, the first notes, pushing into a layback spin, the world a blur as she felt her right leg lift, a ninety-degree angle, her left blade on that spot right between the first spike of the toe pick and the last inch of the straight edge. Arms overhead, a perfect arch. Ten rotations, then a release, backward onto a right outside edge.

Her mind was already ahead to the first jumping pass—the triple-triple combination—when she saw Dawn skating toward her, and behind that image, by the boards, her father, who hadn't been to The Palace for months. It didn't register as she reached the bend that if he was here, something bad had happened.

"Ana!" Dawn called out, trailing behind her on her gold blades. "Stop."

So she stopped and waited for Dawn to catch up, then take her in her arms, inside the blue puffer coat.

"You need to come with me," she said. And then, "I'm so sorry."

Ana followed Dawn off the ice. Grabbing her skate guards, slipping them on. Then up the stairs to her office. Her father was right behind them.

In Dawn's office, she learned her mother had died the night before, in her bed. Carl said those actual words. But he entrusted the rest of it to Dawn. Who said things like *she's at peace now*. And *she's proud of you*. Ana's eyes darted between them, her father and Dawn. For the first time since arriving at The Palace, she truly felt like an orphan.

Carl spent the day with her at Avery Hall. In her empty room, sitting on her bed, talking about what had happened. He repeated what Dawn had said. How Connie was at peace now. In a better place. She'd said her goodbyes over Thanksgiving weekend, and didn't Ana know that was what those moments had been? Wasn't it obvious?

They called Tim and spoke to him together. He seemed to understand all these things about the end having been days away and the goodbyes having come and gone.

"She wrote you both letters, and I'll share them with you next time we're all together," Carl said.

Ana couldn't speak. She couldn't even cry. Again, she was frozen. Not with fear but with something else. Something even worse.

Carl left and told her she should go back to the rink. "*Live your life*," he said again. "*It's the best thing for you. I promise. I love you.*"

So she went, because what else was she supposed to do? She went to The Palace, where Dawn gave her a lesson and she was *a good girl.* Falling, but making the rotations. Fighting the fear. Folding into the puffer coat, extra long because her mother had just died. Inhaling the smell, the makeup, hairspray, stale coffee on warm breath.

"*Don't go home. Come for dinner.*"

She made the stir-fry.

She poured orange soda.

But tonight there were three place mats because "*Emile is joining us for dinner. Won't that be fun? Won't that make you feel better?*"

After the food and the soda, they watched Ana's program, and then it was time to go and Emile said, "I can drive her home."

To which Dawn said, "Great."

But he didn't bring her home. He turned left at the fork, down the dirt road.

Ana had been in the guest cottage just once before. When Kayla was assaulted.

She was here again, after losing all of them, the Orphans, and now her mother.

"Want a beer?" he asked.

Ana nodded.

Emile got up to grab a beer. As he passed by her, he stroked her cheek with the back of his hand, and she felt a sudden release inside her. Tears began to fall.

"What do you need, Ana?" Emile asked her. Then he took her arm and pulled her to stand.

"I don't know," she cried. But this was a lie. In this moment, all she could think was that she needed someone to hold her.

She fell into his body, her head barely reaching the nape of his neck. Wrapped her arms around his waist. Showing him what she needed.

She didn't care that it felt wrong. She was drowning, and he was there, offering a lifeboat. Just like he'd offered his hand as she lay on the ground outside the snack bar.

He moaned then. Made a sound like *mmmmm*. Like her body felt good to him.

"Ask me what I want," he said. His voice was playful.

And she did. She asked, her voice trembling, "What do you want?"

"I want to be the first," he said. "Do you know what I mean?"

It didn't matter if she did or if she didn't. The only thing she knew that mattered in that moment was that she would have sold her soul for the comfort of being held.

"Come on, then," he said. "Take off your clothes . . . lie on the bed for me."

She walked to the bed. Undressed. Hating herself more and more with each reveal of her body. And more when he climbed on top of her, his head above hers so she couldn't see his face.

More, when he moved his knee between her thighs, pushing them apart.

More, when she felt him inside her.

Emile hardly noticed the tears that became a waterfall down her face and onto his sheets as her mind filled with thoughts of warm banana bread and colorful scarves. Of bubble gum lip gloss and red hair and Jack Daniel's.

When it was over, he went to pee, grab a fresh beer, his body moving in the shadows. Ana sat up and wiped her face with the edge of a pillowcase.

"See—it's no big deal," he said as he walked back to the bathroom.

She gathered her clothes while he took a shower, then sneaked out the door in the dead of night, into the woods behind the cottage. The woods that led down the mountain.

Through the trees with their prickly branches, grabbing at her wool mittens. Her sleeves. The thick brush catching her boots. She didn't stop until she got to the field, then made her way back up the access road to Avery Hall.

She took a shower, so hot her skin turned bright red. The burning felt better than what was happening inside her. Emile had betrayed her friends. She hated him. But she also needed him. Just like Dawn, but maybe worse. And the disgust this bred inside her was the very thing that led her back to his door whenever it was open.

Chapter
Thirty-Six

ANA

Now

"Artis!"

I step out of the closet, and he flips on the light in Westin's office.

"Thank God," he says. He holds up his cell phone. "The monitoring station called—they tracked Grace here . . . I've been looking all over."

His eyes scan the room, then land on the open sliding panel behind me. "Where is she?"

"There's an exit through there," I tell him, pointing into the closet.

He looks at me with panic in his eyes. "This isn't good! I have to get her back to the condo within the hour, or they'll take her in. They'll arrest her, Ana. Christ . . ."

Hands on my hips, I drop my head and let out a long exhale. I know how all of this works. We have to find Grace.

"Why did she come here?" he asks now. And I'm about to tell him everything—how Grace heard Dawn fighting with Emile the night he died. How his blood seeped through the wall to the floor in the closet. How his body was moved to the field, Grace's skate cleaned, put back in her locker.

But there's no time. If Artis didn't pass Grace coming up from the rink, that means she went out the back.

"Do you have your car?" I ask.

Artis dangles the keys that are clutched in his hand.

"Meet me at the back exit—by the small rink," I tell him. "I think that's where she went."

And then I leave him there, in Westin's office, as I move into the hallway and away from the arena. I walk the corridor that leads to another passage, then down a set of stairs at the back of the stands, to the level of the ice. I look for Grace in every dark corner.

I remember walking through this corridor, windowless and damp, every step echoing. This was a way to get out of the building without passing by the mothers in the stands, the skaters in the snack bar. Dawn and Emile. I remember wanting it to swallow me up and spit me out a million miles away. Or maybe back in time before I'd felt the speed and freedom of the ice. Before it had sucked me in like an addiction and led me to this place.

I grab my phone and call Jolene. She picks up on the first ring, her voice shaking.

"Did you find her? Please tell me . . ."

"She came to The Palace . . ."

"Why?" she asks, alarm in her voice.

I don't know how much to tell her. Not before I find her daughter.

"She knows something, Jo. And she's scared. She told me, then ran away."

"What did she tell you?"

"We'll find her—Artis is here with the car . . ."

I hear her feet pounding on the thin carpet, a door opening, like she's getting ready to leave.

We have the same exchange as we did before. I tell her she has to stay there in case Grace returns. She makes me promise to find her daughter. And I do. Again, I promise.

I hang up the phone, put it back in my pocket as I reach the entrance to the second rink and push through the double doors.

I smell the rink again. But it's thicker here, trapped by the low ceiling and windowless walls, the plexiglass that sits on the boards.

The second rink was where I practiced spins and laid out choreography because it was too small to get speed for a jump, but enough to feel the ice, feel my body move. It was where we got dressed for the summer show—helped by the skating mothers, who spent more time at The Palace than their children. They had nowhere else to go, their lives entirely vicarious. I think now about Mrs. Finch—Shannon's mother—and then Shannon.

How she told Tammy Theisen about Jolene and the clinic.

How could she do that—knowing it would get back to Grace? She has a child now. I saw the LEGO set. Heard the cartoons. I'm reminded of the lesson I had to keep learning when I was here as a girl. Over and over about the *mothers*. How that word, alone, means nothing.

Memories creep out of hiding. I've woken the dead.

The musty costumes that were rented from theater companies, lingering body odor from the last people to wear them, fabric scratching my neck, hanging on my shoulders like a brocade drapery. Dawn dressing us up like puppets. Pulling us away from our routines and schedules, our alliances and bunkers. Stripped bare without them.

I call out her name.

"Grace?"

My breath encircles my head like a plume of smoke, cutting through the cold. The heat is off in this rink, and it's dropped below freezing.

Panels of LED lights hang from metal beams that stretch across the ceiling. I can see wall to wall, across the ice through the plexiglass in front of me, and behind me to two rows of benches where we used to sit and lace our skates.

I call out again.

"Grace!"

Searching behind the boards, I walk the perimeter, reaching the place where we would hide, me and the other Orphans. We would hide and listen to the mothers' gossip while they set up the racks with the costumes during the summer show, or Dawn with the other coaches. Dawn with Emile in between lessons.

Fourteen years ago, I left this place behind, sorted the memories like files. Put them in a box. I thought I'd done what I tell my clients to do—process, feel, then move on.

But it's all here now, after building for days. Excitement, fear. Longing, fear. Loneliness, fear. Every emotion I cycled through at The Palace was accompanied by the one thing I was supposed to control.

Except for the one that came last. The rage. The same rage that was on Grace's face in that video.

I make my way around the first corner, at the other end of the oval. I can feel the costumes, hear the Broadway music, all of it churning.

Anticipation, fear. The party at the field. The one that always came on the last night of the ice show—before the start of school. The night we parked next to the black van.

That was where it all began to unravel for us, the four Orphans. The second rink with the costumes. Then the show. Then back to Avery Hall to change for the party. What started then is still happening. Emile is dead. Jolene's daughter is about to be charged with the crime, her life ruined.

Suddenly, I catch a flash of movement behind me, then a gust of bitter cold, the prickle of snow on my face. I turn to see a flurry of white as the storm rushes inside through the Zamboni bay.

"Ana!" Artis has pulled the car around. "What's happening?" He can see me through the large metal door that's open in the back. Grace must have gone out that way.

It's dark now. The temperature is dropping fast.

Grace didn't have a hat or gloves, and her coat wasn't made for this kind of cold.

"Grace!" I call out one last time into the rink, though I know she's not here. She's out in the storm. And a wave of panic rises. She'll freeze to death out there.

I can see the face of every child I've tried to save. Even the ones who were charged and tried, found guilty, and sentenced to some form of incarceration. We fought for them like they were our own children, and we never stopped. Appeals, motions for transfer, motions for release. Not one of my clients was discarded, left to slip away into psychosis, left to be abused in an adult facility. We fought for them—no matter what they'd done. Because they couldn't fight for themselves.

That was how I dug my way out of this place.

I've asked myself when it might be enough. When I might see this work as a job and not a lifeline. I don't have an answer. Sometimes I think all I see and hear in this world are the desperate pleas of damaged children. I know I can't save them all.

I look at the white bursts of wind that pass through the beam of the headlights and think, *Maybe not—but I can save Grace.*

I can finish what Emile started. Burn this whole place to the ground.

Chapter Thirty-Seven

Excerpt from Testimony of Bobby Stark

ADA OLSON: When Indy was expelled from The Palace by Dawn Sumner, did she try to contact you?

BOBBY STARK: Of course—we were in touch every day, from the moment she left. She told me the things that happened there—to her and the other girls. When she got kicked out, she begged me to coach her again. She didn't even care about the Olympic cycle being lost—she said being able to come home was a silver lining.

ADA OLSON: But you didn't train her again, did you?

BOBBY STARK: No.

ADA OLSON: Why was that?

BOBBY STARK: When Patrice found out Indy and I had been talking, conspiring to get her home, she accused me of being inappropriate with her. And then she reported me to Safe Sport.

ADA OLSON: That's the organization that protects child athletes from abuse?

BOBBY STARK: Yes. She told them I was grooming her.

ADA OLSON: For sex?

BOBBY STARK: Yes. It was a disgusting lie. Indy was like a daughter to me. I hired a lawyer. I had to tell them about Patrice wanting to have an affair. I had to show them proof—I had her text messages. Still, it was my word against hers.

ADA OLSON: And during that time, did you have any contact with Indy?

BOBBY STARK: Yes. I had to tell her the truth—why I couldn't train her. Why I couldn't even speak to her anymore.

ADA OLSON: You told her about her mother's sexual advances—and how she made false accusations about you to the USFS?

BOBBY STARK: Yes. I wanted her to understand—it had nothing to do with her.

ADA OLSON: But you still cut her off.

BOBBY STARK: Well, yes. I couldn't risk losing my career.

ADA OLSON: Did you tell her to her face? Did you see her one last time?

BOBBY STARK: No—like I said—I couldn't risk it.

ADA OLSON: So you told her over the phone. How did she take it?

BOBBY STARK: She was upset—and angry. Enraged, actually.

ADA OLSON: And then . . .

BOBBY STARK: I think we all know the ending.

Chapter
Thirty-Eight

ANA

Before—Two Years at The Palace

In the aftermath, in the weeks after her mother died, what Ana needed more than anything was comfort. She took what she could from her lessons with Dawn and her nights with Emile.

She worked on the triples, fighting to get the height, to *fight the fear* and go faster, be stronger. She let Dawn pull her into her coat and whisper *good girl* when she finally landed the triple flip clean four weeks before Nationals.

"See! That's the way," Dawn told her. "There's no hesitation now—the fear is gone."

And maybe it was. Because everything that Ana had feared had already happened. She was getting higher, hurling herself into the air with the same abandon that Kayla once had. High enough to make the full rotation, though that wasn't what was driving her. It was leaving the ice, even for a second, that she started to crave. And how ironic, she thought, that being *on* the ice had once been her greatest joy.

It's no big deal.

And it wasn't, sleeping with Emile. It was nothing, really, when measured against the relief that would overwhelm her when they were together and her body had a mind of its own.

And while that mind was busy being tangled in his sheets, beneath his body, another part of her was set free, to float above the bed and be with the others who had brought her comfort, like they were still here, maybe up by the ceiling. Only seeing each other. Kayla. Jolene. Indy. Connie. She could be with them without feeling the pain of having them all gone.

So, yes, she found relief in his bed.

Which disgusted her the moment she left, every time she left, the disgust then fueling the need for greater relief. And on and on in a circle, a giant snowball rolling down a hill, growing bigger and bigger, but enabling her to survive. She was holding on, white knuckled, just trying to keep it together for Nationals, where everyone would see the new triple flip, but also wanting to disappear.

Until the night she wore the baby blue dress with the yellow butterflies to train in the second rink, working on a transition for her spin combination.

The night Emile came looking for her.

He stood by the open boards and called her name. "You need to come with me," he said.

"Now?" Ana asked. "Let me go change . . ."

"No," Emile said. "Right now."

Ana was confused because the session was almost over, and so was his, in the big rink.

"What's going on?"

"Just do what I'm asking."

So she did, following him to the parking lot outside the Zamboni bay, her skates still on her feet, guards on the blades but not even a sweater to keep her warm.

He didn't so much as turn his head as they drove up the access road to the long driveway. Panic rising in her throat because they never went to the cottage during the day. Something was wrong.

He drove past the dirt road to the end of the driveway, parked, and got out. Ana took off her skates and carried them as she followed Emile to Dawn's front door.

They walked inside, then back to the dining room, where Dawn and Dr. Westin sat at the table, nothing in front of them on the coasters and place mats. Not even a glass of water, just folded hands and serious faces, looking intently at Ana, in her tights and the blue dress, her skates dangling from her fingers.

Dr. Westin spoke first. "Why don't you sit down."

Ana didn't answer, and she didn't sit down. White specks floated across her eyes and blood surged in her veins.

Dawn sighed.

"It's Indy," she said. "Please—sit down."

Emile took her arm and led her toward a chair, the same way he'd brought her to his bed. But this time, she pulled away.

"Someone tell me what's happened."

"Maybe we should call her father first," Dr. Westin said to Dawn and Emile, as if Ana wasn't even there in the room.

Dawn shook her head. "There's no time," she said. "It's spreading fast. She needs to hear it from us."

"Hear what?" Ana asked, her throat so dry her voice began to crack.

"Ana, honey," Dawn said. "Indy died."

Ana stared blankly at Dawn's mouth. At the red lipstick caked between the small folds and the cracks in the corners. She stared, waiting for more words, because what she'd just heard didn't make sense.

"Ana?" Emile said. "Did you hear what Dawn said? Indy is dead. It's terrible, I know . . ."

Ana took a step back, away from them as they sat at the table.

"No," she whispered. And again. "No."

"Ana . . ." Dr. Westin said. "I know this is a shock. Maybe it will help if we explain what happened."

"No . . ."

"Just listen," Dr. Westin said. His voice was calm. Clinical.

"Indy drank the chemicals in that bottle—the DMSO mixed with morphine—a powerful opioid," he said. "The DMSO accelerated the absorption into her bloodstream," he explained. "It's not clear if she was trying to make herself feel better, or if she was trying to hurt herself. But either way, she was a troubled young woman. I think you know that."

One light off and another switched on inside her head. A shift, a sudden awakening. None of this was real. Indy wasn't dead.

"You're lying!" Ana screamed, backing away from the table.

Emile reached out for her again. "Just sit down," he said. "Let us help you."

But Ana's feet were moving the other way, and she ran back toward the foyer and the front door. And all of them followed.

Emile got there first and blocked her from leaving. He held his hands in front of him like he was confronting a cornered animal. Dawn and Dr. Westin stood there. Watching.

Each of them said her name.

"Ana . . . calm down," Dr. Westin said.

"Ana . . . let's go back to the table," Emile pleaded.

"Ana . . . be a good girl now," Dawn said.

The dam broke, letting loose an eruption. "You did this to her!" Ana screamed. "You killed Indy!"

"Ana—calm down!" Dawn ordered. "I did nothing but support her! I fought for her appeal . . ."

"That's a lie!" Ana screamed, tears soaking her face. "You gave her that bruise! You're the one who reported her! Everything that happened is because of you! You killed her!"

Emile and Dr. Westin both looked at Dawn, waiting for her defense to the allegations. But she said nothing.

"How did you know what she was doing? Who told you?" Ana demanded, still trapped, with Emile at the front door. Dawn and Dr. Westin behind her.

She looked at each of them, searching their faces for answers. It was then she saw a look pass between Dawn and Emile.

"You? Did you tell her?" Ana asked.

Of course he did, she thought. Hugo was his best friend. And Hugo was the one who'd first given Indy that clear plastic bottle.

"No," Emile lied. "I didn't know anything about it."

But Ana knew the truth.

Emile had told Dawn and she'd reported Indy and now Indy was dead. And all Ana could think was to run.

Pushing past Emile, out the front door, into the frigid air, into the darkness that had descended since they'd arrived, around the back of the house to the tree line of evergreens and bare maples, and to the woods and down the mountain.

Run.

Dr. Westin ran after her, trying to keep up.

She reached the field, Dr. Westin's voice behind her, the headlights of a car out in front. Emile's car. He got out, walked closer, while Dr. Westin approached from behind.

"Stop!"

"It's all right!"

"There's nowhere to go . . ."

She stood only a few feet away when she leveled her accusation again. "You told Dawn. You knew what she would do!"

For weeks, she'd been coming to his bed. Disgust. Relief. The snowball growing with each swell of emotions.

"Come here now, Ana. Nice and easy," Emile said.

"It's no big deal."

She slipped her hand inside the boot of the skate, removed the guard, as the narrative shifted in her head. This place. These people. Indy was dead because of them. Fear finally turning to rage.

It was time to fight.

"Ana!" Dr. Westin was out of breath when he caught up, the two men boxing her in.

"Get away from me!" Ana said.

But they didn't listen. "Calm down. You're acting crazy," Emile said, taking a step closer.

Ana lifted her hand higher, the one with the skate, the heel of the blade angled to strike. She swung it at his head, and he stepped back. She could see the fear in his eyes.

"Everybody, calm down," Dr. Westin said. She could hear the fear in his voice.

All because of the blade.

"Ana," Dr. Westin said. "What do you want us to do? It's cold, and you have no shoes. No coat. Let us take you home. There's nowhere to go."

But their fear had lit a fuse.

"You killed Indy! All of you. Stay away from me . . ."

Emile's voice sharpened. "Come on, Ana—you're acting like a child!"

Disgust. Relief.

She could see things now, in this new narrative, the walls of a cage she'd put herself in. Thinking this was all there was—The Palace, Dawn, Emile—with everyone else gone. Her family, the Orphans. Her mother was dead. Indy was dead. *Dead.* The men kept talking, pleading with her. The cage door open. Freedom waiting on the other side.

Freedom from this tarnished dream and the person she had become, the child trying to hold on to it.

Her eyes turned again to the highway at the other end of the field, the lights from the cars and trucks passing through.

She lowered her hand from the air, picked up her other skate from the ground, then turned, and ran toward the road, toward freedom, the men calling after her but unable to follow. Emile with his limp, and Dr. Westin exhausted from the chase down the mountain.

She didn't look back as their voices faded. Making her way to the edge of the field and under the split rail fence. To the shoulder of the highway. And she kept running, then walking, skates hanging by their blades, clenched in her hands.

Exhausted, feet numb and bleeding, she came to the truck stop after a quarter of a mile.

Black pavement. White painted lines. Bright streetlamps shining on the tops of metal trucks, their sides red, blue, orange, yellow. Their tires as tall as her shoulders when she limped past them. The drivers' cabs dark, the truckers asleep somewhere inside.

Walking between them, she got to the other side, away from the highway, where she might be seen. There was a small structure. The sign read **Facilities**, so she went inside. There she found a row of vending machines that lined the wall to the left. On the right was a broken door, hanging from one hinge. Behind it, a toilet and sink and a stench that made her gag.

But she washed her hands. Wiped her face. Dried them with the sleeves of her dress. Then she leaned her body against the back of a vending machine that was warm and buzzing, the motor inside keeping the drinks cold. She slid down to the ground.

Her head was light, high from the rush. It felt euphoric, this thing she'd done, breaking out of the cage, running from the despair and all she'd lost. And before she could come down and think of what to do next, think of Indy, the door opened and a man walked in.

"Hey," he said. "What do we have here?"

He waited a moment. Let Ana study him. His kind smile. Gentle demeanor.

"Are you okay?" he asked, looking at her torn tights. Bloody feet.

Ana nodded, suddenly aware of how she must look. What he must think.

"Do you need a ride home?" he asked. "I'm headed to Wyoming, but I don't mind stopping somewhere."

He wore a brown coat and jeans. His boots were clean, his face shaved.

"Or I could call someone for you," he said. "My phone's just back in the truck."

He reached out his hand to help her to her feet. And she took it.

Ana followed him to the cab of his semi, where he opened the passenger side door and lifted her up so she could climb inside. He gave her a soda and a bag of chips from the vending machine, and she ate and drank.

"What happened to you?" he asked.

Ana didn't answer. She was in another world, some in-between place her mind had taken her.

"It's okay," he said, starting the engine. "It's none of my business."

He looked out the window, to the front and the back, then switched on the turn signal.

"You're safe now, sweetheart," he said. "I'll take you anywhere you want to go."

He took off his coat and handed it to her.

"Here, take this," he said. "Get warm. Get some rest."

As he steered the rig away from the curb, back onto the highway, Ana pulled the coat over her like a blanket. She leaned her head against the window and felt the soft hum of the engine as they gathered speed.

Music came from the radio, and he turned the volume down low.

Ana's eyes were heavy and began to close. She didn't fight it. Listening to the music, feeling the vibrations from the road, the warmth from his coat.

Smelling the pine from the air freshener that hung on the rearview mirror as she drifted off.

Chapter Thirty-Nine

ANA

Now

Artis is just outside the back entrance to the small rink. I send a text to Jolene.

> Grace left The Palace.
> She might be headed to you.

> She replies. Kayla's here. We have her truck. We're coming to look.

I run to the car through the whipping wind, thinking she must have called Kayla the moment I left the condo. She didn't trust me to find Grace. To keep her safe.

I reach Artis's car and get inside.

"No sign?" he asks, but he already knows. If I'd found Grace, she would be with me.

"She couldn't have gone far." My eyes turn to the road, the exit, the places Grace might be heading. I'm expecting Artis to shift the car into drive and hit the gas.

Instead he looks at me and waits.

"What?" I ask.

"I don't know where to go. Maybe we should wait for the next call from the monitoring station."

"Artis—no!" I protest. "She could freeze to death by then! And what if they lose the signal?"

He hangs his head. "Okay—then where would she be going? What did she tell you in there that made her run away again?"

I think now about what she said, what spooked her.

"She heard them fighting—Emile and Dawn, and possibly Westin, the night he was killed. They were in Emile's office."

Artis goes quiet as he fights to hold an expression. What is it, exactly? Curiosity? Surprise?

"Did you know?"

Now a change, the pull of his cheeks, squint of his eyes. "Know what?"

I rattle off everything I learned from Jill back home and Grace just moments ago.

"Emile was speaking to a reporter about The Palace. He was telling them things about Dawn's training methods and Westin's practices. And about us—me, Jolene, Kayla, and Indy. He knew everything. He wanted to take this place down before leaving for California."

Artis shifts back in his seat. "You think they killed Emile? And then what—moved his body? And now they're letting everyone believe Grace did it?"

Impatience seethes inside me—I need Artis to catch up, to get to where I am in understanding what happened. He doesn't know what they're capable of. I can see it on his face. How crazy I must sound.

"There was something else Grace saw—a car she recognized in the parking lot. But she heard you coming down the hall, and she ran out the back before she could tell me."

"Wait—someone *else* was at The Palace the night Emile went missing? Besides Dawn and Westin?"

"Yes . . . please—just drive. We need to find her."

Artis puts the car in gear and starts to move.

"Who does she think was there? Besides Dawn and Westin?"

"I don't know—just drive toward the condos. Maybe she's going back there."

Artis does as I ask, but I can see his face growing apprehensive.

"It's a little convenient that she didn't have time to tell you—don't you think? Before she ran away again?"

I shake my head, look at him. "No—I don't. She was scared."

He exhales long and hard. "And you're sure it was blood in that closet?"

Now I understand. "You think this is all a ruse? That she's making it up?"

"She hasn't exactly been helpful—until now. Saying, what? That she heard a fight, then someone else coming, and now there's blood in the closet between the offices . . . she's found a way to explain the blood on her skates."

I can't believe what he's saying. But then I think, maybe it's me—maybe I'm blinded by the past. She knew exactly what to tell me to ignite my own fear—that Emile knew a secret about me.

"And what about the dress?" Artis asks. "Someone would have seen them in the dorm if they'd taken it from Grace's room."

"Not necessarily—and what are we even doing? It's their job to prove Grace is guilty. Not ours . . ."

My phone pings, and I reach for it in my coat.

Artis glances over with anticipation. "Is it Grace?"

I shake my head. "It's my office," I tell him. "They've been chasing a lead."

He returns his eyes to the road, hands on the wheel, while I read the text.

Not sure what this means but read the file, it says.

So I click the link and get to a filing in a Colorado court. It's a family matter.

Artis pulls onto the access road, his SUV slipping in the deep snow. "Christ," he says. "This is bad."

I'm reading a court filing in a custody case. Emile Dresiér v. Shannon Finch—PETITION FOR SOLE LEGAL CUSTODY AND RELOCATION OF THE MINOR CHILD, CALEB FINCH . . .

What the hell is this?

I read on, pulling out the facts. The minor child is five years old, the petition says. It recites the history of the legal proceedings. The ongoing custody hearings. The recent decision in Emile's favor. The appeal Shannon filed.

I think about the cartoons playing in Shannon's apartment at Avery Hall. The LEGO set in the corner. Shannon never married, but she had a child—with Emile, the pleadings say. They'd been battling over him for years. And now Emile was moving to California. He was taking his son with him.

And then I hear Artis's question from moments before. About Grace's dress and who might have had access to her room.

There's the answer—right in front of me. *Shannon Finch.*

Artis looks from me to the road. Back and forth.

"Ana," he says, as the car creeps through a tunnel of white. We can't see more than a few feet beyond the hood. Can't even get our bearings from the landscape, the shape of the road, the direction we're heading.

"I know it's bad—just keep going," I say. But that's not what he wants to tell me, about the storm and the snow and the dangerous driving conditions.

"It's about the dress . . ."

Now he has my full attention. "The dress? What about it?"

"Look on the back seat," he says. So I do. I turn and see a clear plastic bag with something inside. A piece of clothing.

Baby blue. Yellow butterflies. The distinct reddish brown of dried blood.

My heart is in my throat as I reach back for the bag. But then I stop. If that's Grace's dress, it's evidence in the crime. There could be prints on the bag, from whoever took it from her room that night. And now from Artis.

"Where did you get that?" I ask, my mind reeling with possibilities as I get another text.

And this . . . it says, with a second file attached—one with supporting affidavits.

But I'm still focused on the dress with the blood in the back seat of Artis's car. I think now that Shannon must have taken it and given it to Artis after we left this morning. Maybe that's where he's been all day.

"Did you get that from Shannon?" I ask him, not sure what to think or do. We have no obligation to disclose incriminating evidence, but Shannon was technically obstructing justice.

And then I have to wonder—why would Shannon take the dress? And why would she give the dress to Artis?

I look back to the files. My eyes dance over the names but now one of them is pulling me back as the pieces fall into place.

Affidavit of Artis Frauhn in Support of Defendant Shannon Finch.

My God . . .

"Artis," I say now. "Why did Shannon give you that dress?"

He sighs, gripping the wheel tighter as the car moves at a slow crawl. Too slow to catch up with Grace if she's on foot.

Then he says, finally, "We're together. Me and Shannon. We're getting married."

Jesus. Yes—this makes sense now. I look back at the documents on my phone but don't say a word about them. I want to hear what he tells me first.

"Did she give you Grace's dress?"

I stare at him, but he doesn't look back. And I try to understand what's happened. Shannon must have given him the dress to help *him*, not Grace. Because Grace is his client. But why is this dress covered in blood?

And right then he draws another long breath. And says:

"It's not Grace's dress, Ana. It's yours."

Chapter Forty

Excerpt from Testimony of Kayla Johnson

ADA OLSON: This man who attacked you in the field when you were training at The Palace—he wore a beaded necklace, correct?

KAYLA JOHNSON: Yes. It was very distinct. Black and white beads.

ADA OLSON: And he smelled of pine?

KAYLA JOHNSON: Yes—like from a car air freshener.

ADA OLSON: And you told all of this to Ana the night it happened?

KAYLA JOHNSON: Yes.

ADA OLSON: But you didn't report it to the police? Or to anyone other than your friends at Avery Hall?

KAYLA JOHNSON: Only Emile Dresiér.

ADA OLSON: When was that?

KAYLA JOHNSON: The next day, when he took me to the clinic for emergency contraception and testing. I told him everything. Including the necklace.

ADA OLSON: And what did he say?

KAYLA JOHNSON: He said hundreds of truckers used the rest stop near the field. He said they'd probably never find him with no physical description—just some necklace the guy probably threw away. I asked him about evidence he might have left—on me. On my clothes. DNA maybe.

ADA OLSON: What did he say to that?

KAYLA JOHNSON: He said he threw my clothes away in a dumpster. They were gone. And he said it was too late to go to the police. It would just be a story, and no one would believe a girl like me. I had no idea at the time that there might have still been evidence on my body—after the bath.

ADA OLSON: How does that make you feel?

KAYLA JOHNSON: I don't really have words for it.

Chapter
Forty-One

ANA

Before—Two Years at The Palace

The truck moved steadily along the highway. The rhythm of the wipers, a swish, then a click, wiping a light snowfall from the windshield. The strong, steady rumble of the engine. Lulling her to sleep.

Bare legs tucked beneath her. The brown coat draped over her body. Pulled all the way up, covering her face.

And in that sleep, her mind let her forget about everything. Indy. Her mother. Jolene. Even Kayla. It brought her back to another time, when she was a little girl and Tim was a young boy. Before she'd put on a pair of skates and felt the blades take her away.

They were in the back seat of her family's car. Carl was driving. Connie was looking out the window for something red. Then her voice called out, "*I spy a red sign!*" And then Tim said it didn't count because the sign wasn't red; it was green. It was just the logo for the gas station that had red in it, and that wasn't the same thing. And then Connie said, "*No fair!*" And Carl let out a big laugh.

Ana felt sleepy, too tired to play the game. Tim popped in his headphones and began tapping his hands on the back of the driver's seat. The beat of music she couldn't hear. A steady *ba-dum-dum, ba-dum-dum*. She leaned her head against the window. Her mother saying, "*I want a rematch*," as Ana's eyes got heavy.

She heard her mother's voice again. *"Ana—don't fall asleep."*

But her eyelids were falling.

Swish. Click. *Ba-dum-dum. Ba-dum-dum.* Swish. Click.

"Wake up, baby girl."

She began to rouse as the engine shifted gears and the brakes squeaked. The smell of the coat filling her nostrils. Tobacco and sweat. And pine. Wafting down from the air freshener that hung from the rearview mirror.

She forced open her heavy eyes.

They burned when the air rushed in. Like they were covered with sand.

She rubbed them gently with her fists. Blinked. Then sat up as the truck slowed and then stopped.

They weren't on the highway.

The headlights shone on a two-lane road surrounded by dense woods on both sides. Not another car in sight.

She told herself it was fine. He'd just pulled over to rest. He'd been so nice to her, and after everything that had happened in the past two years, she thought she knew about people. That she'd learned all the lessons.

Her eyes turned then from the windshield to the man sitting in the driver's seat.

"Hi there, sleepyhead," he said, glancing at her with a smile and big black oval eyes.

He reached his hand across the console between them. Placed it gently on her shoulder.

"Did you get a good rest?" he asked. Moving his hand to the back of her head. He took hold of the elastic tie that was holding it in a ponytail and slid it off.

"Look at you," he said. His eyes widening into circles. "Do you take pretty pills?"

Ana stared at him. Felt the adrenaline burst from the calm, from the sleep that lingered in her muscles and bones. Shock spread across her face, freezing her mouth in a gape. Her eyes in a stare.

This seemed to excite him. Eliciting a suggestive smile.

He tossed the elastic tie to the floor. Returned his hand to her head and ran his fingers through her hair.

"Do you like to party?" he asked.

He leaned closer, grabbing her hair into his fist. His shirt falling open, just at the top, revealing a necklace.

Ana stared at it. The square beads strung tightly together. Just two colors. Black and white.

The pieces coming together.

The smell of pine. The beaded necklace.

The man who'd attacked Kayla in the field two years ago.

She reached for the handle of the door as her mind dug out excuses she'd thought of, just like before. In the field. In the back of the black van.

"I have to pee," she said, pushing the door open and stumbling out, her skates falling beside her. It was a long way to the ground from the cab of the semi, and by the time she got to her feet and gathered her skates in her hands, he was walking around the front.

"Hey," he said. "Where you goin'?"

There was nowhere to hide in the bare trees off the side of the road, so she ran. And he chased after her.

Do you like to party? She knew what that meant. What he was going to do when he caught her.

What he had done to Kayla that night in the field.

There was nowhere to go, except deeper into the woods.

And so she ran, with one skate in each hand, the blades cutting into her palms, heart pounding wild in her chest. The sound of the truck driver weaving through the trees, close behind her. The branches snapping. Click. Click. Click.

It's enough, she thought. Dawn. Emile. Dr. Westin. She hated them all. Hated herself. But she'd broken free. And there she'd been, in the cab of the truck, thinking she was finally safe. That the damage was done, behind her, and now, finally, someone was bringing her home. Taking her away, to safety.

She felt tired. She just wanted to go home to her father, her brother—even if her mother was no longer there. Maybe she would still feel her inside the walls of the house where she was born.

No more. I have to go home.

She stopped running when she felt him closing in. She slipped her hand inside the boot of the skate, the blade angled to strike, just like in the field. Only this time, there was no retreat.

He caught up to her, grabbing her shoulder, spinning her around. For just a moment, he stumbled to his knees.

And that's when her body took over.

With all the strength and speed she possessed, she swung her arm and felt the blade pierce his skull with a sickening thud. Rage bursting from her mouth in a primal scream. Rage for Indy, and Jolene, and Kayla, and for the loss of the wide-eyed girl she'd been when she'd walked through the doors of Avery Hall two years ago.

He reached for her leg, stunned, bleeding. It took two hands to pull out the blade, so the next time she was ready.

One arm to strike, two hands to pull the blade free.

Again and again—four strikes for the four Orphans—until the rage finally left her.

Chapter
Forty-Two

ANA

Now

There it is—on the back seat of Artis's car: *my dress.*

From that night I ran through the woods, down the mountain. Away from Dawn and Emile and Westin because Indy was dead and they were all to blame. The same night I took a ride from a stranger. Desperate to be home.

I left that man in the woods and returned to the cab of the semi. I took his coat from the seat where I'd been sleeping and put it on. I rummaged through the truck, finding a bag for my skates, a pair of boots, and socks.

I shoved the socks into the toes of the boots to make them fit.

Then I climbed into the driver's seat. Turned the ignition. I could barely see over the steering wheel to the road. I pulled the seat as far up as it would go, my toe just reaching the gas. I slid the gear into drive and began to move.

I drove that truck fifty miles straight ahead until I got to the entrance of the highway and a gas station. It was there I left it in the middle of the parking lot because I didn't know how to do more than make it go forward. I found a pay phone and called Mio.

Now, I stare at the dress in the bag. Not Grace's dress with Emile's blood. But my dress with the blood of that trucker. A man named Jeb Clayton, who wouldn't be found until six years ago.

"You come across all kinds of things being a criminal lawyer," Artis says, braking to a stop. "So when these bones were found in the middle of nowhere, north of Denver, in the woods where they were excavating to expand a back road into four lanes, well—I didn't think anything of it. But then the bones were matched to a missing truck driver. And the cause of death was found to be fractures to his skull—four of them, oddly shaped like a skating blade."

I run through the rest of that night in my head. Mio came to get me, brought me back to Avery Hall. We went in through the window on the first floor, then up the stairs to the bathroom, where I changed and showered and Mio took everything I was wearing and put it into a garbage bag and put the bag in the dumpster out back.

"*Do you want to tell me?*" she asked as she scrubbed the blood from my skate in the bathroom sink.

I shook my head. *"No."* I sat on the cold tile, wrapped in a towel, my whole body trembling. I never wanted to speak of it again.

One day, I got a Google alert from the words I'd entered when I started working at my firm. *Truck driver. Remains. Bones. Colorado. Blade.* I saw the picture of the man and learned his name. I ordered a copy of the paper where the article was printed, cut out the report, and sent it, anonymously, to Kayla.

But now a thought rushes in.

"Shannon," I say out loud, but in a whisper. "She was staying at Avery Hall that month. Her mother had gone back home . . ."

Artis nods. "Right," he says. "Her brother broke his leg. He couldn't drive to school. And Shannon didn't want to stop training."

"She lived on the first floor," I remember now. She would have been there . . . that night.

"She heard you and Mio come in through the window. Then she saw Mio go back out—and throw something in the dumpster."

What is going on here? Even if Shannon went to the dumpster to see what Mio had thrown away, why would she keep my blood-soaked dress all these years? Why not give it to the police or Edie? Or even to her mother, who had gone out of her way to destroy the other Orphans?

But then Artis has the answer.

"She went to Dawn the next day and told her what had happened. She gave her the dress. She thought Dawn would do the right thing. She didn't want you to get in trouble."

"How do you know all this?"

His face changes again, this time to something cold. Indifferent.

"We dated in high school, after you left. But then she quit skating and moved home. She came back eight years ago when Edie died and the job opened up at Avery Hall. She started seeing Emile."

My God. Artis and Shannon. They acted like strangers before.

But Dawn had the dress—he just told me that. How did he get his hands on it?

Then I think—Artis, the lawyer. His practice dependent on The Palace. If he has my dress from fourteen years ago, he must have gotten it from Dawn, who's kept it all this time. Which means they're working together now.

Artis is not working to help Grace.

No. He's helping frame her for Emile's murder.

But then why *my* dress? It had to be Shannon who took Grace's dress the night Emile was killed—in his office at The Palace—and his body later moved to the field.

And now I remember about the four cars Grace said she recognized that night. And the footsteps she heard coming down the hall toward Emile's office.

"It was you," I say, staring incredulously at Artis. "You were there when Emile was killed! Did you do it? Did you kill him?"

Artis puts the car in gear and starts to drive.

He says nothing, but I feel myself moving further toward one conclusion.

"It was you. Oh my God, Artis." The custody files are right there on my phone. Emile wasn't just taking down The Palace, then leaving with its skaters. He was taking his son with him. The son Shannon had with Emile just five years ago.

"It wasn't just business—you wouldn't kill over that. You could move your practice somewhere else. It was personal, wasn't it?" I race through the pleading that's still open on my phone. The affidavit Artis filed to try to keep Emile from gaining custody of Shannon's son and relocating to California.

"You stepped in when Emile abandoned her, didn't you? You raised Caleb like your own child. You were planning to marry Shannon, and Emile was ruining everything. Your law practice. Your family. Your entire life."

Still, no answer. Not even a flinch. Which means he has a plan to get himself out of this.

I feel the car accelerate even though the road is buried in a foot of snow, nothing visible from any window.

"What are you doing?" I say, my heart racing as we skid out, then swerve back.

He keeps driving.

"Artis! Stop the car!"

He reaches back and grabs my dress in the plastic bag. He holds it up to my face, and he smiles.

"I don't know, Ana. Did I? You had much more to lose. This dress proves you killed that trucker fifteen years ago. Dawn kept it all this time because she didn't know what it meant—and because she didn't want any of that night to come back to bite her."

Right, I think. Of course—the night they told me Indy died. Because of what they did to her. The falling and the bruise and then having her disqualified. They all played a role.

Artis continues. "When I told her about the murdered trucker and the wounds in the skull, how they were shaped like a blade—she remembered that night you ran away. Right after they told you about Indy. And then she showed me the dress."

I get it now. "So, what, you both kept this secret? To protect The Palace and Echo?"

"We also protected you. All of us. Shannon could have gone to the police when she found the dress in the dumpster. Dawn could have done the same when Shannon gave it to her. And when I read about the body and Dawn told me about that night—I could have gone to them as well."

The car skids again, and Artis goes faster, bringing it back onto the road. The lights shine on the path carved by the plows.

And a figure up ahead. Someone walking.

"You did it to protect *The Palace*. Don't pretend any of you cared about me. I would have been fine. That man assaulted Kayla. He'd been convicted of rape and domestic violence—it was in that article after they identified his body. He was a predator. And Emile convinced Kayla to stay quiet. He took her clothes. He gave her a bath. It could have destroyed her."

I look ahead to the figure, and as a gust of wind clears away the snow, I can make out the coat. The bare head. The ponytail.

"There she is!" I tell him.

But he just keeps driving. "No, Ana. I didn't kill Emile."

And now he starts to move to the right, onto what would be the shoulder if it wasn't buried in snow.

The shoulder Grace is walking on.

"What are you doing?" I ask. He's heading right for Grace, and there's no way she'll hear the car with the wind whipping past her ears.

"Artis!"

"I didn't kill Emile. And neither did Dawn or Dr. Westin."

"It's over!" I scream now. "Grace already told me Dawn and Westin were there! And the fourth car she saw—it had to be yours!"

And now, as he steps even harder on the gas, Grace just yards away, he says, "Maybe you're lying."

"What? Why would I lie?"

"Because maybe you did it," he says. "Maybe you killed Emile."

Chapter
Forty-Three

Excerpt from Testimony of Mio Akasawa

ADA OLSON: What happened the next day—after you drove home from the rest stop outside of Denver?

MIO AKASAWA: Ana woke up at six a.m. for her morning sessions. She went to the rink, skated, then went to school. Nationals were just three weeks away.

ADA OLSON: Back to normal?

MIO AKASAWA: Yes.

ADA OLSON: And did you ever ask her again why her dress, and her skate, were covered in blood? Where she'd been or what she'd done?

MIO AKASAWA: No.

ADA OLSON: Why not?

MIO AKASAWA: Because she asked me not to.

Chapter
Forty-Four

ANA

Before—Third Year at The Palace

The next morning Ana woke up at six a.m. for her skating sessions. Dawn was there in her blue puffer coat. She said nothing about the night before, about what had happened in her house. About Indy. About Ana running away.

About her and Emile having killed Indy.

Instead, she skated over to Ana for a lesson. "Good, you're here," she said. "Let's get to work. Go. Now—the triple Lutz."

Ana stroked around the edge of the boards, past the other skaters, who kept gathering in small clusters to stare and whisper about Indy.

They could all go straight to hell. All of them and their mothers in the stands who'd done nothing to help any of them. The others were gone, but Ana was still here. And she would never let them forget the four Orphans.

She passed Coach Emile, who averted his gaze in shame. And who would do that for the next ten months, until she left. She would do the same to him. Like nothing had ever happened in the tangled sheets, in his bed, in the guest cottage.

Down the center, she gathered speed, as much as humanly possible for a girl her age and with her strength. Left blade. Back outside edge. Right toe pick reaching back, jamming into the ice, so hard she left an enormous divot. Springing into the air for the three full rotations, arms and legs coiled like a spring ready to explode. Into the landing on the right back edge.

She felt the sole of her boot release moisture from the soap and water.

And this brought a flash of memory of the blood that she and Mio had washed off, and from the man in the woods who had smelled of pine and worn a beaded necklace. But that was all she would allow. It was surprising how easy it was, when she put her mind to it, how she was able to keep it in the very back of her mind with all the other things she didn't want to think about.

She had Dr. Westin to thank for the skills this required.

Dawn was waiting for her with open arms. But Ana stopped a few feet away. She was done with all of that. With being a *good girl*.

Three weeks later at Nationals, she landed all her jumps and placed fifth in the junior division—which was a significant accomplishment for her first time out.

Carl and Tim both came to watch. Carl said Connie would be so proud of her—though what did she really remember about her mother, after they'd kept her away for so long? She, too, was tucked far away in the back of Ana's mind.

That March, Carl agreed to let her live with Mio in a new condo complex a little farther down the access road. Mio would train year-round now that she had enrolled in a local college. And sure, why not? Ana was fifteen and had been living as an Orphan for over two years. She was basically all grown up.

For eight more months, Ana returned to her old routine. But then, one morning, she heard her alarm and didn't jump from her bed like she usually did. Instead, she sat on its edge, staring out her window at the dawn. And the mountain. The trees glowing with the florescent colors of dying leaves.

She went to the kitchen and made coffee. Then she sat at the table, sipping it while she scrolled through photographs on her phone. Jolene in her red Jeep, her hair wild around her face. Sunglasses, a sleeveless top. Kayla outside the rink, black leggings and a sweatshirt. Smiling as she held up two middle fingers. And Indy—there were so many images it was hard to land on any one of them. She eventually stopped on a selfie they'd taken outside Avery Hall. A Sunday afternoon, sitting on the bench her mother had noticed the day she'd dropped her off.

"*I'll picture you there,*" she'd said.

Ana missed the morning sessions, then the afternoon, and two full days after that before she finally returned to The Palace. When she did, she said nothing to Dawn, who was waiting on the ice. The expectation contorting her face trickled down to every part of her—folded arms, squared shoulders, feet pulled together in a first position. Ready for Ana to cower over. Make excuses. But instead, Ana barreled past her without as much as a glance. For a split second, Ana saw her push away from the boards, thinking she might chase her down. Ask her what the hell was going on. But then she stopped. Maybe she knew that it was over. Maybe she didn't even care.

After a few more days of this, Ana sat with Mio in front of the TV. They'd made dinner. Chosen a show. But Mio grabbed the remote and hit pause.

"Why do you stay here?" she asked.

"I don't know," Ana said after giving it a thought.

"Well," Mio said. "I do. This is the best place to be punished—for you to torment yourself over whatever happened that night," she said, though she had no idea what *had* actually happened the night Ana called her from the rest stop outside Denver.

"Skating isn't life," she said. "Think of all the other things you can do."

Which was a strange thing for Mio to say, since skating had been her life for her entire twenty years. She'd won the silver medal at the Olympics the year before. The year Indy was supposed to make the team for the United States.

But Ana listened, because like most everything Mio said, it was right.

Ana was gone before Christmas, and she didn't look back. She never saw any of them again. Mio, Jolene, Kayla.

Until the week when they were reunited to save Jolene's daughter.

Chapter Forty-Five

ANA

Now

Maybe you killed Emile.

Artis's words swim in my head as the car picks up speed. But the tires can't grip the road, and they skid, making the car swerve. We slide to the right and bounce off the wall of snow made by the plows.

"Artis!" I scream. "Stop!"

I grab the wheel and push it to the left, away from the shoulder, away from Grace. And the car moves into the other lane, then starts to slide sideways.

You killed Emile.

I see my hand raised, the blade about to strike Emile's skull—but, no. It wasn't me.

Artis was there, with Dawn and Westin. One of them killed Emile, and now they needed someone to take the fall. Grace's skates were on Emile's desk—it was so easy to point suspicion her way. To enlist Shannon's help—taking Grace's dress. Telling the police about the video. But then they must have thought about me, back in Colorado for the first time. Just five hours away in Aspen. Artis knew I'd killed a man fifteen years ago with the heel of my blade. Dawn had my dress.

But Grace—she heard all of them there the night Emile disappeared. She saw the blood on the floor in the closet. She recognized the car in the parking lot—and then comes another thought.

Grace didn't know Artis's car.

Shannon, I think. She had more to lose than anyone. Custody of her child. She knew Grace was with Emile. She'd just witnessed the fight between Grace and Tammy Theisen.

"Was it Shannon?" I ask. "Shannon killed Emile—not you. Artis . . ."

Headlights come from the other direction. We both see them. They don't slow down as we continue to slide sideways, taking up both lanes of the access road.

"Turn!" I scream at Artis. He grabs the wheel and pulls to the right, again in the direction of Grace, who is just feet away.

"No!" I scream. "It's too late—I know what happened!"

His car starts to spin as the truck approaches, then slams into us, airbags exploding from the front and sides. Then everything stops. Dead quiet.

Until I hear Artis moan. And then voices outside.

"Ana!"

"Ana!"

Two voices, ghosts from the past. Jolene. Kayla.

They open my door, pull me out onto the ground. They lay me down in the snow, and then I see Grace standing over me, unharmed.

Kayla is on the phone, calling for help. She's at the car, the open door. She tells Artis to hold on. He's trapped inside, his door mangled by the impact.

I look at Grace as I begin to feel the pain in my chest.

"It was Shannon's car at The Palace that night, wasn't it?"

Jolene looks at her daughter. "What is she talking about?"

I hear Grace begin to tell the story she told me in Westin's office. The closet where she showed me the blood on the floor.

The story she was too afraid to share because of Dawn and Westin. And Artis—hired by her own mother to defend her. Too afraid because of this place. The Palace.

And then sirens in the distance as my vision blurs and voices get farther away.

And then everything is black.

Chapter Forty-Six

Excerpt from Testimony of Grace Montgomery

ADA OLSON: Grace—you've heard the testimony of Dawn Sumner and Dr. Gerard Westin about the events that occurred the night Emile Dresiér was killed, correct?

GRACE MONTGOMERY: Yes.

ADA OLSON: They both claim that following the argument with Mr. Dresiér, they left his office.

GRACE MONTGOMERY: Yes. That's what they said.

ADA OLSON: Ms. Sumner also testified that she saw your skates on his desk.

GRACE MONTGOMERY: Yeah—I don't know how they got there. Maybe Dr. Westin brought them to Emile in his office. I was supposed to meet Emile there.

ADA OLSON: But when you went to meet him, you heard the fighting about Emile knowing things—things about your mother and her friends, including Ms. Robbins.

GRACE MONTGOMERY: Yes.

ADA OLSON: You told Ms. Robbins you didn't hear much more than that. Is that true?

GRACE MONTGOMERY: No.

ADA OLSON: What exactly did you hear through that door?

GRACE MONTGOMERY: Emile said Ana Robbins killed a man in the woods. He accused Dawn of knowing about it. He said Shannon had told him about Ana's dress. That she'd given it to Dawn.

ADA OLSON: So he knew about Ms. Robbins killing Jeb Clayton? And he was going to tell the reporter?

GRACE MONTGOMERY: That's what he said.

ADA OLSON: And then you left when you heard another person coming down the hall, correct?

GRACE MONTGOMERY: Yes.

ADA OLSON: And when you got outside, you saw four cars in the parking lot, correct? Who did they belong to, if you know?

GRACE MONTGOMERY: Dawn. Emile. Dr. Westin. And Shannon Finch.

ADA OLSON: The dorm mother at Avery Hall?

GRACE MONTGOMERY: Yes.

ADA OLSON: And when you got back to Avery Hall on foot, was Ms. Finch there?

GRACE MONTGOMERY: No. And neither was her car.

Chapter Forty-Seven

ANA

Now

I returned to Echo ten months later, for the trial of Shannon Finch in the murder of Emile Dresiér. It was there that my secret was finally revealed.

I had gone through my life as if that night had never happened. I'd had no idea about the dress, and the lengths to which Dawn would go to protect me. Emile, as well, because he'd read about the body being found, the cause of death. Shannon had told him about the dress, and how she'd given it to Dawn. He'd held the secret until it was time to finally make a move against The Palace.

As for Shannon—I don't know why she gave the dress to Dawn and not the police. Or why she didn't tell anyone when she and Artis finally put the pieces together.

I don't take any of this as a sign of affection for me. They all had reasons that served themselves. For Dawn, Jeb Clayton's murder was the end of a story she didn't want told.

And what does that say about me? That I felt no remorse? I feel none now, almost fifteen years later. Maybe from the years of therapy, though I never told any of the shrinks what I'd done. Or from my work, coming to understand trauma responses in children. Defending children who have committed heinous crimes. Maybe because he deserved it.

I thought about this when I was questioned by the same ADA who prosecuted Shannon Finch. When I told her about that night when I was fifteen. Having so recently lost my mother. Having just learned that my best friend had died of an overdose, drinking a strange concoction of DMSO and morphine mixed by a veterinarian. The liquid I'd hid for her in a shampoo bottle so she could take it with her to Nationals, and that had made her smell of garlic. And numbed the bruise she got from falling. It sounds absurd, now that I'm so removed from this place. But at the time, Indy landing the triple Axel was bigger than any of us.

I told her about the man who gave me a ride after finding me alone and scared at the truck stop, and how I thought I might be safe, but then I smelled the pine and saw the necklace as he leaned over to grab my hair. Asked me if I liked to party.

I could not have told it any better, or painted a clearer picture. I was acting in self-defense from this man who chased me after I ran away, this man with a rape conviction and multiple reports by his former wife for domestic violence.

I told the story like the lawyer I am now, and not the girl I was then—and I got her off. No charges were filed.

The story I told was true. Except, maybe, when she asked the final question—about the four puncture wounds to his skull and how hard it must have been to extract the blade and plunge it back three more times. What was going through my mind? What was in my heart? Why didn't I strike once, then try to run away?

"*Did you want to kill him?*" she asked.

As a killer with an excellent attorney, I said, "*No. Of course not.*"

The four puncture wounds to Emile's skull were used to convict Shannon of first-degree murder and Artis of conspiracy after the fact. They built a compelling narrative.

The family court had ruled in Emile's favor days before Shannon killed him. She'd filed an appeal. But then she had a better idea.

She knew Jolene was in town for the holidays. She knew Kayla lived an hour away.

And she knew about the conference I was speaking at in Aspen. Artis had told her—he followed my career.

When they searched her apartment, they found the burner phone with the text message—the one with an emoji of a skating blade. That message had sent me into a tailspin. I didn't leave my room that day, hiding from the world. The second day of the conference—when Westin noticed my absence. No wonder he thought I might have killed Emile.

Tammy Theisen testified that Shannon was the one to tell her about Jolene, Grace's mother, wanting to terminate the pregnancy. And how Emile was with us, how he stopped her by calling Jolene's father. Shannon had told her the night before, sneaking it into a conversation about her time as a skater, years ago. Tammy said it didn't seem unusual. Shannon was always gossiping. Treating the girls more like peers than kids. Like she still wanted to be one of them.

Then came the fight with Grace. Her rage, insisting on seeing Emile. Shannon knew that would be enough to make Grace a suspect, but she made sure of it with the blood on Grace's skate, and the missing dress.

Grace would be a suspect, but also any one of us. The three Orphans whose secrets Emile was about to disclose.

The ADA argued, and the jury believed, that she killed Emile with the heel of a blade to mimic the way Kayla had threatened her mother. And that she intentionally struck Emile four times, mirroring my crime from fifteen years before.

Turning against her to get a reduced sentence, Artis testified that she'd called him from Emile's office, claiming it had all happened in the heat of the moment. He joined in the cause to cover up her crime, helping clean the office, move the body to the field, then advising Shannon on what to say to the police so they would question Grace and test her skates for blood. And about the clothes she was wearing when she was last seen with Emile. And, of course, there was that very convenient video demonstrating Grace's rage.

Getting Jolene to summon me from Aspen was the last part of Shannon's plan.

Shannon and Artis were both sentenced to prison. Maybe not for quite as long as they could have been. But I'm not in any position to throw stones. Shannon's son is now living with her mother, a retired widow in Oregon. I try not to think about the way she was with us, one of the worst bleacher bees, and the woman who raised a sociopath.

I returned to testify in the other trial—the one against Dawn Sumner for abuse and neglect of a child named Indy Cunningham. We had all been subpoenaed. Me, Jolene, Kayla, Grace. I've heard rumblings about Mio and Hugo and even Bobby Stark providing testimony. Our entire story is about to be told in a court of law. Justice for Indy after all these years.

Kayla asked us to come to her farm one day while we waited our turn. We had a lot of sorting out to do about our time here, things we never said back then or any time since. Where all of it has lived inside us, how we managed to move forward.

Which made us all think about Indy as we sat at Kayla's kitchen table, with Grace watching her iPad in the other room.

Jolene wanted to raise a glass to her, so we lifted coffee cups and pretended this was enough. Knowing in our hearts that she would never leave us.

Kayla said, "We didn't know the half of what happened to her."

It was too much for her to bear. We could all see that now. Her mother's motives in sending her away, the falling and the bruise and the suspension. Dawn's betrayal. But the worst, we all agreed, was the fact that Bobby had rejected her. It didn't matter that he had to save his career, or that it was her mother who pushed him into that corner. In the end, she had been expendable. And that made him feel like a lie.

"We couldn't have known. She kept a lot inside," Jolene said.

And that had to be right, because if it was wrong, it couldn't be sorted into a file and put in a box, with the lid closed tight. Right next to the files we had about our time here. About Dawn's abuse, which had made us vulnerable, opening the door for Emile to alter each of our lives. Denying justice for Kayla. Making a life decision for Jolene. Ending Indy's skating career. And me, well. I've said enough about that already.

The files are sorted and locked away in the backs of our minds, because it's just not possible to find peace, let alone joy, with open boxes.

Later, we peel Grace away from her show, and Kayla leads us on a walk through the woods of her property.

Where there is a frozen pond. And four pairs of skates laid out on a wooden bench.

I haven't been on the ice for seventeen years.

Jolene and Kayla never stopped, and this still surprises me.

We sit on the bench and lace up the skates. Mine are new, but somehow the right size. The Orphans have gone to a lot of trouble.

Kayla looks at the soft flesh on my fingers and reaches out with hers. They have the familiar calloused grooves from pulling on nylon laces.

"Do you need help?" she asks with a slight laugh.

I start to say, *No, I've got it,* but instead I tell her the truth.

"I might."

I turn off my thoughts as I slip my feet inside the stiff leather and start to pull.

"Come on," Jolene says. "It's like riding a bike."

We step onto the ice and Kayla takes off, the way she always did. As if no time has passed. And I see the girl who lives inside her as she flies away, looking for a moment of escape.

Jolene takes her time, stroking beside her daughter like a mother hen with her baby chick. But soon Grace takes off, too, chasing after Kayla.

I push away from the bench and feel that first glide. On a new skate. A new blade. And then the other boot drops to the ice, digs into an edge. Left, then right. Left, then right. I gather speed.

And then my arms lift from my sides as my knees bend deeper. I reach the corner and make the turn, right over left, right over left, crossovers to the other side. Then back to the long, curved strokes that build more speed.

Kayla laps me, her ponytail flying in the air, before she cuts down the middle and takes off for an enormous double toe loop. She looks back when she lands, the pond making a loud thud as it resettles.

"Not bad for an old lady, right?"

"Not bad at all," I call out.

"Come on! Catch up!" she says, speeding past me.

She is magnificent, this woman who was once a girl being dragged out of the woods.

And so is Jolene, her life defined by another, but not a hint of what might have been anywhere in her eyes.

"Watch this!" Grace calls out from across the pond. We gather, side by side, and watch as she launches into a huge triple flip, one arm over her head.

"She's such a show-off!" Jolene says, though she's smiling ear to ear.

"No," I tell her. "She's perfect." And I think to myself that she truly is—even if there are still storms inside her that need to be quelled.

"Well," Jolene says. "She's better than we were, that's for sure."

To which Kayla replies, "Speak for yourself."

Jolene gives her a shoulder bump.

I had such a desperate longing when I was at The Palace. Living as an Orphan at Avery Hall while my mother was slowly dying 289 miles away from me. Crawling into Indy's bed. Into Dawn's blue coat, and finally, into those tangled sheets at her guest cottage. I hated myself for a long time, until I found a way to be redeemed—my mission to save damaged children.

As laughter fills my chest, I look at these women who were once girls just down the hall. How they've filled their lives with love, and I know I have more work to do. Starting right here. With them. On the ice.

Grace passes me. "You're too slow!" she says.

So I bend my knees, pushing into the blades, deeper and faster, right arm sweeping overhead, then a three turn and I'm backward. Crossovers around the bend, then forward again. My body moving, making shapes that feel glorious. Not caring how they look to the outside world.

Moving across the ice so fast my eyes begin to water.

Then Grace comes back to skate beside me.

"You're crying," she says. But I tell her no—it's just the wind.

And she looks at me perplexed, like I should know what this is. Don't I remember?

As she skates away, she yells back to me—

"It's not the wind."

And I think, *No. It's not the wind.*

It's the joy of being on a blade, finally returned.

Acknowledgments

First and foremost, I want to thank my agent, Dan Conaway, who saw the potential of this book before I had the courage to write it. Dan—your unwavering support, confidence, and belief in *Blade* (and me) enabled me to sort through my own stories until a new one emerged. Thank you for being in the trenches from start to finish, for always asking me how I was doing before diving into the work, and for understanding how personal this journey was for me. I am so grateful to have you in my corner.

To the fabulous publishing team at Thomas & Mercer—my magnificent editor, Liz Pearsons, thank you for seeing the heart of the story and making it shine; to Miranda Gardner and the production team, thank you for the dedication, keen insights, and honed expertise that flawlessly brought *Blade* into the world. To Angela James, your sharp editorial eye brought the book to even greater heights. To Megan Beatie, for your brilliant skills and tireless efforts getting *Blade* into readers' hands. And thank you, Jarrod Taylor and Olga Grlic, for the gorgeous cover design!

To Rhea Lyons, and the team at Audible, thank you for being the champions of my work. You have given *Blade* a life beyond the page, which is truly spectacular. I can't wait for all that is to come. And to Matt Patterson—thank you for bringing my Audible Original stories to life in a truly unique way!

To my beloved friends in the author community—you are the invaluable antidote to the solitude of this profession. Being in your company is magical. And especially, during the writing of this book, to Lynne Constantine, Jean Kwok, May Cobb, Jeneva Rose, Mary Kubica, Deborah Goodrich Royce, Fiona Davis, Greg Wands, Sandra Miller, and Kate White.

To my early readers—Sydnee Harlan at Writers House, and Jacqueline Wein—thank you for the honest feedback, support, and encouragement. And Sydnee, too, for your diligent attention to every aspect of my career.

To my friends—thank you for being in my life and supporting me in everything I do. Thank you, especially, to Sharon Cohen, Cynthia Briggs, and Pam Peterson—for being with me in the day-to-day shuffles, but also the big moments, both good and bad.

Thanks also to Beth Barsanti, Suzy Ort, Valerie Rosenberg, Kristan Roth, and Deb Schwartz. I am so lucky to call you friends. Thank you for listening and always being at the ready to lend a hand.

To my family—thank you for being there for me, even when we are apart.

To my sons—Andrew, Ben, and Christopher Israel—you are the light inside me, always, but also generous, kind, and caring young men. I am so proud and humbled to be your mom. I love you beyond words.

To Craig Orlando, thank you for putting a smile on my face every single day, and helping me back onto the ice!

To Dr. Joel Fuhrman, for being an exceptional coach, then and now. You were the first to see my potential as a skater, and as a person. Your work as a doctor now inspires me. Thank you for some of the happiest years of my life.

To Darlene Garlutzo, Lisa Marie Allen, Dorothy Allen, and the girls whose paths crossed mine at Beatty Hall. Thank you for helping me through some of the hardest years of my life.

To Figure Skating in Harlem, and again to Sharon Cohen, the work you do transforms the lives of young girls, and I thank you for bringing me back to this beautiful sport.

To Robert Rosenbluth, for walking me through the many ways the sport has changed over the years.

And last, to all of the skaters out there creating art and sport unlike any other—I will continue to watch you with profound reverence.

About the Author

Photo © 2015 Bill Miles

Wendy Walker is the author of the psychological suspense novels *All Is Not Forgotten*, *Emma in the Night*, *The Night Before*, *Don't Look for Me*, *What Remains*, and the Audible Originals *Hold Your Breath*, *American Girl*, *Mad Love*, and *The Room Next Door*. Her work has been translated into twenty-three languages, topping bestseller lists both in the United States and abroad, and featured by the *Today* show, the Reese Witherspoon Book Club, and the Book of the Month Club. Six of her titles have also been optioned for television and film.

Wendy holds degrees from Brown University and Georgetown University Law School. Prior to her writing career, Wendy trained for competitive figure skating, worked as a financial analyst at Goldman Sachs, and practiced both corporate and family law. She resides in Connecticut, where she raised her three sons.